About the author

Jennifer Barrett has worked in the areas of fundraising, communications and marketing across a range of arts companies, schools, colleges, youth mental health charities and other non-profit organisations. She is currently chief executive of a developing world charity based in Dublin, Ireland.

Jennifer divides her time between her own home in West Dublin and the family home in Wicklow, where her large clan gathers most weekends. A keen photographer, Jennifer travels far and wide to photograph and observe whales and other marine life in their natural habitats. Look into the Eye *was inspired by her trip to the Norwegian fjords to photograph wild orcas in 2007.*

Follow Jennifer on:
Facebook *(JenniferBarrettAuthor)*
Twitter *(@JenBarrettEye)*

Acknowledgements

I have many people to thank for first teaching me *how* to write a novel, then helping me to bring this book to life. So let me take a deep breath, and say a very big, heartfelt *thank you* to:

Paula Campbell, publisher of Poolbeg Press. Thank you so much, Paula, for saying yes – that elusive word that we authors-in-waiting long to hear. I'm so grateful to you, and to Sarah, Ailbhe and all at Poolbeg Press for your support, and for your belief in this story.

Gaye Shortland, my editor, who I think at times understood the message of this book even better than I did myself. Thank you, Gaye, for challenging me, and for teaching me a few new grammar rules along the way. (Although I must admit I'm still not *one hundred* per cent sure what a comma-splice is!)

Fiona Quinn – an absolute legend, who is never afraid to tell it like it is. Fo, only you can know how much you helped me with this book at the end. I am forever grateful.

Dave Walsh, one of the inspirational Greenpeace activists who defended the whales against the whaling fleet in Antarctica. Thank you, Dave, for helping me with my research for this book – any errors or inaccuracies in the story are entirely my own.

The Irish Writers' Centre, and to Claire Hennessy, my

writing teacher, who gave me the tools and the confidence to write this story; to Mary O'Donnell for sharing her valuable wisdom on writing with me in those early days; to Vanessa O'Loughlin of www.writing.ie for the advice that proved so pivotal in helping me to fine-tune the story for submission, and to Daisy Cummins for her fantastic support and advice, which helped me to navigate my way around this wonderful world of words.

Sandra Barrett, Kara Flannery, Ruth Flannery and Jessica Kavanagh – thank you all so much for suffering through the various early drafts of this novel, and for your valuable feedback on same. Special thanks to Jessica for the hill-rolling inspiration, and to Cormac Lynch for providing the male perspective, and letting me know that exclamation marks are largely superfluous when men are speaking (!!).

Sue Booth Forbes of Anam Cara Writer's and Artist's Retreat on the Beara Peninsula in West Cork, where I fled many times upon hitting the dreaded writing wall. Oh, how the words always flow at your magical centre, Sue.

Robert Doyle and all at Halpin's Bridge Café in Wicklow, and to the Phoenix Park Visitor Centre Café in Dublin – my friendly 'second offices' where I scribbled vast chunks of this novel over copious cappuccinos.

Aiveen Mullally, my haiku teacher; and to the many Facebook friends who responded to my research questions and pleas for help along the way – thanks for always pointing me in the right direction, guys.

Paul and Noreen Barrett, Chris Barrett, Lisa Burke, Helen Coughlan, Linda and Tom Hickey, my team at ERD, and all the Garglemonsters – thanks so much for your ongoing support, and for your encouragement of this writing whim of mine.

Claire Pyx for your truly invaluable gift of the alarm/light thingie that has helped me to get up and get writing before the sun rises on the dark, wintry mornings.

Suzanne Barrett for your endless encouragement, interest and moral support. And thanks especially for putting up with your *moody-when-writing* sis – love ya loads. x

Maureen and John Barrett, my wonderful parents. You have always been there in good times and bad, never failing in your support of your children's dreams. Without your abiding belief in me, this book would never have been started, let alone finished. I love ye to bits, and am more grateful to you both than I could ever find adequate words to express. xx

And finally, to the whales: thank you so much for showing up when I needed you – for causing my spirits to soar and these words to flow. I am so sorry that people continue to hunt you down and place you in danger from overfishing, pollution, heavy boat strikes, sonar testing and entanglement in fishing nets. And I'm so sad that, even today, in numerous theme parks around the world, we hold you captive, and make you and your dolphin cousins perform inane circus tricks in return for food. Whatever must you think of us?

It is my sincerest wish that some day we will all begin to see sense, that we will stop hurting you, and realise just how much we can learn when we look into the eye.

Until that day, I write.

xJ

Whenever I find myself growing grim about the mouth;
whenever it is a damp, drizzly November in my soul . . .
then I account it high time to get to sea as soon as I can.

Herman Melville, *Moby Dick*

For Daniel, Isabel, Rachel, Liam, Laura,
Marianne, Lochlann
and the whales.
xJ

Chapter 1

MELANIE

May 2007

I couldn't wait to be out of the stuffy function room. I stood there on the edge of the outdoor terrace, desperately trying to breathe in enough of the delicious, tobacco-filled air to ease the pain of the fundraising lunch.

Ah, that's better – at least I can breathe again, I said to myself. Which was when I noticed I was getting some strange looks from the glamorous, fully fledged smokers on the terrace.

I left the second-hand smoke and walked down the few steps to the lawn.

Whatever about the dull event, there was no denying the beauty of the setting of the Wicklow Landon Hotel – it was breathtaking. Freshly cut grass lay green and proud as it swept down the hill towards a running stream and copse of trees. I stared out at the sea in the distance, then kicked off my high heels and took a sip of my gin and tonic. The cool grass felt wonderful beneath my bare feet.

"There you are, Mel!" I turned around to see my best friend Katy walking towards me down the hotel steps.

"Isn't the weather glorious?" She linked her arm through mine when she reached me. "So are you enjoying the day?"

Katy and her boyfriend Frank had invited me along to the fundraiser for a new youth café and counselling service, so I didn't want to seem ungrateful. "Eh . . . yes, thanks, hon. And it's such a great cause." I looked away from her, back out at the view.

Katy touched my elbow. "Come on, Mel, this is me you're talking to."

I turned back. Katy's usually smiling face was sporting a furrowed brow. The game was up. "I suppose it's just not really my kind of thing, that's all."

"What? It certainly used to be your kind of thing, Mel – you used to love going to events like these when we were in college. Why don't you let your hair down a little and enjoy yourself today?"

"It's not the same, Katy. College was a long time ago. We're grown up now, and everyone's all coupled up and sensible these days – most of them anyway."

"Well, the music's just started and Frank has some nice single friends – why don't you come in and talk to a few of them? Maybe have a dance with one? You never know, Mr Right could be waiting for you just inside . . ."

I smiled at her determination. "Sure where would I have time for any man, let alone Mr Right? I've more than enough to cope with, trying to stay on top of my new promotion at work and saving up the money I need to renovate the new house. I want to make sure my future is secure – with or without a man."

"Fair enough," said Katy. "But remember, your dazzling career won't keep you warm at night."

"No, but the new fully insulated roof it puts over my head will!"

"All right, all right, I give up," Katy sighed. "You win."

She went to sit down on the grass, holding up her lovely, long, sea-green chiffon dress that went so beautifully with her wavy auburn hair.

I eased my own tight black dress up slightly and sat down beside her.

"I wish I'd worn something a bit lighter," I said to change the subject. "I'm roasted in this thing. I should have realised that everyone would be wearing bright colours and pastels at a lunch in May."

"Sure you look great in whatever you wear, Mel," Katy said, but she sounded a little distant. I knew she was disappointed in me, and I started to feel a bit bad then. It was nice of her and Frank to invite me along to the lunch. I needed to try to pick myself up and get into it.

"Ah sorry, Katy. Don't mind me. Why don't you go in and find Frank for a dance? I'll follow you when I've finished this." I held up my glass. "I'll even come and talk to some of his friends."

"Right – I'll hold you to that." She gave me a smile, scrambled to her feet, shook her dress out and went back inside.

I rested my head on my knees and just sat there for a few minutes, staring down over the rolling green hill out at the Irish Sea in the distance, enjoying the peace.

"Nice quiet spot you've got here."

I turned and shaded my eyes to look up at the man standing over me, pint glass in one hand, fat smoking cigar in the other. He was tall and broad and looked a little familiar, but the sun was shining directly above him,

3

making it difficult to see him properly.

"Mind if I join you?" He sat down beside me and took a long puff of his cigar.

I stole a brief glance at his face – late thirties, I reckoned, good-looking but not in an obvious kind of way, just something about him. He had sandy-coloured hair, cut short at the sides but already starting to curl on top. Who was he, though? How did I know this guy?

I turned back to the view, and I couldn't help myself breathing in some of the cigar smoke. For the first few seconds it was divine, but either the smoke was very strong or I breathed it in too deeply – either way, I started to cough.

"Sorry, is the cigar bothering you?" The guy flapped his hand around but just ended up blowing more smoke in my direction.

I swallowed the last of my drink and thankfully it seemed to work – the coughing finally stopped.

"Sorry about that – me and my evil cigar can go away if you like?" he said.

It took me a few seconds to get my voice back enough to speak. "Yes, that's probably a good idea." I was already missing the tranquillity of a few moments earlier.

"Ah, you don't mean that really?" He looked at me sideways and grinned.

I just sighed loudly, willing him to leave. But he didn't take the hint – just stayed sitting beside me, alternating between taking a swig of his pint, and a puff of his cigar.

"I haven't smoked one of these in years," he said after a while. "Somebody bought it for me earlier, though, so I thought why not? I need something to get me through – just one of those days, y'know?"

"Yep, I hear you," I said – referring to both the lunch *and* my growing need for a proper nicotine fix.

He must have read my mind. "Sounds like you might need a drag yourself there?" He offered me the cigar.

"No, thanks, I don't smoke," I said, feeling like such a phony. Though there were days like today when I really missed it, I hadn't smoked a cigarette in almost seven years. My ex-fiancé Ian had hated my smoking habit – it was one of the first things he pressured me to change about myself when we got together.

"Dead right too, filthy habit," said the man, stubbing the cigar out in the grass. He parked the pint glass precariously on the grass beside him and looked at me. "I noticed you earlier at the lunch. Did you have somewhere else you needed to be?"

"Sorry?"

"Just that you were checking your watch all through lunch – you seemed pretty uptight, that's all."

He'd hit a raw nerve. "Uptight?" I put my knees down and turned to face him. "Who are you calling uptight? You don't even know me."

"All right, steady on!" He pulled his head back and opened his eyes wide to feign shock at my reaction.

I turned back around to the view.

"You just seemed on edge, that's all," he said. "You couldn't sit still – must have got up from the table at least four or five times during the meal. Either you had somewhere else to be, or you have an overactive bladder!" He raised his eyebrows and smirked at me.

More than anything in the world at that moment I wanted to wipe that irritating smirk right off his face.

"So you were watching me then, were you?" I flicked

my hair behind my shoulder. "I'm afraid I'm not interested." I looked straight ahead at the view, delighted with myself.

He laughed. "You're all right – me neither, darling."

Right, that's it, I thought.

I went to stand up. "Time I was going."

"No, wait, don't." He put his hand out to stop me. "Where are my manners? I'm sorry about the comments. I'm not that bad really when you get to know me. I just can't ever seem to resist stirring things up. It's a personal failing – has got me in a lot of trouble over the years. Please sit back down – you looked happy there."

I settled back down with some reluctance.

He held his hand out. "The name is Richard Blake – pleased to meet you."

"Richard Blake . . . I'm sure I've heard your name before, and you look familiar – have we met?"

"Could have done, I guess. I'm a journalist for the *Irish Chronicle*. You?"

Of course. That was it!

"You're the guy who wrote that article about the Dublin Millennium Centre for the Arts last week, aren't you?"

"Yes, the very man," he said, looking pleased with himself. "Not a bad article that, though it should have been better. I tried to spice it up a bit by throwing in a flavour of my theory about an imminent Irish property crash, but my editor was having none of it – she and I hold vastly differing opinions on this country's economic outlook. In the end, that compromise report I filed was pretty bland – just like the subject matter. I did like my headline though." He leant back on one arm and sketched it out in the sky: "*Another Run-of-The-Mill Development Project* – most excellent, even if I do say so myself. Edith just about let me away with that one – after a struggle."

"Indeed. Well, let *me* introduce *my*self," I said, turning towards him and holding out my hand. "I'm Melanie McQuaid, director of marketing and development at The Mill. I'm responsible for marketing the venue, all public relations and fundraising for any new development at the centre. You'll find that that was my newest building project you were trashing."

"Ah," he said, sitting up straight, looking suitably chastened.

"Yes – 'Ah' is right. Do you have any idea of the hassle your article caused me? I spent all week fielding media queries after it went out – and as for my boss . . ."

I closed my eyes, remembering my boss's reaction – one I would have preferred to have been able to forget. Marcus Boydell, The Mill's CEO and artistic director went nuts when he read the scathing article about his pet project – which wasn't good for me. I'd only recently been promoted to director level and I knew I still had a lot to prove to Marcus, and to all the others who felt that at the age of thirty-four I was still too young and inexperienced to be taking over as second-in-command at Dublin's fastest-growing arts venue. After the article went out, it was all I could do to keep the press at bay and to convince Marcus that the piece wouldn't affect the forthcoming major fundraising campaign for the new wing.

"Correct me if I'm wrong, but didn't The Mill issue a press release on this project?" Richard said. "And isn't the whole point of a press release to get the media interested? You should be thanking me really."

Wise-ass!

"Anyway, you can just be glad I didn't get to file the copy I really wanted to file," he said.

I just stared ahead, almost afraid of what I might say.

"Oh, come on! You have to admit it was a fair piece, Miss McQuaid. There's no way you're ever going to raise all that money – fifteen million euro of private funding to co-fund the twenty-million government grant? No chance! No matter how successful The Mill has become, or how wealthy your clientele, it's completely off-the-scale stuff for a relatively new arts centre."

I sat up straight. "I admit nothing, Mister Blake. This project is sure to be a massive success."

I tried to sound confident but the truth was I'd never really been convinced about the scale of the new project myself. It was a highly ambitious plan, arguably *overly* ambitious. I'd tried to persuade Marcus at least to put off briefing the press until we had the majority of the funding in place, but he didn't want to hear it. My boss was nearing retirement, and now that the dream of running a venue with facilities large enough to stage full-scale opera and ballet productions was finally within his grasp, there was no way he was going to stay quiet about it. In the end it seemed my opinion didn't matter. I had to toe the company line.

"You'll see," I went on, in an effort to convince myself as much as Richard Blake. "In less than three years' time, you'll be standing in a queue along the quays of the River Liffey trying to get in to see a full-scale ballet production in our new state-of-the-art auditorium."

"I wouldn't bank on it." He laughed.

But when he saw I wasn't coming around, he looked

down and nodded slowly in defeat. "Right, I'll just go now then, shall I?" He took a long swig of his pint then went to get up.

"No, you're all right." If I was being honest I'd actually agreed with most of what he'd written – even if I would never admit it to him. "Whatever about the rest of the article, I did quite enjoy the bit you wrote about our chairwoman." I couldn't help but smile.

"Ah yes – the infamous, spoiled Fenella Wright," he said. "That bit was an added bonus." He smiled, then tilted his head down and looked sideways at me. "Any chance we could start again? My friends call me Richie." He held out his hand. "Peace?"

I paused for a second to think about it, then gave in and smiled. "Oh all right, go on then." I took his hand. "Nice to meet you, Richie. I'm Mel."

I scanned his face properly as I shook his hand. It was one of those friendly faces – he looked tired and his eyes were a bit bloodshot, but he had a cheeky smile. I imagined nobody was able to stay annoyed at Richie Blake for too long.

I turned back to face the view and we both just sat there for a minute in silence.

"So what drove you to the cigars?" I asked him after a while.

"Women! What else?" He gestured behind us towards the hotel. "I'm avoiding one, and supposed to be in there celebrating my engagement to the other."

"I thought you said you were at the lunch?"

"Yes, but we only got engaged yesterday, so we just told our friends and families about it at the lunch today. My future father-in-law and fiancée are in there now organising champagne for everyone. Which is a bonus, I guess – she's been trying her best lately to turn me teetotal – reckons I drink too much." He took a large swig of stout from his pint glass.

"Do you?"

He wiped the froth from his mouth.

"What?"

"Do you drink too much?"

He looked at the pint glass. "Ah, I suppose. But I need something to get through. I mean, why is it we all have to conform anyway?"

"What do you mean?" I asked. "Conform to what?"

"Marriage. Why do we all have to get married anyway?" he said. "What's wrong with just staying as we are and enjoying one another's company? Why do we have to give in to convention – to marriage, kids and the like?"

"I couldn't agree more," I said. "I, for one, am never going back there."

"Back? Were you married before, then?"

"Nearly – it's a long story." I changed the subject quickly: "So why are you getting engaged if you don't want to get married?"

"Shagged if I know." He shook his head slowly. "Sometimes I think I must be on some kind of white-knuckle ride that I got led onto – now I'm being carried along on it and I have no idea how to get off – don't even know if I want to. It's all pretty damned confusing." He took another swig of his pint. "The trouble is, I've never been very good at relationships. Sooner or later every one that I've ever been in comes crashing down around my ears."

There's nothing like a fellow-sufferer to make you feel better about your own situation.

"I hear you," I said, warming to the topic. "I'm a bit of a disaster in that department too. In fact, I find it easier these days to just keep life simple and stay single."

"Sounds like I should have spoken to you last week then – before I popped the question. Everyone else kept telling me to make an honest woman of her – herself included. I guess I just caved in, in the end."

"Well, I hope it all works out for you."

"Thanks." He looked at me. "So you're really single then? No boyfriends? Fiancés?" He took my left hand and turned it around, looking for an invisible ring.

I pulled my hand back. "No. I've more important things on my mind at the moment." I flicked my hair behind my shoulders.

"Like what? Fundraising for that daft ego-driven development project?"

I shot him a sideways look. "Yes, actually, that is one thing. But there's more than just that – in fact I've got a five-year plan."

"Oh, you have, have you?" he said, raising an eyebrow. "Now why doesn't that surprise me? Go on then, let's hear it."

I knew he was mocking me, and my five-year plan was one thing I didn't joke about.

"Why would I tell you my secrets?" I said. "You're a total stranger."

"Stranger?" he said, feigning hurt. "Sure you know more about me already than most of my closest friends do."

I smiled – he had a way about him, despite all the talk.

"Why is it that it's always easier to talk to a stranger, d'you think?" I asked. "Is it because there's no baggage there? No past?"

"Maybe," he said. "Or maybe it's because you know you're never going to see them again, so whatever you say can't be used in evidence against you in the future."

"You never know!" I said. "I could turn up at your newspaper some day to sue the pants off you for another of those libellous articles of yours."

"Ah, it'd be worth it to see you again." He gave me a cheeky smile.

I tried very hard not to smile back. "I thought you said you weren't interested?"

"That was before I got hooked by your magnetic personality, and now that I know you're available, well . . ."

I caught him looking down at my legs, and pulled the hem of my dress down to cover my knees. "Eh, you're engaged, remember?"

"So I am. I keep forgetting." He glanced back at the hotel. "Ah, I'm just kidding around." He turned back to me. "Come on, I want to hear about this five-year plan. Tell the nice stranger your innermost secrets."

"No chance. I'd probably end up reading about it next week in the gossip column on the back page of that rag you write for."

"Touché," he laughed. "Go on – our discerning readership wouldn't have the slightest interest in a lowly arts-centre director, so you're safe on that score."

Oh, what the hell, I thought. I'll never see him again anyway . . .

I turned around to face him. "All right then, I'm almost four years into the plan now and I just bought my dream house – or at least the best one I could afford given Dublin property prices these days. I've had some work done to it, but there's still a bit to do. I also now have an

MBA to my name, and I recently got the promotion in work that I wanted. So it's going well so far. In a year or so, when I've finished refurbishing the house and have replenished my savings a bit, I'd like to travel some more, maybe visit a few of the top dive locations around the world."

"So you dive then?" He seemed impressed. "Where would you go?"

"Red Sea, Great Barrier Reef, those kind of places." I started to get into the conversation, warming to one of my favourite topics. "But the trip I really can't wait to do is one I read about in a water-sports magazine last year – it's to the Norwegian fjords to see the killer whales. You wear a drysuit, mask and snorkel and then float on top of the water to watch them swim underneath."

"Killer whales, eh? Wouldn't it be dangerous getting in the water with them? They've killed people in the past, haven't they?"

"In theme parks and aquariums, yes – they can become quite dangerous in captivity. But it's not the whales' fault – they can go a bit crazy after being kept cooped up in swimming pools no bigger than bathtubs to them, away from their family pods, made to perform inane tricks for food. It's so sad." I sighed. "But there's no record of a killer whale hurting a human being in the wild."

Richie raised his eyebrows. "That's good to know, should I ever happen upon one."

"The company running the trip in Norway is fully licensed too," I went on. "They have to follow very strict regulations and safety precautions – to protect both the whales and the people going in the water with them. And anyway," I smiled, "I like a challenge – keeps life interesting."

"I bet you do." Richie smiled back at me. "It's an impressive plan, I'll grant you that, and I get the sense you'll do it all too."

"I most certainly will." I leant back on my elbows.

He took another swig of his stout, finishing it off. "Thing is," he said, interrupting my daydream of sailing through the snow-capped Norwegian fjords, "the good stuff is all a bit of a way off, isn't it? I mean, what do you do for fun nowadays?"

I sat back up straight. "I have fun. I'm bloomin' great fun, in fact."

Richie sucked his cheeks in. "I'm not sure I believe you, girl. That master plan of yours is all about work, doing up houses and saving. The interesting bit – the travel – doesn't come into play for another couple of years."

Why was everyone on my case about this lately? I sighed. Maybe they were right. I had been a bit dull of late.

Then I had an idea. I jumped up.

"What's up?" he asked.

"I'm going to prove I know how to have fun. Now give me those glasses." I took the slim gin glass I'd been holding and the empty pint glass he handed me, then turned and dropped them both down beside the nearest bush.

"*Woah!*" Richie looked shocked.

"Ah, I'm sure they're bio-degradable." I knew he thought I was dumping them but I quite liked the idea of shocking him.

I walked in my bare feet over to the edge of the lawn without a backward glance. Then I knelt down and stretched out so that I was lying flat, face-down at the top of the grassy hill.

14

"What are you doing now?" Richie shouted over. "You're going to wreck your clothes!"

"That's one of the advantages of wearing black – no grass stains." I laughed and rolled myself over until I was lying flat just on the brow of the hill. "My brothers and I used to do this all the time when we were young – it's great fun. Come on – get over here. Or are you all talk?"

Richie stayed sitting where he was. "Most definitely all talk." He looked back up at the terrace. "People are looking at us, y'know? And I'm trying to keep a low profile here today."

"That's fine, Richie!" I shouted back. "Stay there. Be boring. But don't accuse me of not knowing how to have fun!"

"You're cracked!" He got up and walked slowly over towards me.

"Yeah, maybe . . . *wheeeeeee*!" I pushed myself off the side of the hill, and I was off, quickly picking up speed. I was rolling so fast down the soft, downy grass, and laughing so much, that I could only just about make out the blurry shape of the man rolling down behind me.

"This is *craaaaaaz-y*!" Richie shouted, just before bumping into me at the bottom.

We lay there beside each other for a while. I was laughing so hard that tears were streaming down my face.

He sat up then and leant back on his hands to look at me. "All right, I'll hand it to you, Miss McQuaid – that was great *craic*."

"Thank you, Mister Blake. So I'm not so uptight then after all?" I said, wiping the tears away.

"Definitely not. It seems first impressions can be

15

deceiving. You're not one bit uptight, Miss – you're completely stark raving bonkers!"

I laughed.

He shook his head, then started to get up. "All right, that's enough fun and frolics for one day. I'd best get back to the lads, not to mention the fiancée and future in-laws – they'll be sending out a search party for me at this rate."

He held out his hand and pulled me up, and we walked slowly back up the steep hill, stopping every now and then to pick up the loose change that had escaped from his pockets.

"You go on ahead," I said as we got to the top and I sat down to strap my shoes back on. "You might just want to tidy yourself up before you present yourself to the future in-laws though." I nodded at the back of his trousers.

Richie looked over his shoulder at his rear. He grinned, then wiggled his backside from side to side as he brushed the dirt and a few loose pieces of grass away.

I shook my head and smiled.

He turned to go.

"Hey, Mister Blake, any chance you could drop those two not-so-biodegradable glasses back to the bar?"

He grinned and picked up the glasses.

"Catchya again so," he said as he strode off indoors.

Chapter 2

RICHARD

I whistled to myself as I went inside. I was surprised to find that I was actually starting to enjoy the day, considering how much I'd been dreading it. Lucy and I had only got engaged the night before, and had just told her parents about it before the fundraising lunch for the latest project of the family's charity foundation. They both seemed really thrilled at the news – Mr Mac hugged me to within an inch of my life when I told him, and Mrs Mac wasted no time asking about the wedding plans – it was all she and Lucy could talk about through lunch. It was when they started to organise the champagne after the lunch that it all started to get on top of me. I had to escape outside for a smoke and a breather.

Meeting the sultry, crazy, hill-rolling girl was just what I needed to take my mind off things. As I walked into the hotel I glanced back at Mel McQuaid who was still sitting down putting her shoes on. I smiled to myself, then carried on inside. There's more to that girl than meets the eye, I thought. With the long, poker-straight, black hair and the black dress, she looked quite severe at first, but when she loosened up a bit she was actually all right. And she did have the most amazing dark-green eyes – bright, strong and incredibly sexy – a guy could get into serious trouble looking into eyes like that. Not that she'd let him of course – I was sure she'd be a tough nut to crack, that one.

I walked in the direction of the bar, and was just leaving the empty glasses down on a table in the foyer, when I spotted one of my favourite people.

"Jangler! I mean *Father*, sorry," I said. "How are you, ol' fella?"

"Master Blake. Good to see you," he said, shaking my hand in both of his. "I'm a bit late, I'm afraid – I had a wedding to attend to first."

Aside from a few grey hairs and wrinkles, my old economics and music teacher hadn't aged much over the years. Except that since he'd retired he no longer carried the huge set of keys that got him his nickname. On the famous bunch was a key to every door of Ashvale College, the country boarding school that had been my second home for six years. If Jangler ever needed to get a boy's attention he used to lift those keys and jangle them loudly. That was just his first warning – you ignored it at your peril. Jangler was a great guy, one of the best, but he was one of the strictest teachers we had – to this day I still stop in my tracks when I hear the sound of a big set of keys jangling.

"It's great to see you too, Father. There's a big Ashvale crowd here today – we missed you at the meal."

"Yes, sorry about that, Richard. It was the Lockwood wedding – young Paul, do you remember him? He would have been a few years behind you in school."

"Of course I remember Locko. Damn good scrum-half."

"Yes, indeed," said Jangler. "He's into property now like so many of them. There was a time when our boys all wanted to go on to be solicitors and accountants, now all they want to do is buy and sell offices and apartment blocks." He sighed. "Anyway, the wedding was nearby, handily enough."

"Well, it's good to see you now, Father." I stood back to look at him. "You're looking well, it has to be said – retirement must be suiting you? And sure why wouldn't it? Living in a top lakeside location there by the borders of Dublin, Wicklow and Kildare? Sure with all of the recent improvements over the last few years, Ashvale must be more like a mountain resort these days than the tough ol' boarding school we remember it as." I slapped him gently on the shoulder. "It's a great life you lot have."

"Ho ho, now, Richard, easy there." He looked around the foyer. "I was just chatting to Jack MacDonagh a second ago, but he seems to have disappeared." He peered over his dark black-rimmed glasses at me then. "Anyway, how is life treating you?"

"Great, thanks, Father. You heard I made business-and-economics editor last year?"

"I did indeed, Richard, and I wasn't surprised – you always were one of my star economics students. I read all your newspaper reports, you know. In fact, I've been meaning to ask you about one of them – that piece you wrote last year about the whale that turned up in the River Thames. I liked it very much indeed. Not your usual economic or business report though – how did you end up writing about whales of all things?"

"Ah, that piece was just a fluke really, Father. I was

over in Westminster meeting with a guy who was giving me the lowdown on a big property deal there –"

"Anyone I might know?"

"No, no, this fellow wasn't an Ashvale lad. I don't think you'd know him. Anyway, while I was in Westminster I got a call from our news desk to say that a northern bottlenose whale had been spotted in the River Thames. And, let's face it, it's not every day you get a call like that, is it?"

Jangler shook his head. "No, indeed."

"So I got myself down there and was one of the first international journalists to arrive on the scene – even ended up getting taken on board the main rescue boat."

"That must have been wonderful," said Jangler. "They're such awe-inspiring creatures."

"They are, Father. In fact, the piece I wrote that day got picked up around the world, which made my editor happy – and when Edith's happy, I'm happy."

"I'm not surprised she was happy. It was a very touching piece – especially when you described the impact on the rescue team when the whale eventually died. Very moving, and very well written. Your mother must have enjoyed it?"

"No idea, Father. I try to avoid her as much as possible these days!" I laughed, but Jangler didn't.

"That's a pity, Richard. I'm sure she'd like to see more of you."

"Wouldn't bank on it, Father – she's not my greatest fan. I see her once a year at Christmas and that seems to be more than enough for both of us." I looked behind Jangler to see if Mr Mac had reappeared or if any of the other lads were nearby to provide a distraction.

No joy.

"I see," said Jangler. "She doesn't get home from London so much any more, does she? She's quite settled there in Richmond now."

Originally from Wicklow, my parents moved to London in the seventies when my father bought a small site for his construction business there. At the time I was seven and Ed was six. He did well and in time his business grew, so we moved from our rented flat into a house in Richmond in the leafy suburbs of London. It was a big step up for us, and I'll never forget the excitement of the move. My mother was ecstatic about the new house – she still lives there to this day. But as my father's business went from strength to strength, my parents' relationship started to crumble. He spent more and more time at work, coming home late or drunk, often both. And it was then that the arguments would start – they'd scream at each other for hours on end, followed by even longer periods of silence.

The one thing that my parents did seem to come together and agree on at the time was our education. They both wanted Ed and me to go back to Ireland to my father's old secondary school. I loved Ashvale from day one. It quickly became a home away from home – a welcome retreat from the tense atmosphere that clouded over my parents' house. I felt a bit bad at first leaving Ed behind on his own with my parents, but he joined me at Ashvale a year later and, aside from his brief period of travelling, we've both lived in Ireland ever since.

I really didn't want to get into a discussion about my family with Jangler, but he wouldn't let up.

"And we haven't seen your father at the annual

reunion in many years," he was saying. "Is everything all right with him?"

I started to feel uneasy with the line the conversation was starting to take; whatever about my mother, there was no way I was going to get into a discussion about my bloody father. I'd barely seen or spoken to him since he left my mother over twenty-two years earlier.

"I don't know. I haven't seen him in years myself – we're not in touch at all." Seeing Jangler's raised eyebrow, I threw in: "Ed sees him the odd time though. I believe he's still living over in Windsor with Louisa and the twins. But you know all this, Father – nothing much changes with my parents."

"No, indeed," said Jangler, pushing his glasses up further on his nose. "Anyway, I believe congratulations are in order? Ben MacDonagh's sister no less?"

I'd somehow managed to avoid meeting Jangler since Lucy and I bumped into each other again for the first time in years at my twentieth Ashvale reunion the previous year. She wasn't long back in Ireland from New York, and she'd come along with her father on the night to thank Ben's old school friends for our past support of Ben's charity foundation. Living in New York over the years had clearly suited Lucy MacDonagh – she'd lost the braces and the puppy fat and had turned into an absolute stunner. I asked her out that night and we'd been seeing each other ever since, give or take a few breaks. Of course, my brother and a few of the lads told me I was mad to start going out with Lucy, with her connection to Ben and all of the history there. But I assured them there was nothing to worry about, and they came around in the end.

"Yes, Father. You've heard right. I expect we'll be calling on your services soon."

"I see. Well, congratulations to both of you."

Here it comes – no doubt I'll get the whole marriage-preparation speech now.

But instead Jangler looked quite solemn, then caught me unawares by what he said next. "Poor Ben, may God rest his soul. He would have enjoyed this day out – especially with all of the Ashvale crowd back together for it."

"Eh, yes, I'm sure he would have, Father," I said.

"It was such a terrible, terrible shame. I wish I could have done something for him that day." Jangler shook his head slowly. "Too many of our young people taking their own lives – it's such a sad waste." He looked directly at me then. "You must find it a comfort being so close with Lucy and the MacDonaghs after all this time, Richard. He was your best friend after all, and you took his death very hard at the time. Does being around his family again now somehow help you to deal with his suicide all these years on?"

I stared at Jangler. Ben had died over twenty years ago – why couldn't he just leave it be? Why did he have to bring it all up again, and today of all days? Why was it that everyone wanted to talk about something that happened so long ago? When we'd started going out last year, Lucy kept wanting to talk about Ben as well – asking me questions like how did I feel about his death? Or how did I deal with life after the funeral? She'd regularly ask me if I had any theories about why Ben had done it, or about what we might have done differently to stop him. But I didn't want to go there and, after she'd pushed me one too many times, I made it clear that I wouldn't ever be discussing the topic with her. I knew she was hurt, and we even broke up over it all for a while, but she let it go eventually and we got back together.

And now I had to deal with Jangler's questions, on a day when all I wanted to do was kick back and enjoy a few pints with the lads.

I looked right at Jangler. "That was over twenty years ago, Father – and you were really great about it at the time. I don't know how I'd have got through it without you, but I'm absolutely fine now."

"Yes, it was a long time ago. Only . . . I'm just wondering . . . why Ben's sister?"

"Sorry?"

"Why, of all the women in the world, Richard, would you choose to date Lucy MacDonagh? Let alone marry into the family?"

"Eh, have you seen her lately, Father? She's an absolute knockout!" I laughed.

Jangler frowned.

"*Richie Blake*! There you are, ya bollix!" A big hand rubbed my head roughly from behind.

I swung around. It was my good mate Jonesy. He'd been sitting at another table throughout lunch and I hadn't had a proper chance to catch up with him yet. I was never so glad to see the big lug.

"Where the hell did you disappear to after the rugby last weekend?" Jonesy asked. "And what's all this shite I'm hearing about you getting engaged? Is it true?"

"A bit of respect, Jonesy." I nodded at Jangler.

"Sorry, excuse me, Father." Jonesy looked suitably contrite.

"Don't mind me, Peter. I've long since given up trying

to put manners on you lot." Jangler held his hand out to shake Jonesy's.

"Good to see you again, Father." Jonesy pumped Jangler's hand, shaking the old fella's entire body in the process.

"And you, Peter." Jangler straightened his glasses with his index finger and thumb. "I'll leave you two to catch up." He put a hand on my arm as he went to leave. "Try to see a bit more of the parents, Richard, if you can. They do their best, you know."

"Eh, right, Father." I looked after him for a second.

"Seriously, man, where did you get to after the match?" Jonesy asked once Jangler was out of earshot. "I thought we were going to grab a kebab, but you disappeared from the pub without a trace."

"Sorry, man, I was absolutely wasted," I said, keen to move on from the topic of Saturday night. "Any sign of Dec? I've been trying to catch him to talk to him about that oversized property portfolio of his. He needs to start selling some of it off – the signals are all there for a shock in the market soon."

"He's around somewhere," said Jonesy. "But hey, can't believe you got engaged, man – what happened there?"

"Took your advice in the end," I said. "Just decided to bite the bullet."

Jonesy patted me on the back. "Good on ya, Rich – I never thought I'd see the day."

"Yeah, well, life catches up with the best of us." I turned to walk over towards the bar.

Jonesy followed. "So Saturday night – what happened to you? We were all wasted. Come on – spill! Did you cave in and head over to Lucy's in the end?"

I gestured to the barman. "Two pints of stout, please." I turned back to Jonesy. "Nah, I told you then – Lucy was in a strop all last weekend. She'd been banging on for weeks about moving our relationship on – gave me grief about it again on Saturday morning before the match. No way was I going back for more of that."

"So where did you go then, if not to Lucy's?"

I looked around to make sure nobody was about, but it was just me and Jonesy by the bar at that stage. So I turned back towards the counter, lowered my voice and spoke out of the side of my mouth. "All right, if you really have to know. I ended up with Sonya. Don't remember much about it – it was all a stupid mistake. Just wish I could forget it ever happened."

"What the f–? *Sonya*? Your brother's *girlfriend* Sonya?"

"Keep it down, will ya, Jonesy? Ed's here. He'd kill me if he found out."

"No shit! What the hell were you doing with feckin' *Sonya* of all people? We don't even like her – I mean, she's smokin' hot 'n' all, but you're always saying what a cow she is to your brother. What were you playing at, Rich?"

"It wasn't intentional, believe me," I said. "She came on to me, then dragged me out the back of the pub. I was completely wasted, remember? Didn't stand a chance."

Jonesy raised his eyebrows. "Back of the pub? Classy."

"Yeah, well, it happened, man. I'm not particularly proud of myself, but it was all over before it began, and she hasn't mentioned anything to anyone since, so hopefully that will just be that. A stupid mistake, never to be repeated."

26

The barman put one pint of stout down in front of Jonesy, and went to finish off the other.

"I don't get you, Rich." Jonesy shook his head slowly. "Why would you want to mess a great girl like Lucy around? If you get a move on, you could have your own sons starting at Ashvale someday – best thing I ever did was marrying Karen and having Petey Junior."

"Yeah, yeah – I've done it, haven't I? I felt so damned guilty about messing around on Lucy that I went and spent a fortune on a ring, then proposed last night." I grabbed Jonesy's pint and took a very welcome mouthful of cold stout.

"*Oi!*" he said.

"Snooze, you lose," I smiled and wiped the froth from my upper lip.

The barman placed the second pint in front of Jonesy.

"You know your problem, Rich?" said Jonesy. "You're stuck in the past, man. You still want to be the big man about town, playing the field, screwing all those beautiful women."

"Nah, that's not it –" I tried to interrupt.

"Just settle down, man. Enjoy where you are with Lucy – stop resisting it. You're not getting any younger. We're pushing forty now, remember?"

"Get lost. We're still only thirty-eight." I sighed. "Ah, maybe you're right."

"Right about what?"

I swung around to see Ed behind me. I shot Jonesy a warning look.

He got it.

"I'm just congratulating your big brother here on his engagement, telling him it's the best decision he'll ever make," said Jonesy, slapping me on the back.

Ed looked unconvinced. "You disappeared pretty sharpish after the meal, Rich – Lucy was wondering where you'd got to."

I rolled my eyes. "What's new?"

"Getting the jitters already?" Ed asked. "How long you been engaged now, bro? Five minutes, is it? Or ten?"

My brother was irritating me even more than usual of late. He'd been a thorn in my side since he'd jacked in his solicitor's job to go off travelling just over two years earlier. As soon as he got back he'd started studying to be a teacher and with no income he'd been scrounging a rent-free room in my house ever since. All right, so shagging his girlfriend was probably going a little far – I wasn't proud of myself on that score – but it didn't mean I could let him away with being an annoying git.

"Get lost, Ed. I'm very happy with my decision as it happens," I swirled the foamy liquid around the pint glass, "and I can't wait to settle down."

"Well, I'll believe that when I see it," Ed said. "My brother? Make an honest woman out of someone?" He laughed. "That'll be the day. Soon enough I'm sure you'll mess things up with Lucy, the way you've done with every other woman you've ever gone out with."

"Laugh all you want, man," I said. "I'd do it, if only just to get you out of my house."

Ed smiled. "You moving a wife in wouldn't bother me one bit, Rich. I'd be quite happy living with Lucy as my sister-in-law." He looked around. "In fact, she couldn't be any worse to be around than my own girlfriend at the moment. There's no pleasing Sonya these days. She's been drinking for Ireland since we arrived, she's half-trashed already and has been in a right mood all day. I

28

can't seem to do anything right."

Jonesy flashed me a knowing look, but I was careful not to react.

"Ah, there's Dec now." I'd spotted him walking across the foyer. I threw a tenner on the bar, grabbed my pint, and escaped out of the bar.

As I walked towards Dec I realised one of the people in the group talking to him was Mel McQuaid. She of hill-rolling fame was standing on the outskirts of the group. She looked up and smiled at me as I approached.

I smiled back and had started to walk a little quicker towards them when a voice suddenly shrieked out across the foyer:

"Well, would you look at who it is? Big Brother himself!"

I didn't have to look around. I knew the voice well.

Sonya.

Shite!

I glanced over at Mel who was staring behind me at Sonya. She looked back at me, then caught my eye for a second, before quickly looking away.

I stopped dead in my tracks. Sonya caught up and stood straight in front of me. Her face was bright red, and so were her eyes – she looked like she'd been crying. And Ed was right: she'd obviously been drinking – the girl was actually swaying.

"So does Lucy know you were out rolling around in the grass with some trollop earlier?" she shouted.

I looked over at Mel to see if she'd heard.

She'd heard all right – her eyes were out on sticks. She looked mortified.

"I wondered how long it would take you to start messing around again, Richard," Sonya said.

"Cool it, Sonya. This is not the place." I took her arm, but she shook me off.

"Sonya, what's going on?"

I swung around to see Ed standing beside me.

"Will you please tell me what in God's name is the matter with you today?" he asked her.

"Ed, man, don't worry about it – go on back to the bar," I said. "Everything's fine."

"Oh, *everything's fine*, is it?" Sonya said, her voice shaking. "I was very surprised to hear the news about your engagement today, Richard." She straightened up to her full height. She glanced quickly at Ed then, before looking back at me. "Especially considering you were screwing *me* last week."

I closed my eyes. When I opened them I glanced over at Mel again – she, along with just about everybody else in the foyer was standing rooted to the spot, staring at us.

Ed stepped forward and shook Sonya by the arm. "What is *wrong* with you, Sonya? Why would you say something like that?"

She pushed him off. "Uh, I don't know . . . *maybe because it's true*?"

Ed let go of Sonya, stepped back, and turned to look straight at me. That one look made me feel like a complete nothing.

"I-is it true, Rich?" he asked.

"No. Well, look, Ed, I was going to tell you. It was just the once. I was hammered drunk and she –"

"Stop!" Ed held up his hand. "Just stop talking!"

Sonya started up again. "Oh, come on, Ed. You can't pretend to actually be surprised. It's not like you give a damn. You're not interested in me, not really. I've had an excruciating year and a half listening to you wittering on about the meaning of life and all that other crap that you read. You're just *so* bloody boring. Richard, on the other hand – your brother here – he knows exactly what a woman wants."

She moved towards me again.

"Just face it, Richard – it was always going to happen between you and me." She looked completely desperate. "It was just a matter of time really."

Ed slumped back, his face completely drained of colour.

I felt like murdering bloody Sonya.

She latched herself tightly on to me then. "He knows about us now, Richard," she said, staring wide-eyed up at me. "We can tell Lucy now too – end this stupid engagement charade and be together properly." She went to try to kiss me.

I pushed her off, but held her at arm's length. "Let's get this straight once and for all, you misguided cow. You and I were never meant to be together. Nor will we *ever* be together again. It was a mistake. A once-off, stupid, drunken mistake. In fact, *fucking you was probably the biggest mistake of my life!*"

There was a sudden loud smash behind me.

I spun around.

Lucy was standing frozen to the spot a few metres from me, arms outstretched, hands empty. Two broken glasses lay shattered over the marble tiles at her feet; her pale grey dress was splattered with dark wet patches. At her side, her father stood holding a champagne bottle, his mouth wide open.

"Lucy! Mr Mac!" I moved towards them. "It's not what you think. I can explain."

31

I never would have expected what happened next.

Before I could get over to Lucy, my younger, smaller brother pulled me back roughly from behind. Then with ears red and eyes wide and wild, he pinned me by the shoulder, drew back his arm and hit me full force in the face.

Then everything went dark.

Chapter 3

MELANIE

I put the phone down and dropped my head into my hands. I just wanted to cry.

He'd pulled out – the new sponsorship manager I'd been working for months to find had decided to accept the raise and promotion offered by his current employers. Damn it!

I was already in mourning for the slick, successful salesman I'd set my heart on to take over my old role.

I stared at the phone in my office in despair. I couldn't spend another eight months covering the position on top of my current role – I was up to my eyes as it was. And Marcus was already on the warpath about the new-season programme sales – he was going to freak when he heard about this.

I closed my eyes and rubbed my temples for a minute – to no effect. The throbbing headache was still there when I opened my eyes again.

Drat, drat, drat! That guy was the only decent stand-out candidate we had. God only knows how we were going to find someone now. Damn these boom times – it never used to be so difficult to find good people.

I'd just reluctantly picked the phone back up to call Marcus to tell him the news when my assistant Grace popped her head around the door.

"Sorry to interrupt, Melanie – just dropping in the camera for those dance shots you wanted to take. The rehearsal starts at three and the company's manager confirmed they're happy to be photographed." She placed the camera on my desk.

I put the receiver back down. "Okay, thanks, Grace." I took the camera out of its case to look it over.

I knew I probably should really have hired a professional photographer for the job, or at least delegated the photography for the Dance Festival sponsorship proposal to one of my team, but I loved taking photographs and it was so rare for me to be able to find the time to get along to a performance or rehearsal these days that I seized on the opportunity.

"I must get one of these cameras myself someday – they take such great pictures," I said, turning over the top-of-the-range SLR. "I tell you, Grace – between the proposal we're putting together and the addition of the few killer dance shots this baby is going to take for me, those potential sponsors will not be able to say no."

"You said it, boss!" Grace said as she shut the door behind her.

I sighed, then reluctantly put the camera back in its case, picked the phone up and dialled Marcus.

I could have sat there and listened to Prokofiev's dramatic *Romeo and Juliet* all day. I got some great shots of the

Nua Dance Company's two lead contemporary-ballet dancers at the beginning of the dress rehearsal, but soon became so engrossed in the elegance of the performance that I forgot about the camera altogether. It was such a relief not to be rushing around, or getting an ear-bashing from Marcus, that I just sat back in my seat in the middle of the empty auditorium and allowed the music and the haunting performance to wash over me. The director and technical crew were busy taking notes, fixing lights and adjusting sound equipment around me, but I barely noticed. I was completely lost in the make-believe world of true love and innocence. The contemporary set and costumes made it seem all the more real and the whole experience was like a luxurious massage for the soul.

In fact, I didn't remember my mission again until Juliet had taken the poison and Romeo was cradling her desperately in his arms. Real tears streamed down the dancer's face as the music of the company's small but excellent orchestra built towards a dramatic climax. I wiped away my own stray tears, then took a couple of beautiful shots of the closing sequence before slipping quietly out of the hall.

As I walked to the office I thought back to when I first joined The Mill five years ago. I went along to as many concerts and shows as I could squeeze into back in those days – and I loved every single one of them. They were such a welcome retreat from my home life at the time.

Ian had always hated the idea of me leaving my marketing-manager job at the insurance firm where we had both worked. He could never understand how I could be happy to take a pay cut to work at an arts centre. When I told him I was applying for the job at The Mill he even threatened to finish with me. I did it anyway and he didn't follow through on his threat – of course, in time I realised that that may not have been such a good thing. At the time I was happy I'd stuck up for myself though – it was one of the few shows of strength I made against Ian during our three-year relationship – until the end. I should have had the courage to finish with him years earlier, of course – should never have let it go so far.

I sighed, and pushed open the door of my office.

After Ian and I broke up I threw myself into my work, and I attended countless beautiful productions at The Mill. But I didn't get to steal into as many performances as the pressure in work built up and I had to spend most evenings and weekends studying for the MBA.

Oh well, no time for all that at the moment, I thought. I'm sure things will calm down soon enough.

I sat down at my computer and uploaded the photographs, sorting through them to edit the best for use, eventually finishing off the dance-festival proposal just before seven o'clock. I was just proof-reading it when my office door swung wide open.

Marcus.

What few strands of hair he still possessed were dangling carelessly down from the left side of his head, his glasses perched on top of his now fully exposed bald crown.

I sat bolt upright.

"Melanie, you're still here. Good." He let the door slam behind him.

I rummaged around in my in-tray, and pulled out the new sales report. "I know what you're about to ask, Marcus, and, just to put your mind at ease, sales of the new season have picked up this week. We also have a couple of great promotions about to go live which I think will make quite an impact."

Marcus held up his hand and came right over to my desk to stand over me. "That's good to hear, Melanie. I was actually quite concerned in that regard. But I'm not here to discuss the sales figures." He threw a couple of stapled pages on my desk. "I've sorted our sponsorship manager problem." He nodded at the document.

"What? Already? Our preferred candidate only pulled out this morning. How?" I picked up the document – a curriculum vitae.

"No need to look through it," Marcus said. "I've gone over it in detail myself and she's perfect – exactly what we need. *And . . .*" his eyes widened as he took a dramatic pause, "she's Fenella's niece."

Oh dear God, no! I thought, in a panic.

Fenella Wright was my other main source of stress at The Mill – she seemed to enjoy making our lives difficult. It was especially irritating because my boss was nauseatingly deferential to his darling chairwoman, and the whole Fenella-Marcus routine was difficult to stomach at the best of times. Fenella had been furious about Richard Blake's article a few weeks' earlier. It had laid bare her dramatic rise through the social ranks. Just a few years older than me, before becoming the second wife of the much older, ludicrously wealthy William Wright, Fenella had been a relatively unknown actress. Her career hadn't exactly been dazzling, and in the early years she'd even appeared in some rather dubious art-house movies. Since her marriage, though, Fenella had finally managed to get the leading-lady roles she so desired: those of glamorous socialite and trophy wife.

Marcus smiled at me – the uncharacteristic good humour was unnerving in so many ways. "Wonderful, isn't it?" he went on. "I was just speaking with Fenella this afternoon and I mentioned that your candidate had pulled out."

My candidate? Marcus was on the interview panel too. Why was it always my problem when things went wrong?

"And Fenella once again saved the day by emailing me on her niece's details," Marcus was saying. "As luck would have it, young Shirley is ideal, and is free to start straight away. No need to waste any more time on recruiting and interview panels – we'll bring her in for a few months on trial and, if she works out, offer her the job altogether."

Oh.

My.

God.

I looked back down, and glanced through the CV which was riddled with spelling mistakes – my pet hate. Normally that alone would be enough for me to file it under 'B' for bin, but in the circumstances I read on, picking out the salient details: Shirley Delamere . . . lives Foxrock . . . two years out of college . . . Interior Design Certificate . . . part-time work during college as a model, including appearance on fashion segment of *Good Morning, Ireland* breakfast show . . . most recent role: four months in an estate agent's . . .

Prior to that, and I quote: **"Carrear brake to travel around the world, and Austrailia."**

Please, please, let this be a joke!

I closed my eyes, praying to see the hidden cameras when I reopened them, but no such luck. I took a deep breath, then looked up at my boss.

"I really don't think she's right for the role, Marcus. I mean, I know we've been trying to recruit for months now, but we still have a number of other avenues to explore. We haven't tried to headhunt yet, and there are a number of other recruitment agencies I'd like to contact now. This is a very important position in the team, a pivotal role. I really need someone experienced and talented who can hit the ground running."

Marcus snatched the CV out of my hands. "What are you talking about? She's ideal!" He flicked his hand at the page. "Look at this – '*direction of property sales team, responsible for new housing-estate promotions*'."

More like directing tea-making, and responsible for new biscuit selection.

Marcus went on: "You keep telling me you want someone with direct sales and promotions experience, Melanie! Well," he waved the CV in my face, "here she is!"

I stood up and took a few steps back from him. "That girl has less than five months' experience in an estate agent's office, Marcus – it hardly makes her Saleswoman of the Year. It's not even an estate agent I've ever heard of before, and she wasn't the one selling – from the looks of things she was a temp who set up a few showings." I held my hand out for the CV to show him what I meant, but Marcus held onto it and pulled his arm back, that familiar look of steel in his eyes. I put my arm down. "Marcus, this is crazy. We can't recruit someone just because she's related to our chairwoman."

But I'd overestimated my boss's sense of reason. He just glared through me for a minute before slowly putting his hand through his few long strands of greasy hair and pushing them back over the top of his scalp, patting them down into place behind his right ear. Then he calmly placed the CV back on my desk, and turned for the door.

He stood in the open doorway and, still with his back to me, said, "I told Fenella that we will bring Shirley in on trial for a few months, and that you will train her up to management level. Make it happen, please." He strode out the door, allowing it to slam shut behind him again.

I flopped back in my seat and picked up the damned CV.

Make it happen . . . make it happen, you say . . . I glared at the door.

All I really felt like doing right then was shoving the wretched CV down his scrawny, nepotistic throat.

I turned back around to my desk. Oh, sod it anyway, I thought. I'd had enough. All I ever got landed with was problems. It was all work, work, work – and I was tired of it. That journalist Richie Blake from last weekend had been right – I needed more fun in my life.

I sat back and smiled as I remembered the roll down the hill with Richie that afternoon. It really was good fun, and I'd surprised myself by quite enjoying the day in the end. Richie's altercation in the foyer had added an element of drama I hadn't expected – enough to reassure me that I was doing the right thing keeping my life simple, staying away from guys like that and staying single – for now at least.

But all that aside, the banter and the roll down the hill with Richie was the most fun I'd had in ages. I dreaded to think how long. And I'd missed fun – until the last weekend I hadn't realised how much.

I threw the CV down on the desk and picked up my phone.

It had been a while, but I knew exactly who to call.

Chapter 4

MELANIE

"Oh my God, that was divine," said Orla, finishing off her first fruity cocktail of the evening. "Let's have another."

I nodded. "Count me in. It is Friday after all."

I was enjoying the buzz of the busy hotel bar and already feeling re-energised by the good company and tasty cocktails after a stressful week in work. And it was so great to see Orla again. I might have all but retired from the Dublin night-scene, but my old diving buddy was still a regular – Orla always knew exactly where to go, and how to have a good time. I couldn't think of anyone better to have a fun night out with.

"Niamh is coming too," said Orla. "She should be here in a minute – I'd better order her one." She tried to catch the waiter's attention.

"Oh right. I haven't seen Niamh in years," I said, with as much enthusiasm as I could manage.

Niamh Delaney and I used to be in the same tennis club in Greystones in Wicklow where we both grew up.

We had a friendly rivalry – *kinda*. Niamh and I were both pretty good at tennis and always seemed to end up facing off against each other in the various tournaments at the club. I didn't like losing to anyone really, but I absolutely hated losing to Niamh. She and Orla had been in college together, so Niamh and I usually managed to put our on-court rivalry aside on nights out with Orla – just about.

"Is she still playing tennis?"

"You can ask her yourself," Orla said, nodding over at the door. "*Cooo-eee! Over here!*" she shouted to Niamh just as a very cute waiter arrived to take our drink order. Orla turned back to him. "Can you give us a minute, please?" She flashed him a big smile.

"Sure thing," he said, giving her a quick wink before going off to collect some glasses from the next table.

Orla had a way with men. I'm not sure if it was her long, wild, curly blonde tresses and voluptuous good looks the men loved, or whether it was the way she so openly flirted with everyone she met. Whatever it was anyway, she always had guys eating out of her hand. In fact, Orla and Niamh were a great double act. Orla would reel the poor unsuspecting men in, and Niamh, a petite brunette, would keep them hanging on her every word.

Niamh sat down and took her coat off. "Melanie McQuaid! You're still alive! I was beginning to think you'd emigrated. I haven't seen you down the club in years now." She laughed. "Not that I'm complaining, of course – I've been Club Champion for four years in a row."

I did my best to stay smiling. I would have loved nothing better than to have made it to Club Champion. I just never quite got there before I quit tennis.

42

"Good to see you, Niamh," I said. "Ah sure, I haven't really had time for tennis for ages now. I bought a new house in town earlier this year, so I don't get down to Greystones as much any more."

It wasn't really the reason I'd given up tennis. I was up and down to Greystones to visit my folks all the time, and I'd been living in an apartment in Dublin for years before I bought the new house. Becoming Club Champion wasn't part of my five-year plan though, so tennis just had to give.

"So what's it to be, ladies?" the cute waiter interrupted.

"Well, hello again. My friends and I would like more sex on the beach, please," Orla said with a wicked grin.

"Right you be, ladies," he said. "I'll look after that for you straight away. And what would you like to drink?"

Orla and Niamh shrieked with laughter. The waiter winked at me this time, then started to collect our empty glasses.

Oh God, I'm so out of practice with all this, I thought.

"Cheeky beggar!" Orla watched him walk away before turning back to me. "It was so brilliant to get your call, Mel – we never see you anymore. If it wasn't for the odd email or text message over the years, we'd have thought you were dead – or worse, married! What have you been up to?"

I started to fill the girls in on my new house and some of the things going on in work. They listened attentively – or so I thought – until I'd almost brought them up to date. "So we're in the final stages of recruiting for a new sponsorship manager to take over my old job that's been vacant since I was promoted. It hasn't been easy – there's not so many good people to choose from –"

Niamh held up her hand, interrupting me mid-flow: "Stop! Stop right there. I can't listen to any more of this." She glanced over at Orla, who just looked down into her glass. Niamh turned back to me. "Mel, it's Friday night, forget about all that – how's the love life, girl? Any men on the scene? Please tell me you're not still with whatshisname?"

"Who? Ian? God no, we split up almost four years ago now," I said, staring down the straw into my drink.

"And good riddance," said Orla. "I never did like that guy. I mean, he was charm personified in the beginning – he wouldn't give up until you went out with him. But he was so boring underneath it all, and he hated you coming out with us. Not that we saw you much after you two got together. In fact, first it was the man, then it was the MBA, wasn't it?" She laughed. "We've been ditched more than once by you, Mel."

"Yes, we have," said Niamh. "But hey, we're not proud – we're always happy to welcome back the prodigal. Once you're not planning a return to the tennis courts, that is." She laughed.

I smiled. "No, I've no plans to go back to tennis at the moment. And I'm sorry I haven't been in touch in so long, ladies, but I'm back now, and I'm ready to party!"

"Good for you, Mel," said Orla. "We'll have to find three nice, eligible men to help us have fun. I haven't been near a man in weeks!"

"Weeks?" I smiled. "Try years!"

Niamh looked shocked. "Sounds like we definitely need to get out there tonight so, girls!"

"To be honest, I'm not really all that interested in men at the moment," I said. "I've enough complications in life right now – between all the hassle at work, family commitments and the new house. I just want a fun night out with you girls tonight – keepin' it simple."

"*Pfff!*" Niamh said. "We'll see about that, eh, Orla?"

"Absolutely!" said Orla. "The night is young, and the unsuspecting men of Dublin await. After all, Mel, what better way to get your mojo back than by chatting up a few nice fellas?"

"Oh yes. Come on, Mel, it'll be fun," said Niamh. "Just like the old days."

"No way – I'm completely out of practice. Any of the flings I've had over the last few years have been disastrous. I don't think I'd even know *how* to chat anyone up any more."

"Ah, sure, all you have to do is show you're interested in a guy – hold his gaze a little longer than normal, and smile a lot." Orla did the actions as she spoke. "Then when you have his attention just approach him and ask him something about himself. Act like everything he says is interesting, and that you agree with him about all things."

I frowned. "Hmm . . . I think I'm beginning to see where I'm going wrong."

Orla and Niamh laughed as I began to wonder what I'd let myself in for.

I enjoyed catching up with the girls and hearing about their recent holiday to Thailand over dinner at a nearby Italian restaurant. Orla had invited me along on a few of their trips over recent years, but I was always too busy with work, studying, helping my folks with their dog kennels business in Greystones, or going along to one of numerous family events. With three sisters, two brothers, one brother-in-law, one sister-in-law, my little sister's on-off boyfriend, and at last count, eight nieces and nephews – soon to be nine when my sister-in-law had her second baby, there was nearly always a McQuaid family birthday, christening or other family event to attend.

By the time we got to the late-night bar after dinner, it was heaving. There was a long queue of people waiting to get in, and the usual crowd of smokers and socialites milled about out front. I went to stand at the end of the queue, but Niamh just gave me a look of disdain, and marched on past me, followed by Orla who beckoned to me to follow. I scurried along behind them. The girls took off their jackets, held their heads high and walked straight up to the door.

"Evening, ladies," said the bouncer as he undid the rope across the entrance. "You're looking well tonight." He looked us up and down as we passed by. "Have a good night."

"How did you manage that?" I asked Orla.

Niamh gave Orla a knowing smile.

"Regulars never have to queue," Orla said to me.

"Usual spot?" Niamh asked Orla once inside.

"Absolutely," said Orla.

I could only just about hear them over the throbbing sound of eighties music that was reverberating through the Greek and Roman themed bar. It was all fake gold statues and tall marble pillars – everything was overstated and large.

We followed Niamh who strode off in the direction of the bar, pushing her way confidently through the hordes of Friday-night revellers. I noticed several men check the girls out as we passed and a couple of them tried to strike up a conversation, but Orla and Niamh just said a word or two in reply to each and walked on.

We got to the end of the bar and stopped by a tall pillar, watched over by a large gold statue of a naked Adonis.

"Jackets, ladies?" said Orla, holding her hand out.

I duly handed her my black cotton jacket, and Niamh passed on her red trench coat. Orla stuffed them between Adonis's legs. "Look after them, babe," she said, patting his golden bottom, before turning back to us. "All right, girls, what's it to be?"

She went off to the bar, while Niamh and I kept Adonis company. I felt a little naked myself in my black strappy summer dress. It was the first time I'd taken my jacket off all night, and my dress was a little more revealing than I was used to. I pulled up the bodice a bit, then stood holding my arms tightly around my chest.

"Will you relax, Mel? You'll put the men off," Niamh laughed.

"Sorry, sorry," I said, putting my arms down and trying to loosen up a bit.

I watched as an Italian guy came over to chat to Niamh. I stood on the outskirts of the conversation as they chatted and flirted effortlessly. I wasn't even in the game.

Thankfully Orla arrived back with our drinks before too long. She poured my tonic mixer into my gin and handed it to me: "All right, Mel, get that into you. Then your mission for this evening is to get out there and get chatting someone up!"

"Oh no – I couldn't, Orla." All I wanted to do was to curl up and hide between Adonis's legs under the coats.

"Shall I show you how it's done?" Niamh draped herself all over the Italian guy who grinned inanely back at her.

"No, thank you!" I couldn't bear to let Niamh beat me at everything. She might have been Club Champion, but that didn't mean she could beat me at this game.

I took a deep breath.

"Oh, all right then, I'll do it."

"Go, Mel!" said Orla.

I smiled and stood up straighter. After all, if Niamh Delaney could do it, so could I. I'd chatted men up before – I used to do it all the time.

I flicked my hair over my shoulders and looked around for a target to better Niamh's skinny Italian. I spotted an interesting-looking guy standing near the bar. He was tall and broad, dressed all in black, with dark stubble on his chin that made him look quite rugged and very sexy.

Perfect.

"Right, here goes nothing." I took a deep breath. "See that guy over there? The one dressed all in black? Prepare to lose to the better woman, Miss Delaney."

"Huh?" said Niamh.

"Good luck!" Orla called after me.

"*Ciao, bella*," said the skinny Italian.

I started to walk over to the bar and was just thinking of something interesting and flirtatious to say, when someone bumped into me from behind. The collision caused me to spill most of my gin and tonic down the front of my dress.

"Mel?"

I turned around, and there, with faded black eye and dishevelled hair, stood Richie Blake. The last time I'd seen him was two weeks earlier as he was being carried off in an ambulance.

"Fancy meeting you here? You look great." He grinned at me. "Sorry for bumping into you there." He noticed my dress then. "Crap, did I make you spill your drink?" He proceeded to dab my front dry with his shirt sleeve.

"It's all right, Richie, don't worry." I pushed his hand away just in time to see the sexy stranger grab his drink and move along the bar.

I sighed. "Probably just as well."

"What's that?" asked Richie.

"Oh, nothing." I looked back at the girls.

Niamh was laughing, Orla just looked disappointed.

I glanced back at Richie. The girls didn't know I'd met him a couple of weeks earlier . . . Maybe I could make it look to them as though I was chatting him up? I just couldn't let Niamh think she'd won this round. I'd never hear the end of it.

I flashed Richie a wide smile. "So how have you been keeping, Mister Blake?"

"Ah, I've had a rough couple of weeks, Miss McQuaid, as you can imagine," he said, rubbing the back of his head.

And indeed he did look rough. He wasn't quite drunk yet, but it was pretty clear that he was well on his way.

We moved up to the bar and he took a long swig of his pint before plonking the near-empty glass down on the counter beside me.

I leaned in to look closer at his eye. "Looks quite sore still?" I did feel a little sorry for him – he'd taken a nasty blow that day.

He nodded, squinting to accentuate his pain and I momentarily forgot about my plan.

"I'm sorry about what happened to you, Richie, but, if you don't mind my saying, it sounded like you deserved it."

"What?" He looked hurt for a second, then he just nodded his head slowly in resignation. "Ah, maybe you're right, Mel. I'm sorry you had to see all that. Not my finest hour." He gave me a weak smile. "But hey, guess what? The good news is – I'm single now. No more wedding planning to avoid, no fiancées or in-laws to keep happy."

I glanced over at the girls – they were still looking over with interest.

Oh well, if he's single . . . It can't hurt to flirt a little.

I smiled at him. "That's great, Richie – that was what you wanted all along, wasn't it?"

"Yeah, I suppose it was – to some degree anyway," he said, picking up his pint from the counter and finishing it off in one gulp.

"Would you like another drink?" I smiled up at him through my eyelashes and leaned both elbows back against the bar, pushing my chest out.

Richie looked me up and down slowly, seeming confused. "Eh . . . no, it's all right," he said eventually. "I'll get them in. What's it to be?"

I sighed. "Forget about the drink, Richie." I stood back up straight. "I need to ask you a favour. See those two girls over there?" I rolled my eyes discreetly in Orla and Niamh's direction. "I need to convince them I'm back in the game. Y'know? I need to look like I'm chatting you up here. All *interested in you* like."

He laughed. "Ah sure, we both know you're interested in me, Mel." He patted his chest with his hand. "Come on, admit it, you can't get enough of the ol' Blakester."

"Mmm," I said, taking a step back.

He looked a bit more serious. "Wait a minute – you're not joking, are you? You actually *were* trying to pick me up to impress your friends?"

I felt like a bit of an idiot then. "No, not *pick* you up exactly . . . just chat you up a bit."

But the more I spoke, the more stupid and embarrassing the whole thing sounded.

"Oh just forget about it, Richie – stupid idea." I turned around to look for an escape route.

"No, no, no," he said, taking my arm to turn me back. "Let's not forget about it actually. The thing is – I don't mind being used and abused so that you can appear to be whoever it is your friends want you to be. To be honest, it's probably about what I deserve right now." He looked straight at me. "I just wonder, Mel . . . why is it you're always trying to be something you're not?"

"What?" I stared at him. "What are you talking about?"

"When we met at that lunch a few weeks ago, you started off all stiff and on edge, then you went to great lengths to prove to me you were something else altogether. Don't get me wrong," he laughed, "I enjoy rolling down a hill after a beautiful woman just as much as the next guy – but now, here you are, trying to prove to that pair over there that you're looking for love." He leaned in closer to me. "When we both know that's the last thing you want."

I couldn't believe the nerve of him. "You can talk. You're the one who gets engaged, then cheats on your fiancée so you don't have to go through with it."

Richie glared at me. "That's not what happened. I didn't become engaged until *after* I'd been with Sonya."

"Oh, well that's all right then!" I glared back at him. "You try to come across as all charming – Mister Nice Guy – when really you're just like all the rest of them."

So it was a pretty nasty thing to say, but the more I got to know Richie Blake, the more I was coming to realise that he was one of those guys you were just meant to stay well away from.

He stared at me for a few seconds, then looked down. "You're probably right." He seemed almost beaten and I felt bad then. "Maybe I'm just a bit of a shit who can't hold down a relationship to save my life. But at least I know who I am. I'm under no illusion at the moment." He straightened up and looked at me. "Who is it you are exactly, Mel? Are you the driven career woman with the five-year plan? Or are you the cool chick who rolls down hills and hangs out with whales? *Or* . . . are you this phony night-clubber who picks up random blokes in bars on Friday nights?" He took a step closer to me. "*Or*, Miss McQuaid, are you something else entirely? Tell me – I'd love to know, because quite frankly I'm confused here."

I was furious. Who the hell did this guy think he was? He didn't know me – what right had he to talk to me like that?

"Maybe I'm all of those things?" I said, sticking out my chin. "And more besides."

"Is that so?"

I tried to stay calm, not rise to it.

"Who are you really, Mel? What do *you* want from life?"

I thought about it for a second. "Honestly?"

He nodded.

"Right now, all I want is a bloody cigarette!"

52

He looked surprised. Then he smiled a bit, took a pack of cigarettes out of his pocket and offered it to me.

I took a cigarette. "How come you have these? I thought the cigars were a one-off last time?"

"I smoke on and off – and I'm leaning on all my bad habits at the moment." He handed me a box of matches. "Keep 'em."

I put the cigarette and the matches in my pocket, then stood up straighter. "Thanks for the cigarette, Richie. You've actually been very helpful."

"Glad to be of service. See ya around then." He turned to get the barman's attention.

I looked at his back for a second then swung around and walked back over to Niamh and Orla. The skinny Italian was wrapped around Niamh and Orla was talking to what looked like his taller, broader friend.

I grabbed my jacket from the pile between Adonis's legs.

"Are you leaving with that guy already?" asked Orla, glancing over at Richie. "Go, Mel! He's a fox – and he's not going to let you get away – he's staring over." She nudged Niamh, who peeled her eyes away from the Italian to look. "Maybe our Mel is not so rusty after all, eh, Niamh?"

I glanced over my shoulder at Richie, and as I did he turned back to the bar.

I looked at the girls. "Thanks for a great night, ladies, but, Niamh, you remain the champion."

Niamh looked confused. I didn't bother to elaborate.

I walked the long way around the bar to avoid passing Richie again, and was very thankful to finally get out into the night air.

I took the cigarette and box of matches out of my pocket, lit up, and took a few drags. It was nice at first – very, very nice in fact. But then the smoke caught in my throat. I started to cough, and went on coughing until tears fell from my eyes.

"You all right there, love?" the bouncer asked.

I nodded as I wiped the tears away. "I'm fine, thanks," I managed to say eventually. Then I went over and stubbed the cigarette out in the ashtray by the door.

At least that was one good thing to come from my relationship with Ian – those things were pure evil.

I sighed, then walked to the side of the road to hail a taxi.

As I travelled home, Richie's words kept going around and around in my head: *"Who are you really, Mel? What do you want from life?"*

The guy had such a nerve.

I sighed. But to be fair to him, they probably were good questions. Who *was* I? And what *did* I want?

I sighed again as I stared out the taxi window.

The truth was – I honestly didn't know any more.

Chapter 5

RICHARD

I turned my head on the pillow and immediately regretted it. Not only was my head killing me, but Barbara – or was it Brenda? – well, whoever – the intern I'd brought home after the pub – was snoring loudly on the bed beside me.

Shite!

What a difference a few months can make: I'd started drinking the morning after the fight with Ed, and for the next six months I stopped only occasionally to work and to sleep. It was about the only way I could live with the guilt of screwing over just about everyone I gave a shit about.

I turned back around and pulled the sides of the pillow up around my hung-over ears to try to drown out the snoring of the stranger beside me.

Why the hell did I have to bring her back with me? Now I'd be stuck with her all morning. I glanced at the clock by my bed – 11.22 a.m. Ah shite, now I was late for work again too. At least Ed wasn't around any more to give me grief about it – that was something, I suppose.

Ed had moved out by the time me and my broken nose and stitched-up eye got home from hospital after the lunch. I'd been dying to get him out of my house for two years, but not like that – definitely not like that. I hadn't spoken to him or Lucy since that day – neither of them would take any of my calls, and I wasn't surprised. I knew they'd never forgive me, so I drank to try to forget about it, to get through the days.

I hadn't seen much of the lads since that day either. I knew I was a miserable git to be around, so rather than inflict myself on anyone that mattered to me, I withdrew. No doubt they all thought badly of me for messing with Ben's family anyway.

I did think about trying to get in contact with Mel McQuaid a couple of times. I thought I should probably try to apologise for getting personal the last time I bumped into her a couple of weeks after the lunch. I was in particularly shite form that night, and she pissed me off by pretending to pick me up – all for her friends' sake. A guy has feelings after all! But all that aside, I was actually kind of happy to see Mel again that time – even if things hadn't finished up particularly well. So I did mean to try to get in touch with the girl, but like so many other things over those six months, I never quite got around to it.

About the only thing that gave me any meaningful link to the rest of the world around then was work. It wasn't always easy getting my act together to go in every day, but I forced myself to do it – I needed to work. At least, I needed something.

It was just before lunch by the time I got in to work that day. I almost wished I'd stayed in bed – winter had really set in, the rain was pelting down and it was freezing cold outside. I was glad to get into the office and get a hot cup of coffee and a couple more painkillers into me, and was just going through my emails when Jeff, our junior business correspondent, popped his head around my office door.

"Hi, Richard, Edith's looking for you, said to drop in to her as soon as you get in."

Shite.

"Right, okay, thanks, man."

Edith Maguire had been in the newspaper game for over twenty-seven years and I'd worked with her at the *Chronicle* for fifteen of them. Her husband Kevin and her son Jason were both past pupils of Ashvale. Jason was arguably Ashvale's best-ever full-back – he ended up playing for Ireland for well over a decade, lucky sod. I've no idea where he got his stocky build from though – his parents were both tiny. But you couldn't let Edith's size fool you – she was the best in the business, a tough old bird, and we'd had more than our fair share of run-ins over the years – most of which she won.

Well, she can't have a go at me today, I thought. I'm sure I filed my article on time before hitting the pub last night.

At least I think I did.

"It was too late, Richard. We went to press over an hour before you filed your copy. I couldn't hold it any longer. Why the hell didn't you answer your phone?"

"Ah sorry, Edith, mustn't have heard it."

Which may have had something to do with the all-night bender I'd been on the previous night as well. Edith's

PA had emailed me the tip-off in the morning, but I didn't get round to opening my emails till lunchtime, and didn't really start digging around on the story proper until later in the afternoon.

"We can get it into tomorrow's edition, can't we?" I knew I was grasping, but it was worth a try.

"Yes, indeed we can, Richard, but, you know, there's just one catch. The one small thing I think you might be forgetting about the news – it sort of needs to be, eh, *new*?"

I hated when she did the sarcastic thing.

She took off her glasses. "*The Times*, *Indo* and every other paper in town are going to be all over this story today. This should have been ours, Richard – it was on a plate for us. It's not often we get a leak on a good lead business story like this." She threw her pen down on the desk. "No wonder our readership figures are slipping."

Crap. The readership figures. When she started on about those, I knew I was in trouble.

"All right, Edith. I messed up. Won't happen again." I stood up to go.

"Really? It's not going to happen again? Because it seems to be happening a lot lately, Richard." She got up from behind her desk, and walked around to face me. She had to stand several feet back from me to look me in the eye. Edith hated looking up at people.

"Can you sit back down, please, Richard?"

"Sorry, Edith, no can do. I've got to get going, busy schedule today."

"Perhaps you might have tried coming into the office on time then?" She pointed to the chair. "Sit, please."

I flopped back down. I knew I was behaving like a

petulant teenager, but I didn't care. The painkillers hadn't made much of an impact on my headache, and I was not in the mood for Edith's crap.

She sat down on the front of her desk next to me, and then, surprisingly, her tone changed. "Richard, are you okay?"

"Ye-eees," I said, trying to work out where this was going. "I'm fine."

"Really? Because you're looking pretty rough. When was the last time you had a haircut?" She reached out and ruffled my hair as though I was a kid. "And would there be any chance you might remember to shave before coming into work?"

I swatted her hand off. "Would there be any chance you could lay off, Edith? Not being my mother and all?"

Edith laughed. "Rose would have something to say about the hair too, I'd imagine."

She was really beginning to piss me off. I'd always hated the fact that my boss and my mother were friends – the Ashvale Mothers' network was way too close for my liking.

Edith cleared her throat. "And I heard that you missed the Ashvale golf outing last week. You normally go every year, don't you?"

"It clashed with something else, that's all."

"Mmm." She squinted at me, as though she was trying to make out some small print. "Well, maybe you should consider laying off the booze for a while? Take some time out?"

I shoved my chair back. "Jesus, Edith, I'm fine, okay? Everything is absolutely fine. Sorry about the story – won't happen again."

She held her hand up to stop me.

I may have been pissed off, but I wasn't stupid – I sat back down.

"Forget about that now, Richard." She paused and looked at me for a few more seconds, then walked back around to her chair and sat down. "I have a new assignment for you, Mr Blake." She put her glasses back on and picked up a piece of paper from the desk. "I want to try you on something different for a time. You've mentioned to me on several occasions that you'd like to do more feature work, so I'm asking Jeff to take on the business-and-economics desk for a few weeks."

"You're what? No way, Edith!"

But she was taking no prisoners. She fixed me with a stare that assured me as much.

"What's going on?" I asked.

"Do you remember the whale-in-the-Thames piece you wrote last year?"

"Yeah, what about it?"

"It was good, Richard. Very good in fact. I'd like to see more."

"Come on, Edith. Enough already. I'm busy, I don't have time for this."

She just smiled and looked at the page in her hand. "In a few days' time the international environmental protection agency, Greenpeace –"

"The Save the Whale brigade?"

"Yes, indeed, Richard, the very ones." She cleared her throat, and continued reading. "In a few days *Greenpeace* –" she glanced up at me over her glasses, "expect to be leaving Shimonoseki in Japan to tail the whaling fleet down to Antarctica. The Japanese persist in whaling out in the Southern Ocean despite a 1986 moratorium – apparently the whalers operate under some legal loophole that allows them to hunt a quota of whales under the guise of scientific research." She tapped the page. "Greenpeace point out here that thousands of whales have been killed through this loophole, but no credible research findings have yet been produced. They say that, in reality, scientific whaling projects are just poorly disguised commercial operations and attempts to see a return to full-scale commercial whaling." She put the page down. "So Greenpeace will be tailing the fleet in order to throw a spotlight on the whaling programme, and to communicate to the world what the Japanese are doing. The publicity will help Greenpeace to advocate for an increase in pressure from international governments and people doing business with Japan. The whaling controversy is severely damaging Japan's image both at home and abroad, and the hope is that growing pressure from the international community might even cause the hunt to be cancelled or scaled back this year." She paused, took off her glasses and looked at me. "Anyway, I've been thinking for a time that we need to cover more environmental issues, so I want to run a short series of features on this expedition – not the usual 'vulnerable whales versus big-bad-Japan' type of thing. I want us to come at it from a different angle, to explore the human side to the story. On board the – eh –" she picked the page up and put her glasses on again, "ah yes, on board the *Illuminar* . . . that's the name of the ship Greenpeace are sending down there." She looked up at me with a smirk.

I just stared at her. I was sorry about the whaling, but I had no idea why she was telling me about it, or what it had to do with me. I didn't for one minute buy her line about my whale-in-the-Thames piece.

But she was still rambling on. "On board the *Illuminar* will be a young Irish couple – newlyweds. They're part of the crew that will be going out to publicise the actions of the whaling fleet and, if needs be, to get between the whalers' harpoons and the whales themselves," she looked up, "which all sounds very dangerous to me, to be honest. These activists really do place themselves in such risky positions. Remember what happened with the sinking of the *Rainbow Warrior* in 1985? And that poor photographer that was drowned? That was really shocking." She shook her head. "Anyway, I want to know what makes a couple of young newlyweds from Ireland travel halfway around the world to spend months at sea and put themselves in grave danger from harpoons and the elements. Is it for the love of the whales? For the love of adventure? Or for the love of each other?"

She must finally be losing it, I thought. Had to happen eventually, I suppose. Tough game, the newspaper business – the old girl's done well for twenty-seven years – sad to see her start to fall apart really.

"This story potentially has it all, Richard," Edith was saying. "Young love, heroic adventures, majestic leviathans. It has the making of a great epic!" By this stage her eyes were almost popping out of their sockets.

Yep – the old girl had definitely lost it.

"*Ri-iight*. Okay, Edith," I said, nodding slowly. "That's very interesting."

But she ignored me. "Greenpeace expect to be joined by a TV crew in about two to three weeks' time, so they'll need the space on board back then. They're planning to make a stop somewhere like Tasmania or New Zealand to refuel and pick up the TV crew, before heading south to Antarctica – so wherever the refuelling stop is will be your drop-off point."

She sat back in her seat and flashed me a big smile. "So what do you think?"

I laughed. "I think if you're finished with the whaling waffle, Edith, I need to get back to my actual work."

"Mmm . . . So anyway, Richard," she picked up an envelope from her desk, "your London flight is tomorrow evening for an early Thursday-morning flight to Japan – everything you need to know is in here."

She threw the envelope at me, and my old rugby reflexes kicked in – I caught the damned thing.

"You'll need to get to know the newlyweds, Ray and Sinéad. Dig deep. I'd like to know exactly what it is about these whales that has them and . . ." she looked at the brief again, "'millions of people worldwide coming together to save a thousand whales, including fifty humpback whales'. They say the humpback whale is actually an endangered species."

"Are you finished now?" I asked.

Edith nodded, and sat back in her chair. She had a smug grin on her face that needed to be eradicated as quickly as possible.

I leaned forward. "*No!*"

But she just kept smiling.

"No bloody way, Edith. If you think for one minute that I am going to go to Japan of all places to interview two idiot whale-huggers, then you have completely lost it!"

Edith just sat there, looking amused.

63

"Why? Just tell me. Why the hell are you asking me to do this? Surely one of your fluffy supplement freelancers or *actual* feature-writers would jump at this one – a nice jolly overseas? An ocean cruise at that? They'd be happy as pigs in shit."

Edith still didn't react. But there was no way I was taking this lying down.

"Why do you want me to go anyway?" I said, this time a lot louder. "What? Just because I wrote some sentimental crap a year ago about a whale who was stupid enough to swim up the wrong channel? It doesn't add up, Edith. Why the hell are you sending me?"

She stopped looking amused, leaned over her desk and fixed me with a stare. "*Because*, Richard. It may surprise you to know that I have a quota of depressed, irritable, overdrinking, lecherous journalists on my staff. And right at this moment, I am at my absolute limit." Her own voice got louder then. "I am tired of picking up the pieces of your sloppy work over the past six months. I am sick of signing off P45s for lovelorn interns that you've seduced and tossed aside."

I tried to interrupt to defend myself, but she was on a roll, driving the knife deeper and deeper into the carnage of my pathetic life.

"But most of all, Richard, I am fed up of having to look at your unshaven, miserable mug every morning. Actually no, sorry, I mean *afternoon* – I can't remember the last time you actually made it into the office before noon." She walked around the desk, leaned over and put her hands on each arm of my chair to eyeball me a few inches from my face. "So, Mr Blake, if you *don't* get your sorry ass out to Japan, and if you *don't* send me back a series of shit-hot features from the Pacific Ocean, then you can kiss your beloved business-and-economics desk goodbye once and for all."

She drew herself up to her full height, all five-foot-nothing of her. "*Do I make myself clear?*"

She had me. I was furious, but I knew when I was beaten.

I looked away from her. "This is a pile of shite, Edith, and you know it."

"Good. I am so glad to hear you're on board, Richard." She laughed. "See what I did there? *On board?* Brilliant!" She cackled away to herself as she went back over to sit at her desk.

"Yeah, hilarious." I stood up. "So can I go now? Or would you like to stab me in the leg too? Or perhaps the arm? You'll be glad to hear you've finished on the back." I walked to the door.

"Well, there is just one more thing, Richard –"

I turned around. "What now?"

"Don't forget to pack your thermals. I hear it can get pretty chilly out at sea at night."

"Fuck off, Edith!"

"Thanks, sweetie. You can close the door on your w–"

But I'd already given it a good slam. It was about all I could do to salvage the last remaining shred of my manhood.

Chapter 6

RICHARD

She didn't relent. I don't know if Edith even read the lengthy protest email I sent her, but the following evening I found myself packed, pissed-off and passenger in a taxi on my way to the airport. And as if bloody Japan wasn't bad enough, as about the only person who would actually care or even notice that I'd be out of the country for a few weeks I'd called my Aunt Sheila the night before. *Which* proved to be a big mistake – she'd guilted me into going to see my mother on my stopover in London on the way.

These bloody women were ruining my life.

I rang the doorbell of my mother's house, and waited for a few seconds before turning my key in the door and letting myself in.

She met me in the hallway. "You're very late, Richard – I thought you said you'd be here by eight?"

"And hello to you too, Mother. Nice to see you."

I walked past her down the hall into the living room which led into the small galley kitchen. It was, as always, just like stepping back into my childhood – nothing had changed in all the years. The electric fire was still burning in front of the fireplace, my mother's armchair was perched beside the fire, and the living-room table was already set for the next meal – two places.

My mother followed me in. "Where are the rest of your bags? I thought you were going for a few weeks?"

Almost a year since we'd spoken and my bags were all she could ask about.

"Did you not pack more than that? Sheila said you were going for at least two or three weeks. You'll need more than that, Richard. At least one more jumper in case it gets cold."

I handed her the bunch of flowers I'd picked up at the airport. Then I took off my coat, put it on the back of a chair and rested my daypack down.

She sighed and put the flowers down on the table, then picked up my coat and went out to hang it up in the hall. Coming back into the room, she took the flowers and walked into the kitchen. I heard her rummage in the cupboard then run the tap.

I followed her in, then said as patiently as I could manage: "I left my big bag at the airport – they have a left-luggage area there. So how are you, Mother?"

She swung around from the sink – vase in one hand, flowers in the other. "At the airport? Oh dear, now really, Richard, is that wise? Anyone could take it – you just don't know what goes on in those storage places. I watched this documentary once where –"

"Any chance of a drink?"

"I'll put the kettle on." She put the flowers in the vase and started to reach for the kettle.

"No tea. I need a drink-drink. What have you got?" I went back out into the living room to look in the drinks cabinet.

"Well, I think there might be some sherry there." She scurried out after me and placed the vase of flowers on the table. "Or there could be some of that Irish Cream left over – the bottle that Sheila brought over at Easter – but would you not prefer a nice cup of tea? I have some sandwiches made, and there's some teacake."

"Nah, I'm okay. I ate on the plane, thanks." I rummaged in the cabinet for whatever alcohol I could get my hands on to help sustain me through the next couple of hours. The bottle of sherry was about the only thing that looked vaguely drinkable so I grabbed it and a glass, flopped down in one of the armchairs, and poured myself a large measure.

My mother tutted her disapproval, then went back out to the kitchen. I could hear her moving about, making the tea. After a few minutes she came back and sat down in her armchair opposite me, cup in hand.

It was a few minutes before she said anything. "It's a bit late to be drinking really, Richard, isn't it? Don't you have a very early start in the morning?"

I chose not to react – I knew I couldn't win the argument, so I took a huge swig of the sickly sweet liquid. It slid slowly down my throat like treacle. I coughed.

My mother frowned, but didn't say anything else for a minute or two. But, as suspected, the peace didn't last too long – pretty soon she went for the jugular: "So have you heard from Ed?"

"No." I looked up at her. "Why? Have you?"

"Yes, a few weeks ago. It was good to talk to him . . .

68

he'd been very distant since . . . well, since . . ."

I waited for her to say it.

Her hand went to her neck. "Since you two fell out at the start of the summer. I don't know all that happened, Richard, but he took it very hard. Don't you think you should try to sort things out with him?"

I tried to stay calm. "I've tried, okay, Mother? I called him after it happened. He didn't want to know me then, and he won't want to know me now. He moved out, and I can't say I blame him."

But she wouldn't let it go. "He might feel differently if you tried again now, a few months on. He's doing a lot better. You boys were so close at one time. Just call him, Richard."

"No. I'm not bothering him again. Ed knows where I am. If he wants to get in touch he can."

My mother sniffed, then blew her nose with her cotton handkerchief. I hated when she did that, it was just one step away from tears.

"Fine, okay," she said. "I'll be over myself in a few weeks' time for Christmas anyway. I'll see him then. I take it you'll be at Sheila's this year?"

I didn't want to think about Christmas. I didn't know where I was going to spend it. "I don't know. I might still be out in the field working on this story then." The Greenpeace gig was starting to look more attractive by the minute.

"In the field? I thought it was the sea you were going to?"

I smiled. "It's just a phrase, Mother – *in the field* means working on location."

"Yes, well, I hope you can do what you have to do out

there and get back in plenty of time. I want us all together for a nice family Christmas." She stared straight at me. It was like a battle of wills.

"We'll see," I said.

She pursed her lips. "I assume you haven't heard from poor Lucy? Or the MacDonaghs since –"

"No, Mother – I have not heard from any of the MacDonaghs since I let them and everyone else down earlier this year. Is that what you wanted to hear?" The MacDonaghs were the last people I wanted to talk to my mother about.

"All right, all right, sorry I asked." She got up and turned on another bar on the electric fire.

"I don't know why you won't let me get you central heating," I said, watching her. "It'd be a lot warmer than that thing."

She just sniffed. "No need to go spending your money on me."

I shook my head, wishing she would just let me do something nice for her for once. I picked up an old newspaper from beside the chair and started to flick through it.

She sat back down. "So are you seeing anyone else now?" she asked after another short silence.

"Nope."

"Oh, *Richard*, you need to be getting a move on."

"Leave it please, Mother."

But of course she wouldn't.

"Is there anybody you like even?"

I'm not sure why, but the image of Mel McQuaid rolling down the hill in Wicklow flashed before my eyes. But a lot had changed since that day.

"There's no one. And I'd rather not talk about all this anyway if that's okay?"

She looked away from me to the fire. "You're just like your father – can't bear to talk about anything that matters."

But that was taking things one step too far. I dropped the paper down beside me. "I am *nothing* like that man!"

My mother stared at me as I stood up, knocked back the end of the sherry, then marched over to the drinks cabinet for the bottle of Irish Cream.

I looked at my reflection in the mirror over the fire an hour or so later while my mother boiled the kettle for her hot-water bottle. By that time she'd managed to get several more digs in – not only about Ed, but also about my drinking, about my approaching forty (in *two* years!), and finally about my weight – which was a new one. I squashed the loose skin under my chin together with one hand, then looked down and pinched my belly with the other. Okay, so maybe I'd put on a few pounds over the last couple of months, but so what? I'd lose it all in no time after a few sessions at the gym.

I turned away from the mirror, then I poured myself another glass of the putrid alcoholic cream.

"I'm off to bed, Mother," I shouted in to her in the kitchen. "I'll pop my head around your door to say goodbye before I leave in the morning. Don't get up – it'll be very early."

And before she could object, I went upstairs to my old bedroom.

It was just before five o'clock when I came down the next morning. I'd had less than six hours' sleep, and was already dreading the journey ahead. I went into the kitchen to grab a quick glass of water, and was surprised to see my mother up and cooking. I was eager to get going, but the taxi still hadn't arrived and the smell of sausages was very appealing.

My mother turned around from the cooker. "Oh good, sit up there now at the table. You'll need a good breakfast before that long flight. I've made some sausages, bacon and scrambled eggs – runny – just the way you like them."

I checked my watch, I only had a few minutes at most before the taxi arrived, but the breakfast smelled great. I couldn't leave without tasting at least one of those sausages. And runny eggs? Superb.

"Okay, thanks, Mum, but I've got to be quick."

I was just mopping up the last of the eggs with some fried bread when I heard the taxi horn outside. "Right, I'd best be off. Thanks for the breakfast, Mum. Appreciate that." I picked up my plate.

"No, no, leave all that – you'd better go," she said, shooing me out to the hall.

She took my coat from the hook and held it open for me to put on. I turned around and crouched down to fit my arms into the sleeves, then turned to face her as I buttoned it up. She handed me my scarf. "Don't forget this, it might be cold out there." She leant up on her toes and wrapped the scarf around my neck, patting it down when she was finished.

Then she stood back to look at me, both hands on my arms.

"Take care of yourself over there, Richard. You haven't really been yourself lately, I hope this trip helps you to get back on track. Do make sure to stay safe, won't you?"

Her eyes looked a little watery. I looked at the old, grey-haired woman standing in front of me in her pale-blue fleece dressing gown and matching slippers. She seemed quite frail and harmless. A small part of me almost wanted to stay and just look after her.

I choked a bit. "Yeah, I will, Mum, thanks." The moment must have got the better of me then, but before I knew what I was doing I put my hand on her shoulder then leant in and gave her a quick kiss on the cheek. She didn't flinch or pull away so I put my arms awkwardly around her to hug her, and she let me, even putting one arm around me herself.

The taxi driver blew his horn again.

My mother patted my back to break the hug.

"All right, all right, man. I'm coming!" I shouted at the closed front door, then stood back from my mother. "Best be off, I guess."

She nodded, with a sad smile.

"I'll see you at Christmas then," she said, handing me my bag.

"Yes, okay, see you then, Mum." I took the bag and walked out to the taxi, followed by my mother. She stood watching me from the garden gate, waving as the taxi moved off.

I smiled and waved back until the house disappeared from sight.

I settled back in the cab. That wasn't too bad actually, I thought. Maybe I won't leave it so long next time.

Chapter 7

MELANIE

I was twelve metres below, finning hard to fight my way through the strong current. I kept hitting off the jagged rocks on my left side, and I couldn't get my buoyancy right so I had to struggle to maintain my depth. After a while I managed to fin out of the current, and into a calmer piece of clear water. I turned around to check on my dive buddy's position, but I couldn't see him anywhere. I was alone underwater.

I checked my air gauge – under seventy bar left – it was just about enough air to dive through the calmer water for another few minutes. I knew I should have resurfaced and tried to find my buddy as per diving code, but if I did I wouldn't have had enough air to get back down and enjoy the better conditions. I looked ahead – the coral looked so beautiful and colourful, and the surrounding water was calm and clear. I was a bit scared of going on alone, but decided to risk the dive club's wrath, and finned on.

Within seconds I was gliding through the crystal-clear, warm water. It was blissfully quiet aside from the soft release of bubbles escaping from my diving apparatus. I managed to get my buoyancy right, so that I floated effortlessly through the multi-coloured coral gardens, barely noticed by the multitude of fish happily munching away on the abundant coral. Any fear or apprehension melted away as calmness washed over me with every gentle flap of my fins.

Just then I spotted an enormous fish, the biggest I had ever seen. It was swimming straight towards me, out of the darker, deep water. As it came closer, I saw that it was black and white.

Wait! That's no fish!

I squinted to make sure I was seeing clearly.

Bloody hell, it's a killer whale!

The whale swam right towards me. My heart started beating faster. It was an incredible sight, yet I was terrified, frozen to the spot. Then, just as the whale was about to collide into me, he changed direction. He circled around, passing by so close that I could feel his tail shift the water. He swam all the way around me, then stopped right in front and appeared to look straight at me. He opened his enormous mouth. I could see the small pointy teeth lining his jaw, his huge pink tongue resting within.

Then, with no warning whatsoever, he threw back his head and started to sing.

What the –?

Then he started to dance – standing up erect on his tail, he swayed from side to side, fins flailing to the strange tune he was singing. I couldn't believe what I was seeing, and hearing: it just wasn't possible.

That's when my buddy reappeared. He swam up from behind the whale and I realised who it was then – that journalist Richie Blake. He was almost suspended in the water as though he was sitting in it. He had a black eye and his nose was broken and bleeding, but he didn't seem to care. He started to laugh, causing more and more bubbles to escape from his regulator up to the ocean surface above.

I began to laugh myself, as the whale danced on. It was at that moment that my alarm finally woke me up.

"Grace – have you ever seen whales?" I asked my assistant as she handed me the morning post.

"Huh?" she grunted.

Grace wasn't much of a morning person.

"Whales. I had the strangest dream about one just before waking up this morning. I've never seen them in the wild – I'd love to though. I did see a killer whale in Windsor safari park in England once when I was visiting with my family as a kid, but it's not the same really, is it?"

"Eh no, I suppose not," she said, looking at me as if I was half mad.

"I mean, it's just plain cruel to keep such large animals in parks simply to keep people amused," I said. "Why don't we go to them – visit the animals in their natural environments, not in those fake theme parks? We have lots of wild dolphins and porpoises off the coast here in Ireland – you can even see whales if you're lucky."

But Grace wasn't in the mood to indulge my marine mammal musings. "Yes, well, *anyway*, Melanie, reception just rang to say that the first of the board members has arrived. He's gone upstairs for the meeting."

"Already?" I looked at my watch. "Drat, he's early. All right, I'll head up there now – thanks, Grace." I grabbed my presentation notes and left.

I was glad when I arrived up to the boardroom to see that the early arrival was Father O'Mara – one of my favourite board members. The author of a number of celebrated classical music books, he was widely regarded as one of the country's most informed experts on Irish composers. And he was a real sweetheart. Father O'Mara and I often ended up in a corner chatting during some of the dull receptions and occasions we were called upon to attend at The Mill.

He was standing by the long mahogany side-table. His long black coat was dangling across his arm and he was holding his black trilby hat in one hand while pouring himself a cup of coffee with the other. Father O'Mara was one of that generation that never left home without a hat, and it suited him – together with his white priest's collar, it gave him a certain presence when he entered a room. He hadn't aged a bit since I'd first met him six years earlier, even though he must easily have been into his seventies.

"Ah, Melanie, lovely to see you, child," he said, putting down the coffee-pot and coming to greet me.

"You too, Father – welcome." I took his outstretched hands and gave him a kiss on the cheek. "Let me take your hat and coat."

"Why, thank you, Melanie, very kind of you." He handed them to me and I hung them up on the coat stand in the corner.

"I'm a bit early," he said. "I wanted to avoid the worst of the traffic. Don't let me keep you now if you need to finish up anything before the meeting." He went back to the side-table to pick up his coffee.

"No, not at all, Father. I'm as ready as I'll ever be. Marcus is waiting for Fenella downstairs, but he'll be up soon, I'm sure." I followed him over and poured myself a coffee.

"Well, that's good, gives us time for a bit of a catch-up ourselves. Tell me now, how are you keeping?"

I smiled. "I'm good, thanks, Father. I'm getting settled into my new house – I'm there almost a year now – it's hard to believe how the time flies. Lots still to do, but it's really starting to take shape now."

"Congratulations. You must be delighted."

"Yes, I am pretty chuffed – and it's a great house. It's just that since the promotion I've barely had time to enjoy it really."

"I do hope you're not overdoing it here, Melanie. You work very hard, don't you? Perhaps a little too hard sometimes?"

Bless him for noticing.

"A bit, I suppose, but I'm trying to get the balance right, and it won't be forever. This is a very exciting time for the Millennium Centre. We're very excited about the new fundraising campaign for Phase Two." I churned out the company line and tried to sound enthusiastic.

Father O'Mara nodded. "Mmm, yes, that's good. Tell me, though, have you been doing any of that – what is it now you called it again? Sub-aqua scoobing, was it?"

I smiled. It never ceased to amaze me how Father O'Mara remembered the details of all his conversations, considering he must have talked to hundreds of people in a week. "It's *scuba diving* I mentioned before, Father; but no, sadly I haven't been able to go diving in quite some time. I've been so busy with work, the house and various family commitments that I haven't really had too much spare time. Still, it will all be worth it in the end –

hopefully later next year I might be able to take more time for travel and the like."

Father O'Mara peered at me over his coffee cup as he took a sip. He put it back down on the sideboard then and said: "Remember, Melanie, to travel is often a better thing than to arrive."

"Sorry, Father?"

He smiled. "It's important to enjoy the journey that is life, as much, if not more, than the destination, don't you think? Better to enjoy life today, than to be always striving for something else in the future."

"Yes, I suppose it is, Father," I said. But I probably needed to think about what he was trying to say a bit more. I was just about to ask him to elaborate when the door opened and Fenella and her lapdog Marcus sailed in.

Father O'Mara gave me a wink before turning to greet them.

"Thank you, Melanie dear, for that proposal," Fenella said when I'd finished my presentation on the new campaign fundraising strategy to the board.

Fenella was wearing her trademark false smile, but I could tell something was bothering her. All I could do was to sit back and wait for the fallout.

"Some sobering issues to consider there." She nodded at the screen. "But thank you, dear, for the research you undertook and for the proposal you made. Let's open the discussion to the floor now." She reconsidered then. "Actually, I have a question myself to start us off if I may?" She looked around, and the heads of the board members all bobbed their assent.

Yep – here we go, I thought. It's never bloody simple with you, is it, Fenella?

"While I do understand, Melanie dear, that we have a very considerable amount of money to raise, to be honest I would have to question the proposal of hiring an expensive external consultancy firm to run this campaign. We have so many prospective donors right at our fingertips, and I would be quite certain that, even around this table, between us we would have dozens of contacts we could approach. Marcus has a lot of experience of this work from the Millennium Centre's Phase One campaign, and I am very confident in your abilities too, Melanie dear." She flashed me one of her toothy smiles.

If she calls me 'dear' one more time . . .

"I know that you would do a wonderful job in coordinating our efforts," she was saying, "without the need to recruit additional expertise."

I stared at her. Was this woman for real? For a start, the only one with any halfway-decent contacts around the table was Fenella herself, and no doubt she'd be too busy instructing Marcus on how to deliver the new artistic programme to raise as much as another brass cent for the project. And for another thing, where the bloody hell was I to get the time to raise fifteen million euro *and* run the marketing and development department? Especially as I had been lumbered with her dimwit, useless niece as my right-hand person for the last six months?

I was just about to put some of these thoughts into some vaguely more diplomatic words, when Marcus finally relocated his backbone. He raised his hand, and Fenella nodded, graciously allowing him to speak.

"With the greatest of respect, Madam Chairwoman –"

He sat forward, but bowed his head in deference as he spoke.

I couldn't believe what a crawler he was.

"I wouldn't be entirely sure that we could manage this campaign internally within existing resources to be honest," he said, almost afraid to look at Fenella. "The staff are quite overworked as it is – I'm not sure we can ask any more of them."

I nodded vigorously, but Fenella shot him a look and he immediately recoiled into his seat.

Fenella gathered herself then, lifted her chin and looked around at the other board members as she said: "The time has come now to put aside any individual concerns, to come together for a much greater purpose. This is a once-off opportunity for the Dublin Millennium Centre of the Arts to shine on the world stage. We are all going to have to pull together on this – the staff included."

I couldn't believe what she was saying.

Who did she think she was? She wasn't going to be *pulling together* on anything – we were the ones who were going to end up in early graves from trying to keep the place afloat.

Yes, please do excuse those individual concerns of ours, Fenella – those of pure exhaustion and almost certain failure. How very selfish of us.

I was absolutely fuming. I stared at Marcus, willing him to speak up for the staff, but he just coughed and sat back in his seat.

Gah! He was so bloody spineless. Well, if he wasn't going to fight our corner, I'd just have to do it myself.

I took a deep breath, then spoke. "Just to be clear, The Mill's staff certainly do *not* have the capacity at the moment to manage a fundraising programme of this scale in-house without additional resources. The reason I proposed the use of professional fundraising consultants was because we have to raise such a significant amount of private funding in a relatively short space of time. This may be expensive, but each of the firms proposed for our consideration have an excellent track record of success in major campaign fundraising. I would question our capacity to do the job ourselves whilst maintaining current activity levels. It would at a minimum require the recruitment of additional professional development staff, which we know from recent experience are very difficult to find."

Marcus shuffled in his seat, giving me a filthy look. He clearly wasn't happy with me pushing, but I didn't care – we couldn't take any more on.

"All in all, I believe bringing in consultants would be our most sensible option," I went on, "and that the costs involved will be recouped many times over by the significant funds they will raise for the campaign."

But Fenella was not going to back down in front of her board. "Yes. I understand what you're saying, dear."

Argh! All right, stay calm, I told myself. Do not lose it now. Breathe in. *Breeeeathe* . . .

"But to reiterate my point," my nemesis was saying, "we have all of the necessary contacts ourselves. That is a fact. I myself can right now think of at least four or five people who would be prepared to support this project. In fact, who are *looking* for a project just like this as a vehicle for their philanthropy. Really now, how difficult can it be to ask a few people for donations for such a wonderful cause?" She smiled, displaying every one of her whitened teeth, and looked around the table at the other board members for their support.

They looked uncomfortable, unsure what to do or say. A few pairs were mumbling to each other around the table.

I was just about to speak again to try to persuade them, when I heard Father O'Mara's voice. "Through the Chair?"

Fenella gave him a sickly sweet smile. "Yes, Brendan?"

"I believe it is one thing to raise a few hundred thousand euro for a charity project," he said, "but it is quite another thing entirely to raise fifteen million euro within three years for a building project of this scale. It took us over seven years to raise the ten-million-euro funding to co-fund the public funds needed to build the first phase of the Millennium Centre, and that was even before we had an existing artistic programme to promote and sell. I have learnt just how challenging it can be to raise large funds from other fundraising initiatives I've been involved in over the years. I think as a board we must listen to the suggestions and the concerns of our management team. They are the experts in this area."

There was a rumble of approval. I looked around the table, this time relieved to see the other board members bobbing their heads in unison to the voice of reason.

Fenella looked furious, Marcus was clearly uncomfortable beside her, but I was beyond caring about that pair.

Unfortunately, though, there was one other board member not nodding – Hugh McWilliams, another honorary member of the Fenella Wright fan-club. A retired opera singer, Hugh ran the country's largest music school and the Wrights were large benefactors.

"With the greatest of respect to Brendan," he said, "I think the chairwoman has a valid argument. We should explore all of the options. We have only been presented with one solution today, that of hiring an external fundraising consultancy. We need to consider all of the issues involved in doing this in-house, and there may indeed be other options that haven't yet been presented. Perhaps Marcus's team could research the matter further, and present us with a fuller picture of *all* of the options at the next board meeting?"

"Yes, indeed – that makes sense," Fenella interjected before anyone else had a chance to disagree. "All in favour?"

The board bleated their approval.

I couldn't believe it: they were like bloody sheep.

I caught Father O'Mara's eye. He shrugged his shoulders and raised his eyebrows in resignation. I gave him a faint smile, but all I could think of was that I was going to have to research and write another damned presentation, no doubt to bring us all back to the same conclusion I'd just presented.

Arghhh!

As soon as I could escape the boardroom I strode as fast as I could down the corridor outside, pushed open the dividing door and marched quickly down the main staircase, taking the steps two at a time over the four flights of stairs. I walked through the foyer, not even saying hello to Gail on reception.

My mind was so distracted that I didn't enjoy the sounds of the baroque group through the open rehearsal-room doors, and I didn't notice Dave, one of our lighting men, standing beside the backstage stairs with a drill. As

I marched past the staircase, I tripped over a trailing drill cable and fell hard and fast, smacking both my knees off the cold stone floor.

Dave rushed over. "Are you okay, Melanie? That looked nasty. I'm so sorry – I had no way of avoiding trailing the flex – there's no power point this side of the stairs."

The pain was intense – it shot through my entire body, but I managed to shuffle myself around into a sitting position on the floor. I looked at Dave but couldn't speak – just sat there in shock, gently rubbing my knees in a daze as the pain grew steadily worse. I drew in a sharp breath, and was very surprised to find that when I did finally manage to speak, my voice was barely audible.

"I-it's okay, Dave. I should have been watching where I was going."

Poor Dave looked pretty shaken. The Mill's health and safety policy was very strict – he could get in serious trouble for trailing a cable across an access route. It was a big mistake, but he was just a young lad, a good guy, and he hadn't been in the job too long.

"Honestly, it's fine, Dave. Don't worry about it. I'm grand. Look." I held onto the wall and stood up, very shakily.

He stepped forward to support me. "Are you sure? You don't look great, Melanie."

I managed a weak laugh. "Probably nothing to do with the fall, Dave. Just this place taking its toll."

"Are you sure? I could call a doctor for you? Or let Grace know?"

"No, no, honestly, I'm grand thanks. Best get back to work."

I made a move to go. The pain shot through my legs with every step I took and I was still shaking, but I didn't want to make too much of it in front of Dave, so I tried as hard as I could to walk through it. Thankfully, he let me go, and I made it as far as one of the ladies' dressing rooms backstage.

As soon as I walked in and made sure no one was there, I collapsed onto one of the dressing-table chairs in front of the mirrors. I held out my hands in front of me: they were shaking. I rolled up my suit trousers to survey the damage to my poor knees. They had already reddened and were starting to swell into lumps – it looked almost like I had four knees.

I struggled to walk over to the tap in the corner of the room, pulled some paper towels off the dispenser on the wall and wet them under cold running water. As I moved, the pain in my knees caused me to gasp. I went and sat back down then in front of the mirror and held the cold, wet towels alternately to each of my knees. My back was aching too, so I tried to straighten up and stretch it out a bit.

As I sat there the tears started to fall. At first just a trickle – but they quickly built up until I was sobbing uncontrollably, barely stopping to take a breath. When I finally did stop crying, I just sat staring straight ahead, holding one lump of soggy paper towels to my knee and another to my eyes.

I got up and looked at my sorry reflection in the long mirror. It was truly pathetic.

You know you can't carry on like this, McQuaid, don't you, I told myself as I stared at my image. Katy's always telling you to get more balance in life, and the family are forever on at you to enjoy yourself more. Even that journalist Richie got you in one, months ago, wondering why you were putting off travelling and all those other things you wanted to do – and he didn't even know you.

So what did you do about it?

Oh all right, so you tried for a few weeks, went out a couple more times than usual, but then when that didn't work you just got swept back up in work again. Pretty soon you were back to normal – only this time pushing yourself even harder.

Is it any wonder this is where you've ended up?

There, in the mirror in front of me, stood a pitiful creature: a grown woman in rolled-up trousers, with swollen eyes and bruised, lumpy knees. I looked like a four-year-old who'd tripped in the school yard.

Pathetic, absolutely pathetic.

It was like Father O'Mara said – I needed to enjoy the journey too, and I wasn't – I was most definitely *not* enjoying it. In fact – I looked at my face in the mirror as the tears started again – I was absolutely miserable.

Something had to change.

And that's when it came to me. That's when I decided what to do.

I took a few seconds more there staring at myself, before wiping my eyes, rolling my trousers back down, and limping back to my office to make the booking.

I knew it wouldn't solve everything, but it would be a good start.

Chapter 8

RICHARD

I thought I would never get to Shimonoseki. A quick glance at the reflection in the mirror of my room at the Plaza Hotel in the Japanese city confirmed that I looked as bad as I felt after the journey – if possible, even worse.

My one saving grace was that, as it was November, it wasn't too hot in the city – just a mild twelve degrees. I switched on the shower and stood underneath the warm water to wash away some of the grime and exhaustion of my twenty-five-hour journey. All I could think of was bed – tomorrow morning I'd take the helicopter ride out to board the *Illuminar* at sea. But that night I was going to sleep – and sleep for a very long time.

The sheets were soft and cool, and the hotel bed was one of the most comfortable I had ever laid on. I wanted to sink down deep into it, to sleep for a whole week.

I turned over to find a comfortable position – just as my mobile started to ring.

I didn't budge.

Should have turned that off, I thought – well, whoever it is can wait.

The phone finally went dead, but five seconds later started ringing again.

"Come on! What's the bloody story?" I shouted out, still without moving.

But the damn thing wouldn't give up. It just kept ringing, stopping intermittently for a couple of seconds before starting again. "All right. *All right!*" I sat up and reached out to answer it.

"Yes?" I said with as much frustration as I could convey in a single word.

"Richard? Is that Richard Blake?"

It was a bad line. I could just about make out the words.

"Yeah, who's this?"

"Where are you? Sorry, it's Ray here, Ray Kelly from Greenpeace. Have you arrived in Shimonoseki yet?"

I sat up a bit. "Yeah, I'm here. Just arrived to the hotel. I'll be out to the ship there in the morning. Helicopter's booked for eight o'clock." I rubbed my eyes.

"Sorry, Richard, that's just it. We expect to be on the move before then. We've received intelligence to say that the whaling fleet may in fact be pulling out to sea today at some stage. They usually have a big ceremony at the port first to wave the ship off, but we now expect them to pull out unannounced. They seem to want to make sure to deflect any international attention this time, not to mention try to catch us off-guard. Anyway, it means you gotta get yourself out here as soon as possible. Right away. Can you sort it?"

I sat up and swung my legs over the edge of the bed.

"Eh – I don't know. Maybe I can reschedule the helicopter or something. I'll give the guy a call."

"Good – well, this is where we are currently laying." I grabbed a pen and wrote down the coordinates he gave me.

"You have the ship's number," Ray went on. "Any problems, just ring through and ask for me. Good luck." He hung up.

Bollox. Fuck. *Sheee-ite* anyway!

I rooted around in my hand luggage to find my itinerary and list of phone numbers, then rang the number of the helicopter charter company. The *Illuminar* was laying out at sea, well outside the port of Shimonoseki. Helicopter was the only way to get out to her.

Thankfully the pilot was pretty amenable, and for a few extra dollars agreed to meet me at the helipad in an hour's time.

I got up and used every curse in the book as I got back into my travel clothes, threw my stuff back into my bag, and within two minutes was walking out the door.

The helicopter circled as it came in to land. I looked down at the ship that was to be my home for the next few weeks – she was actually a lot bigger than I had expected her to be. The hull was painted a strong, royal blue. Over this, the familiar multicoloured Greenpeace rainbow symbol arched dramatically across the front of the hull from one side of the ship to the other. The words '*Defending our Oceans*' were painted beside the rainbow on either side of the hull. The rest of the ship was painted white, save for a few blue whales painted here and there. I counted at least two orange inflatable boats tied up on deck. A tall mast stood high on the deck, and I noticed a big aerial-type structure at the front of the ship – or the bow. I should probably start using nautical terms, I thought.

Overall, the ship actually looked to be in pretty good shape – from above, at least.

I could make out a number of people milling around on deck below. One of them was waving a flag. We circled in to land and, when we touched down on the deck, the guy with the flag approached, bending down low to avoid the whirling helicopter blades.

"Richard Blake, I presume?" He had to shout to be heard above the engine.

"Yeah, in the flesh!" I shouted back.

He waved me away from the helicopter to the side of the deck. We watched it take off again and disappear into the setting sun.

"Welcome to the *Illuminar*. I'm Ray Kelly, communications officer for this expedition – we spoke earlier." He held out his hand for me to shake.

Ray looked younger than I'd expected – late twenties, I reckoned. He was wearing a dirty grey Billabong T-shirt and green board shorts. His ginger hair was escaping from underneath his baseball cap, and his face was covered in large freckles – there was no denying the guy's Irish roots, but he actually looked surprisingly normal, not quite the hippy environmentalist I was expecting.

He went ahead of me, leading me up a couple of flights of steel stairs and along the deck, introducing me to a couple of people on the way. They all seemed a bit preoccupied though – nobody hung about to talk.

"We're getting ready to haul anchor and follow the Japanese whaling fleet out of port," Ray explained as we walked along an inner corridor. "Once we hear they're on the move, we'll be off." He pushed open one of the doors and stepped over the door-frame. "Watch your step there," he said. "This will be your crib – you're sharing with Takumi, our Japanese campaigner – a good guy."

The cabin was small, but quite well fitted-out. It had a desk and lamp in the corner, a telephone on the wall, and a small sink. There seemed to be a decent amount of storage, with a large double cupboard in a recess of the wall. The bunk beds looked small though, very bloody small in fact. A small porthole just above the top bunk was letting in a blast of sunlight. The room was stiflingly hot and stuffy; I could see what looked like an air-conditioning unit in the wall, but it wasn't turned on.

Ray patted the top bunk bed. "This is the only reason me and Sinéad got married – so we could get one of the few proper beds on board!" He checked the bunk below. "Looks like you're on top – Takumi's taken the bottom one."

I hadn't shared a room with another bloke since school. I wasn't impressed, but right at that moment I could have slept standing up.

"You can put some stuff in here if you can find any room," Ray was saying. He opened up the cupboard door. "Jeez, he's one neat-freak – Takumi." He nodded at the two piles of perfectly folded T-shirts and fleeces. "He's left you a few free shelves in here anyway so make yourself at home. I'll give you a few minutes to settle in, then pop back to show you around the rest of the ship."

"Actually, man, d'you mind if I grab a bit of shut-eye first? I'm wrecked – been travelling now for over twenty-seven hours straight."

"Oh yeah, sure. No worries. I'll call you if there's any action from the whaling fleet."

I nodded. "Great, thanks." But I couldn't have given a shit about the whaling fleet; right at that moment, the ghost of Moby Dick himself could have jumped up out of the Pacific Ocean, performed a series of acrobatic manoeuvres and swallowed the entire whaling fleet whole for all I cared. I just wanted to sleep.

When Ray finally left, I tried to turn on the air-conditioning unit. I twisted every knob, flicked every switch, but nothing. I thought about going to find someone to fix the blasted thing, but I was so exhausted that I didn't have the energy. What little I did have went into the kick I gave the dysfunctional metal box. I finally gave up, took off my boots, combats and T-shirt and struggled up onto the top bunk. It was very narrow, and must have been designed for a child – it was far too small for a big fella like me – I had to curl up to fit into it.

"Edith, you damn well owe me one!" I shouted, before falling into a deep sleep.

Chapter 9

RICHARD

I woke up to sunlight streaming through the porthole. I was soaked in sweat, and could barely breathe. Disorientated, I sat up, and promptly banged my head off the ceiling.

Fuuuck!

I rubbed my scalp and looked around. It wasn't a bad dream then, I really was stuck on a steel hell-house off the coast of Japan.

I was absolutely parched – my throat felt like sandpaper. I got up and splashed some water on myself from the sink in the cabin – then I tried drinking some, but it was warm and tasted awful, so I pulled on some clothes and went outside. I walked down a short, narrow corridor until I got to a doorway which looked as if it might lead out onto the deck. I walked through, then immediately recoiled from the sudden force of the sunlight outside. When I finally readjusted to the brightness of the day, I realised that the ship was moving.

So that's what that noise was. I recognised the hum of

the engine then, as my full senses finally began to kick in. I leaned out over the railing. All I could see was sea – flat, calm and blue: in front, behind and all around. There wasn't another ship in sight.

I wondered if they had lost the whaling fleet. But I didn't spend too long wondering; my need to find a toilet and a drink quickly took over. I went back inside and found two small cubicles a few feet down from my cabin. Each cubicle doubled-up as a toilet and a shower – another sharp reminder that I was no longer at the Plaza Hotel.

My quest for drinking water brought me upstairs to another short corridor of doors. I could just about make out some voices coming from one of the rooms at the end, so I walked down and looked around the door.

Inside, Ray was sitting at a long table working on a laptop. Beside him was a young woman with long matted dreadlocks and several nose-rings – much more like the eco-hippy I'd expected to come across on this trip. The woman was laughing and talking in French on the phone. Ray was busy tapping away at his laptop.

"Well, well, the dead arose!" Ray said, then turned to the woman on the phone. "Jules, quit chatting up that journalist – we've got a live one right here."

Jules looked up, smiled and waved at me. "*Pardonez-moi un moment, Michel*," she said to the person on the phone.

"This is Richard Blake, our long-lost *Irish Chronicle* journalist," Ray said, then turned to me. "Jules writes the campaign blog. She also deals with some of the foreign press when my language skills fail me."

I held out my hand to shake hers.

"Nice to meet you, Richard," Jules said. "We were starting to get worried – you were asleep a long time, my friend." Her English was perfect, though her accent was foreign – but not French. Scandinavian perhaps.

"Really? What time is it now?" I asked, taking off my watch to adjust to local time.

Ray pointed at the wall behind me. I looked around but all I could see at first were dozens of photographs of whales, large maps and Greenpeace posters. Then I saw the clock – it was a quarter past three.

I couldn't believe it – that meant I must have been asleep for almost a full day and night.

"You missed it all," Ray was saying. "We had to get the engines going late last night. The whaling fleet left the port of Shimonoseki unannounced as we thought they might. We did intercept them, and George, our captain and the crew put in a valiant effort to stay with them, but it was dark and they must have used a lookalike lead ship as a decoy. Anyway, they managed to give us the slip somehow. I tried waking you as it was all happening, but you were dead to the world."

"Right, sorry about that, man." Truth be known though, I was actually bloody glad that he hadn't managed to wake me for the second time in two days. I needed the sleep. "So what happens now then? Are you trying to catch up with the whaling fleet again?"

Ray jumped up from behind the desk. "Why don't we go grab a coffee and I'll fill you in? We can go via the bridge and I'll show you how we operate."

The bridge, I learned, was the operational hub of the ship. The front of it was a slanted glass window which ran the whole width of the space. Under the window were the many controls and navigational devices needed to operate the ship. Inside, Ray introduced me to George, the

Illuminar's captain. Tall and lean, he looked to be in his late forties, and from his tanned, weather-worn face I could tell that he'd seen a lot of days at sea. He barely looked up from the map to acknowledge me. The guy exuded authority, and you could tell from the way Ray's voice hushed when showing me around the controls near to him that the captain had the full respect of his crew.

I also met Ally, the expedition leader. She was from the Netherlands and was leading her third Greenpeace expedition. Neither she, nor the few ship's mates Ray introduced me to, stopped to chat. Everyone was milling around the numerous radar screens, peering into the horizon through binoculars and scopes or poring over maps and charts. Nobody paid me too much attention; in fact, I felt a bit in the way. Ray lingered for a few minutes chatting with George and Ally about coordinates, and discussing various moving spots on the radar. It was vaguely interesting, and on any other occasion I might have tried to listen in and work out what was going on, but right at that moment I was absolutely gasping for a drink of water, beer and coffee – in that order.

I finally managed to drag Ray away and down to the galley, where the smell of cooking made me realise I was also starving.

"Heya, babe, what's cooking?" Ray asked a skinny girl with blonde wavy hair and a pretty face who was busy peeling potatoes. That face lit up when she saw Ray arrive. She bounded right over and jumped up on him, wrapping both legs around his waist.

"Hello there, lover," she said after they kissed.

His wife, I assumed. Either that or he had a pretty open marriage.

"It's vegetable frittata and chicken stew today," she said.

"Mmm, fantastic," Ray said, before landing her with a massive wet kiss. I could actually hear the slobbering, and almost puked into the spud peelings.

I was beginning to think I was in fact invisible on board this ship, when Ray said, "Sorry, where are my manners? Sinéad, this is Richard Blake, journalist from *The Irish Chronicle* – remember, the guy I told you about yesterday?"

"Oooh, yes, of course. It's so exciting," she said, and shook my hand. "Welcome on board, Richard. I hope you're hungry, 'cos we've got loads of food tonight. I think I may have overdone it this time."

I began to take a liking to this woman.

"Great, I'm absolutely starving. I can hardly remember my last meal. Any chance of a glass of water in the meantime?"

Ray filled a plastic cup with water from a tap in a large container and handed it to me. "Head on into the mess there next door and I'll bring you in something to eat. Help yourself to coffee and whatever's there."

I drained my cup of water, filled it up again from the container, and went next door into the mess. It was a large dining room, filled with tables and benches, and the walls were adorned with murals of whales lest you should forget the ship's raison d'être. I made myself a coffee and climbed over one of the benches to sit down to wait for my food. After what seemed like an eternity Ray came in holding a plate of sandwiches. You had to hand it to the guy, he had it good – shagging the cook on board a ship definitely reaped its rewards.

He put down the plate of ham and cheese sandwiches

and climbed over the bench opposite me at the long table.

"That was some sleep you had," he said as I munched hungrily.

"Sure was, but I needed it." I swallowed the bite I was eating. "To be honest, I'm surprised I slept so long – the beds remind me of the bunks at my old boarding school."

"Yeah, but I think they were bigger at Ashvale." Ray reached out for a sandwich.

I stopped eating. "What did you say? How do you know Ashvale?"

"Class of '99." Ray saluted. "Didn't Aunt Edie tell you?"

"Aunt Edie? Hold on a second." I put down my sandwich. "Do you mean Edith? Edith *Maguire*? My editor?"

Ray nodded. "She didn't tell you? She's my mother's sister."

I didn't trust myself to speak. I just shook my head. Edith was his *aunt*? What the hell was she playing at?

Ray laughed. "You know, I must admit I was surprised when she called to say she was sending someone out here at long last. I've been on at her for months, years even, to do something on our anti-whaling campaign in her paper. 'Not quite our thing, dear,' she'd tell me each time. She kept palming me off until a few days ago when she rang me out of the blue and asked if we could take one more on board. 'One of our top journalists,' she said. We jumped at it, of course – once there's space on board, and the paper pays your way, we're happy to get whatever positive coverage we can for the campaign. Hey, are you okay, Richard?"

I just sat staring at Ray. I couldn't believe what I was

hearing. Why hadn't Edith mentioned that he was her nephew? And why had she suddenly decided to cover this issue? In fact – not just cover it, not just run a rehashed article from a press release, or conduct a telephone interview. Why had she gone to the expense and trouble of sending me – her *business-and-economics editor* for Chrissake – out off the coast of Japan and into the Pacific Ocean to follow a group of sea-hippies? Even if one of them *was* her nephew.

"Did Edith mention why she changed her mind on covering the story?" I asked Ray as calmly as I could.

"No, though it may have had something to do with that awesome press release we wrote last week about the humpbacks being included in the hunt this year. It was good stuff even if I say so myself."

Ray started to rabbit on about his journalistic skills, but my mind was racing again.

There was only one logical explanation for this. Edith couldn't care less about whales or about giving her nephew's cause coverage in the paper. No, the only explanation that made any sense was that she was trying to shaft me. She must have wanted me out of the way for a few weeks so she could try Jeff out in my job, see if she could sideline me into Fashions or the bloody Social Diary, or even if she could get rid of me altogether. Shit, I knew I'd been a bit out of line in recent months, maybe been drinking a bit too much, screwed one or two interns too many, missed the odd deadline. But this was not on.

I stood up, stumbling backwards when the bench didn't give way.

"You okay, Richard? You'd wanna watch that – most

of the furniture is nailed to the floor – stops it rolling when the weather's bad."

I stepped over the damned bench. "Yeah, I'm fine, man. Can you show me how to make a phone call?"

"Edith?"

"Yes, hello, Richard. What has you calling me so early? It's just turned seven in the morning here."

"I'm terribly sorry to be calling so early, Edith. It was just to let you know that we've set sail now – me, the crew of the Good Ship Lollipop . . . oh, and your sprightly young *nephew,* Ray Kelly."

"Oh, that is good, Richard. I'm delighted you've connected," she said.

"What the bloody hell is going on here, Edith? Why didn't you tell me he was your nephew?"

"Would you have gone if I did?"

"No, I would not have. I'd have known it was a bloody set-up and I'd have held firm on it. So why did you really send me down here, Edith? Do you want to get rid of me, is that it? Are you hoping that I might get speared by a stray harpoon perhaps? Or swallowed whole by a whale?"

I could hear her laugh at the end of the phone.

"Wouldn't that be handy?" I went on. "Then all your troubles would be over. You could instate bloody Jeff in my job permanently and never have to worry about missing a deadline again."

"All right, just calm down, Richard." She sighed. "Yes, look, okay. I sent you there to research and write a series of features about my much-loved nephew and his lovely new wife. Have you met Sinéad yet, by the way? Sweetie, isn't she?"

"Yes, she's a real honey. Bloody hell, Edith, *this is a pile of fucking shite and you know it*!"

Her voice turned quite stern then. "I told you why I sent you out there, Richard – I want this story, and I want it from first-hand experience. I have no other agenda. Just grow up and write the damn feature articles, will you? Throw in a few whales to keep the environmentalists happy, and try to give me something a little bit different. Is that so difficult?"

I went to answer but she wasn't finished yet.

"And before you say anything else, let me be quite clear here. Mess this up, Mr Blake, and we will have some serious talking to do when you get back to Dublin. In fact, getting harpooned out there will seem a rather attractive fate in comparison with what will greet you on return if you don't deliver. Do I make myself clear?"

I felt like murdering her, but I knew when I was beaten. "Yes, all right. You'll get your damned features, but I want my job back when I get home. No games, Edith. I mean it – I'll sue you and the paper if you try to shaft me on this one."

"I understand. Thank you, Richard. So is that it then?"

I grunted.

"Well, good luck with your features now, and give my nephew and Sinéad a big kiss for –" She stopped short. "Actually no, on second thoughts stay away from Sinéad." She actually sounded like a witch as she cackled down the phone. "Toodles!" she said before hanging up.

I slammed down the receiver. "Stupid, bloody b–" I stopped as Ray walked into the office.

"My aunt?" he asked.

"Don't ask." I shoved back my chair and walked past him to get back to my cabin.

Chapter 10

RICHARD

I tried to put the Edith issue to the back of my mind and put on a good front when I met the rest of the crew. It was an effort, but I had at least two, if not three weeks ahead with these people – I didn't want to be known as a total grouch for the whole trip.

"Ah, there's your cabin-mate Takumi now," Ray said as we walked over to join him at the end of the dinner queue in the mess that evening. "Takumi, I'd like you to meet Richard Blake. He was the guy snoring above you for a whole day and night yesterday."

I was instantly envious of Takumi's small frame – he must have found the *Illuminar's* miniscule bunks practically *spacious*. Clean-shaven, with tightly cut, black, spiky hair, he wore a smart, navy polo shirt with a Greenpeace rainbow logo on the chest pocket, and a matching pair of navy shorts with brown sandals. Small black-rimmed glasses framed his dark-brown eyes, and his high-set eyebrows made him look surprised.

"Ah yes, hello, Richard," Takumi nodded.

"Just be careful not to shorten his name," Ray said to me.

"Why, what do they call you? Taco? Or is it Tacky?" I asked, in an admittedly very lame attempt to break the ice.

But Takumi didn't laugh. He immediately stiffened up, and glared straight at me. "Richard Blake, you bring great dishonour to my family."

"What? No, sorry, I didn't mean anything by it, man."

Shit, I've done it now, I thought.

"Takumi – I know that's your name." I looked at Ray for a dig-out, but he just shrugged and looked down at the ground. Then he looked slowly up and caught Takumi's eye, and they both burst out laughing.

Dickheads!

"Yeah, yeah, yeah. Hilarious. You're funny guys," I said, more annoyed with myself for being such a twat as to fall for the new-guy joke.

The two just went on laughing. Takumi had tears rolling down his cheeks as he held his stomach. "You should have seen your face, Richard – you looked so worried." He almost choked he was laughing so hard.

I just nodded, and forced a smile. It wasn't *that* funny. Oh well, at least the ice was broken.

I let them laugh it up and turned around.

Behind me in the queue was the ship's researcher, Hilary, a cheery, skinny marine biologist from Iceland. She wore the requisite whale-themed T-shirt, and her long mousey blonde hair was caught up in a messy pony-tail. She had a pencil behind one ear.

They ran out of food just before we got served so we had to wait for fresh supplies to be brought through from the galley, so I asked Hilary about her work.

"I'm tracking and researching humpback whales," she said. "The project I'm working on is actually being sponsored by Greenpeace's online supporters – they've been fundraising and sending donations in to keep us going."

I nodded and tried to look interested, but I was distracted by the new batch of chicken stew that had just arrived.

"Our project provides an alternative to the scientific research methods of the Japanese – where the whales are killed and a post mortem carried out. We track the whales' migratory movements through tagging, and we monitor their behaviour and breeding patterns – it's all harmless for the whales and we're getting some interesting results."

"Mmm, that's good," I said, spooning a large portion of stew onto some rice on my plate, whale research the last thing on my mind.

We all sat down at a table with Jules. I'd pretty much had it with being social, so I just ate my food and listened to them talk amongst themselves. It seemed that George and Ally had decided to abandon efforts to try to locate the whaling fleet again and tail them down to Antarctica. They felt it could waste too much fuel and time. Instead, they decided to change tactics, and to refocus the campaign spotlight on direct action – intercepting the whaling fleet in the act of whaling in Antarctica. So they had decided to get down to the Southern Ocean as quickly as possible. It was a risk apparently – it could prove a lot harder to locate the whaling fleet in Antarctica as the *Illuminar* hadn't stuck with them from the start, but the crew seemed cautiously optimistic that they had the ability to find the fleet again using their helicopter and sophisticated radar equipment. So the plan was to head for Auckland, and to refuel there before finally heading down to the Antarctic shelf.

This was all good news for me – it would cut some time off my leg of the trip, even if it did mean that I most likely wouldn't get to actually see the whaling fleet.

"It should only take about ten to fourteen days in total to get to Auckland now, depending on the winds of course," Ray was saying.

Most excellent. I could get these features written in that time, get off this tug in Auckland, and get back to Dublin to salvage the wreckage of my career. The thought cheered me up a bit and I cleared my plate and went up for seconds.

They were still talking about the campaign when I got back.

"So it's definitely going to be Auckland where we pick up the Japanese television crew?" asked Takumi.

"Yeah. Can you confirm that with them?" said Ray.

Takumi took a very small notebook and pen out of his shirt pocket. He slowly wrote a few Japanese symbols on the page in meticulous penmanship, then put the lid back on the pen and slid it back in the side of the notebook. Every move he made was definitive and thorough – the guy was so together that he made me feel like a total scruff. I rubbed my coarse chin, and felt my belly spilling out over the top of my combats. Maybe I should cut out second portions for the rest of the trip, and take a shave after dinner.

"So, it's a Japanese TV crew you have joining the ship?" I asked Takumi. "I wouldn't have thought there would be much appetite in Japan for this issue?"

Takumi put his notebook back in his pocket. "It is changing in my country, Richard." He looked at Ray, who nodded to him to go on. Takumi's whole demeanour changed – there was no fooling around this time – the whaling issue was clearly something the crew took very seriously. "We've seen big increase in media interest in my country over last two years. Many Japanese people love whales and want protect them – but they do not know full detail of whaling in Southern Ocean. They do not know Japanese government subsidise whaling activities with the tax money of my people."

"I didn't realise that either." I took my own notebook out of my back pocket to make some notes.

"Yes," Takumi nodded. "Is only a small group of people involved in whaling industry, and Japanese people only now beginning to understand potential damage it cause reputation of whole of our country abroad. Our businesses also starting to get concerned about effect on international trade relations. So we work on this expedition, and on land in Japan, to increase Japanese media coverage of the issue. We want expose the corruption, and wasteful nature of whaling industry. And I want show Government and Japanese people that is possible study whales without necessary to kill." He looked around at Hilary, Ray and Jules. "I think we are starting to make difference?"

"Definitely," said Ray. "This was the first year that the whaling fleet left port without a big ceremony. They wanted the departure to be invisible, to avoid the international media. And this year, the UK, United States, New Zealand, Australia, even the European Commission, have called on Japan to stop hunting. If we can just get the Japanese people to join them, we think we could really see an end to this someday." Ray put his arm around Takumi's shoulder. "And this guy, and his colleagues back on land in Japan, are our secret weapons. The Japanese people seem to be beginning to listen to us now – it makes a difference to be hearing the message from one of their own."

Sinéad arrived at the table with her dish of food. "Any room there for your wife? Or have you completely thrown me over for Takumi?" She squeezed in between them on the bench opposite me.

"Thanks for dinner, love, superb as always," Ray said and gave her a high-volume slobber of a kiss.

"Maybe the Japanese attitude could be an angle for one of my features?" I said to Takumi.

He nodded.

"And maybe I could work in some information about your project too, Hilary?"

"Ooh, fantastic! Thanks, Richard," said Hilary. "I'll make sure to give you a shout next time we get out to work with the whales themselves."

"That'd be great thanks." After all, I was damned if I was focusing the whole thing on the two sickening honeymooners. Sinéad and Ray were whispering and giggling to each other – it was enough to put anyone off their chicken stew.

"We've also been working on some angles for the humpback media and PR campaign," said Jules. "There's quite a lot going on at the moment."

"Great – well, I have to write at least two features, so it sounds like there's a few hot issues to –"

I was interrupted by Ally, who was standing up at the next table and had started to bang a spoon on a metal bowl to get everyone's attention. "All right, guys – after wash-up we're going to be showing the new campaign video down in the lounge. Can everyone who's not on duty report down to check it out? Ray, Jules and the team back at Greenpeace International have worked hard on this one and we're very pleased with the result. We're going to be releasing it to the international media next week so we'd like to get your feedback on it before then."

The journalist in me knew I should go to watch the video and try to start getting to grips with the campaign, but the lazy bugger in me just wanted to go back to my cabin to sleep off my jetlag.

Ray, Jules and Takumi stood up when Ally finished speaking, and started to gather up the dishes.

"See you downstairs for video, Richard," Takumi said, catching me off guard.

"Huh? Eh yeah, okay, see you down there, man," I answered before I knew what I was saying.

Ah, sod it, I thought. No harm in having a drink with them before hitting the sack, I guess.

The video opened with a sequence of a humpback whale and her calf swimming underwater. The sea was so clear that you could make out every feature of both whales – even the bumps and scratches on their skin. The calf was swimming along on top of its mother's back one minute, the next he was rolling off and gliding along underneath her.

Ray's voice came in over the pictures: *"Humpback whales are one of the world's best-loved breeds of whales. Known for their acrobatic skills, they have thrilled millions of people around the world. But the humpback whale is now considered vulnerable to extinction. There are approximately only 80,000 left in the world today."*

Then the sound of the whales took over. It sounded quite eerie at first – like a series of high-pitched grunts, squeals and groans. I sat forward to try to make them out. But without warning, the images switched to a fast-moving montage of clips – picture after picture of harpoons being shot, struggling whales and the chilling reality of the blood-red sea.

I was actually pretty shocked. I knew this was going on, I knew whales were being killed, but I'd never thought about what that really meant. It wasn't pleasant – these animals died hard. I watched as one whale was hit by a harpoon, then struggled and flailed about manically for what seemed like a very long time, before finally giving up. Then the carcass was hauled up onto the ship on a winch – a final humiliating act of cruelty. I looked around the room. Everyone looked shaken; even the hard-nosed Captain George was wiping an eye.

Then came a sequence of images of the Greenpeace inflatable speedboats – they were dwarfed beside the whaling ships which towered above them in the water, but regardless they were zipping in and out between the ships and the whales. The Greenpeace crew in the inflatables were being pounded with water cannons and jets from the ships as a loud Japanese voice repeatedly ordered them to stay away from the ship and to stop interfering with their work – over and over again the voice droned through a loudspeaker.

In the next scene some of the Greenpeace crew were standing up in the inflatables, holding up placards saying *Shame* and *Research?* beside the whaling ships. Takumi was one of them: he was holding up a Japanese character painted on a large sign.

He was sitting beside me so I turned and asked him: "What does it mean?"

"It means *fake*," he said. "It refers to their scientific whaling pretext."

The footage finally switched back to the earlier sequence – the mother and calf swimming underwater. I watched them with a feeling of unease this time, almost wanting to stand up and shout at the screen '*Get the hell out of there, lads!*' I looked around the room again. There were a couple of criers – Sinéad was sniffing beside Ray, and George was now openly crying and blowing his nose.

The video finished, and Ray turned to me. "So what did you think?"

"Eh yeah." I nodded a few times to get myself together, then coughed to clear my throat. "All a bit shocking though, man. Hard enough to watch, but well made."

"Thanks," said Ray. "The humpbacks are going to be a big focus for us over the coming weeks. There's been huge public outcry about their inclusion in the hunt this year. You've joined the *Illuminar* at a good time, Richard – we'll be upping the campaign pressure from here on out. I think – well, at least I hope – that there's going to be a lot of attention on this story, so it'd be great if you could write about it in one of your features – useful to get an outside view on it. If it's any good then we'll send it out to our international media contacts."

I hadn't had any international recognition since the whale-in-the-Thames story, and I knew a successful feature or two would do my career no harm. What was it with me and whales though?

"Course I know Aunt Edie wants you to write about Sinéad and me," Ray was saying, "but I think the humpback campaign would be more interesting, don't you?"

I nodded. "Yeah, but maybe we can work it all in together, keep the old lady sweet, and still raise some awareness for your campaign."

Ray smiled. "You're a wise man, Richard, I wouldn't want to get on the wrong side of Aunt Edie. We can start work in the morning after my watch. I'll show you more of what we're working on at the moment, take it from there."

"Good stuff, man."

I sat back in my seat, and cracked open another beer. Right, Edith, I thought. You asked for a couple of good features. Well, my evil tormentor, you're going to get exactly that, and more besides. I'll show you that Richard Blake has still got what it takes. You might be expecting me to fall flat on my face out here, but you've got a surprise in store. I'm going to write the best bloody series of features I've ever written in my whole damned life. I'll wipe the floor with Jeff, and any other pretender to my job. "*Mwah ha ha ha ha!*"

"What's that?" Ray asked.

I realised I'd actually pantomime-laughed out loud. "Nothing, man, sorry."

I looked back up at the screen where they'd started to play some more whale footage.

And if it could help those poor suckers in the process, so much the better.

I reached for my notebook and clicked on my pen. "Hey, Ray, why wait till morning, man? Tell me, why did the Japanese decide to include the humpbacks in the hunt again this year?"

Chapter 11

MELANIE

It was a long way to go to see whales. In fact it was a long way to go to see anything. I'd been travelling for nine hours and had already taken a taxi, an airport bus and two flights to get as far as the Norwegian capital of Oslo. I sat in a café in the airport sipping a cappuccino, and waiting for my third flight of the day – to Evenes. After that I still had a ferry ride and another bus trip before I would get to Tysfjord, my final destination. I was tired, but so happy.

Of course Marcus hadn't been one bit happy when I told him that I'd be taking a few days off. He'd scowled and muttered about there not being enough time as it was to prepare for the next board meeting. But it was only a couple of days, and even he couldn't refuse me that. And so I used the money I'd been saving to do up the bathroom and I'd done it – for four glorious days I had escaped.

Not only did I not have to think about work for four whole days, but I would also soon be getting to see the fjords and those killer whales.

I smiled to myself, stretched, and looked up at the departures board.

The entrance to my gate was quite close, so I had time to stop and buy a glossy magazine as I sauntered towards it. I was walking along and glancing at the mindless headlines on the front cover, when I heard my flight announced. I went to put the magazine away but dropped it when I opened my bag. As I bent down to pick it up, I noticed some large words in gold lettering written on the floor tiles in some sort of art fixture. I stood up and took a step back to read what it said:

If you cannot be
Where you are
Go to where you can be
And I will be there waiting for you

I turned around and strained to look back at the floor behind me in the terminal building to see if there were other quotes I hadn't noticed, but there were so many people milling around that I couldn't really see the rest of the floor from where I stood. Just these lines:

I stood there and read it again.

If you cannot be
Where you are

That's it – that's exactly my problem, I thought. I can't seem to rest and just be where I am. I'm spending every minute of every day trying to get somewhere else – that's what Father O'Mara meant, I suppose. And it's probably why I'm already feeling so relieved to be here, away from the chaos of my life.

I read the lines again.

Go to where you can be
Norway maybe?

And I will be there waiting for you
Who's *I*?

Just then somebody bumped into me. I looked around and realised where I was. I was getting a few strange looks, and I had a flight to catch, so I tucked my magazine into my bag and walked on to find my gate.

Tysfjord Inn was a welcoming, down-to-earth lodge hotel in a beautiful waterside setting. I arrived there with a coach-load of fellow tourists just after ten o'clock. It was very dark outside but there was a glimmer of light coming from the moon and I could just about make out some mountains and a small bay behind the building. Just inside the entrance, a somewhat intimidating ten-foot-high stuffed polar bear stood watch over the arriving guests. It added to the atmosphere, but nonetheless I scuttled past him to the reception as fast as possible.

While I waited my turn to check in, I scanned the foyer. Beside the reception desk was an unassuming, cosy bar area where a big log fire was burning furiously in the grate. I imagined myself warming up and enjoying a nice drink in there after a chilly day out at sea. There was also a small gift shop opposite the reception area which was still open and selling the requisite postcards, T-shirts and souvenirs.

I must stock up on a few of those stuffed orcas for the nieces and nephews before I leave, I thought.

"Long line, isn't it?" the woman in front of me in the queue said, interrupting my thoughts.

"Yes, it sure is," I said, instantly intrigued by her straight, snow-white hair, which she wore loose over her shoulders. It was so long that it almost reached her waist.

She appeared to be in her late fifties, or early sixties, I couldn't be sure. She looked great anyway. Her face was almost completely free of lines, and if it hadn't been for her waist-length long white hair and her hands, I would have thought she was a lot younger.

She turned around and shouted up to the receptionist in a deep southern-American accent. "Hey, honey, if this is the line for the bar, can you make mine a bourbon?"

The girl looked up, smiled and nodded, before returning to deal with the young couple she was with.

The white-haired American woman let out a huge deep, throaty laugh punctuated with a couple of great nasal snorts. I couldn't help but laugh too. It was one of those infectious laughs – if you stood within a few feet of it, you caught it. The people in front of her and behind me were all smiling too.

She turned back to me then, and held out her hand. "I'm Angie. Pleased ta meet ya, honey."

I smiled. "You too, Angie. I'm Melanie – my friends call me Mel."

"Well, honey, Mel it is. Looks like we're gonna be gettin' to know each other real well before we reach the top of this line."

I took an instant liking to Angie. Large as life, she wore a long blue shirt over beige cargo trousers. She was slightly overweight with a big personality that you couldn't help but be drawn to. We struck up a conversation, and I didn't notice how long the queue took. It turned out Angie was a horse breeder from Texas, in Norway as part of a world tour that had started in Africa five months earlier – a year to the day since the death of her second husband.

"Damn fool – I loved the bones off the man for thirty-one years, but he drove me crazy. Always so darned careful with money, never wantin' to spend any more money than was absolutely necessary in case there was some emergency or other around the corner. Then he ups and snuffs it on me – 'n all before we got to enjoy our retirement, before we got to grow old together." Her eyes seemed to drift away for a minute. Then she gave herself a quick shake. "Well, I ain't makin' the same mistake. I'm gonna spend every cent while there's still breath in my body and fire in my belly – you betcha, the whole, darn, tootin' lot of it. The kids encouraged me to take this trip – told me they didn't want no inheritance. So that's what's payin' for all this – damn, but they're good kids!" She smiled. "Anyhoo, I'm gonna do every single thing now that me and Ron said we'd do together some day." She put her arm around my shoulder. "I tell ya, Mel, never put off till tomorrow what you can do today. Read that someplace – damn clever words, those."

"They sure are." Angie's laugh wasn't the only infectious thing about her, I found myself picking up the American twang myself.

"So!" She took her arm away, and stood back to take a long look at me. "You here on your own too, honey?"

"Yes. I decided to take the break at quite short notice."

"No husband or guy back home then?" asked Angie.

"No, no men at all," I said, standing up straighter. "I'm here on my own."

"Well, I'll have to take you under my wing then. You're about my younger daughter's age – mid to late twenties, right?"

I laughed. I knew I was going to like this woman.

"Mmm . . . thereabouts."

Angie's turn at reception came, and true to her word she waited for me after.

"So you on for a nightcap, honey?" she asked after I'd got my key. "If I don't get a shot of bourbon before bed, I don't sleep."

I had planned to sink straight into bed with my book. But what the heck? I was on holidays after all.

"Why not?" I said. "I'll just drop my bag in the room and see you back here in a few minutes."

Most of the other passengers from our coach had also decided on a nightcap, so the small bar area was quite full when we arrived in.

"So what made you come on this trip then, Mel?" Angie asked as we settled into a corner of a table beside the fire.

"I just love the sea and marine animals," I said. "I do a bit of scuba diving, well, I used to anyway . . . So when I found you could actually get to see killer whales underwater here, I had to come. I've always had a bit of a fascination with whales in particular – they're such beautiful animals. I did some whale-watching a few years ago in Ireland."

"So you've seen whales in the wild before then?" asked Angie.

"Well, no, not exactly. I took a weekend course with the Irish Whale and Dolphin Group down in West Cork. We learned about whales and dolphins, and about how to identify the different species in the wild – it was really interesting. During the weekend we went out in a boat to do some watching, but sadly the weather was so foggy and overcast that, other than one small harbour porpoise, we didn't get to see anything."

"Jeez, I hope now, Mel, you're not going to jinx us on this holiday. If we don't get to see whales now we'll know who to blame, eh?" Angie gave a loud guffaw and a snort.

I hadn't even considered that we might not get to see whales on the trip. I just sort of assumed they'd be there if I travelled halfway across Europe to see them.

"Do you think there's a chance of that?" I asked.

"*Hakuna matata!*" shouted Angie so loudly that the rest of the people in the bar turned around for a few seconds. She picked up her glass, and saluted them all before finishing off her drink. Then she leant in close to me. "It means '*There are no worries*'," she whispered. "It's a popular phrase in Africa – learnt it when I was in Kenya a couple of months back."

"I thought it was from *The Lion King*," I said.

"Huh?"

"Nothing, it's all right," I smiled.

Angie leaned back from me. "Listen, honey, we either will, or we won't, see whales on this trip – that's about the only thing I know. There sure as heck ain't no point worryin' about it."

"You're so right, Angie," I said. "We'll have a great time no matter what happens."

"That's the spirit, honey!" She held up her empty glass. "One more for the road?"

I was so tired and groggy from the nightcaps when I got up at five thirty the next morning that I couldn't decide what to wear. After breakfast we were to have a lecture at the Inn, before being taken out to try to find whales in a large whale-watching boat for the day. The heating was on in my small bedroom, so it was quite snug, but I knew it was going to be very cold out on the water. I finally settled on a pair of thick black combat trousers, thermal leggings, a thermal vest, a long-sleeved T-shirt, a heavy, woollen polo-neck jumper and a warm black fleece – I wasn't going to risk getting cold. I put my warm puffer jacket and white woolly hat and matching gloves with my camera equipment by the door to collect later. Then I made my way down to breakfast.

We were due to meet in the lecture room after breakfast. Angie was sitting a few rows from the front beside an elderly couple I recognised from the bar the night before. And lest we should forget why we were there, the lecture room was dominated by a life-size model of a killer whale, which hung from the ceiling.

I stared at it for a few seconds.

It really *was* big. Seeing one of those was going to be quite something, let alone getting in the water with it. I felt a wave of excitement wash over me.

"Over here, Mel!" Angie shouted to me.

I went and sat down beside her.

"Mel, this is Tanya and Bert, they're from England," said Angie.

"So have you ever seen whales before, Mel?" Tanya asked after we'd all said our hellos.

Angie let out another of her loud guffaws. I wasn't expecting it this time and nearly jumped out of my skin.

"Don't ask!" she said. "Mel here is a bit of a jinx when it comes to whales. Ain't that right, honey?"

I smiled. I couldn't help but smile around Angie, even when she was teasing me.

"That's right, Angie, but I'm hoping you'll help me break my streak of bad luck."

We were interrupted then by a bell.

"Hello, everyone, can I have your attention, please?"

A woman with short black hair and very red cheeks stood at the front of the room, smiling profusely and shaking a small silver bell.

"I'm here to tell you the story of killer whales. It all starts with a very fishy love story."

And we were immediately hooked.

Odile, our guide for the day, enchanted us with the story of the killer whales of Norway and the mating herring (the lovers of the story) which were the whale's food source.

"Here, in fact, we prefer to call killer whales by their other name – orcas," she said. "They sound a lot nicer that way, don't they?"

We smiled and nodded our agreement. Odile could have given lessons on how to charm an audience. She had such a captivating presentation style that it would have been impossible not to agree with everything she said.

"Orcas are part of the dolphin family." She clicked through the first set of slides as she spoke. "In fact, they are the largest species of dolphin. The adults typically range from five to eight metres in length, the males being bigger than the females. They are very intelligent, sociable animals, living together in small family pods. They spend about a quarter of their time feeding, and the type of orcas that come to Tysfjord only have one thing on their minds – the herring that meet and mate here!"

Odile pointed to the screen behind her where a sequence of photographs showed the whales using what she called "the carousel feeding method".

"This is when a pod of whales surround the fish, and slap their massive tail flukes through the shoal of herring, thereby stunning them." Odile turned around to face the room again. "Then – and you may be surprised by this – they eat the fish one by one. Yes, even though they are such big animals with such huge mouths, they just eat one small fish each at a time. Can you believe it?"

Now, normally, I would be put off by Odile's approach – it might have seemed more suitable to a group of schoolchildren than adults, but this woman clearly loved her job and the whales, and her passion was wholly infectious.

I sighed as I thought of Marcus, Fenella and the stress of my job at The Mill. I wished I could go back to the time when I felt more like Odile did about my own work – back to the days when I bounced into the office every day at The Mill.

The last slide was a photograph of a line of three orcas – their heads popping out from the water.

"Such a beautiful spy-hopping photograph, isn't it?" Odile said. "'Spy-hopping', as you may know, is when they rise vertically from the water and scan the area around them, rotating as they do so. They are such curious animals as you can see."

I nodded – I longed to see them in action.

"And so, the number of orcas coming to Tysfjord each year goes up and down," said Odile, "but it is thought that between four and five hundred hunt the herring and live in the fjords here between the months of October and January each year."

"That should be enough to see at least one or two on a clear day in November, shouldn't it?" I whispered to Angie.

"Absolutely, honey," she whispered back with a wink.

Chapter 12

MELANIE

The *Nordic Dream* was a large cruising boat with three decks and ample vantage points for spotting whales. Angie, Tanya, Bert and myself found a spot on the upper deck where we could sit outside and take in the scenery and after a quick safety briefing we were under way. The others all went inside to the cabin to get warm a few minutes after we set sail, but I didn't want to leave. I took a deep breath as I gazed out at the scenery. The air was very cold and sharp, but it felt so fresh and clear that after inhaling it my lungs almost didn't want to let it go again.

I went up to the front of the ship where I could feel the sea spray on my face. It was freezing, but I didn't care. I was well wrapped up and I didn't want to leave. It felt so good to be out on the water again – to inhale the salty air, to feel the vibrations and hum of the ship's engine. We snaked through the narrow channels of water, passed by jagged cliffs, rocks and snow-capped mountains. And we were blessed with the weather – the sun shone down on us, creating kaleidoscopes of colours as it bounced off the mountains and shone down onto the dark water below. I took out my brand-new camera to capture the scene – and the whole effect was so stunning that I couldn't stop it clicking away, almost by itself.

"Good for the soul, eh, honey?" Angie appeared beside me. She was all bundled up in a white puffer jacket and matching white faux-fur hat.

"It certainly is," I said.

"So what kind of equipment have you got there?"

I took my camera off over my head and handed it to her. She inspected it. "Ah, Canon 400D – nice. Good all-round camera, this one. Are you getting any decent shots with it?"

"A few, but it's new so I'm only getting used to it. I'm just using it on the automatic function at the moment."

Angie made a face. "You've a great camera here, and you're using it on auto? For shame!" She shook her head. "Well, kid, you're in luck. I took a couple of advanced photography classes before this world trip – one of those things I'd always wanted to do. Want me to show you some of the basics?"

"Absolutely – that would be great, thanks, Angie."

I looked over my photos on the small camera screen while I waited in the foyer for Angie and the others to arrive down for dinner that evening. I'd enjoyed myself out on the water, and I felt thoroughly invigorated from the fresh air and the scenery – so much so that I almost didn't mind that we didn't get to see any orcas from the *Nordic Dream*. Almost.

The talk over dinner was all about orcas – whether we would see any orcas the next day, where we might see orcas, what we would have to wear to see them in the water, and so it went on. Like most of the people there, I was enjoying everything about the trip, but seeing the orcas was what it was all about.

One day on the water down, just one more to go.

We'd been warned that it would be very cold out on the small Zodiac speedboats the next day, so this time I put on six layers of warm clothing underneath my dry suit. Angie and the staff at the Inn had enjoyed a good laugh at my expense as we struggled to find a suit big enough to fit over all my clothes, but I didn't care – I was determined to stay warm.

There were three Zodiacs going out on the water that day. Each had between twelve and sixteen guests on board. They sliced at speed through the waves, which was great fun at first but in time the combination of the icy air and the chilling spray cut right through my layers of clothing – right down to the bone. Angie and I huddled together in the middle of the boat to try to stay warm.

By one o'clock we'd been at sea for over three hours and we still hadn't found any orcas. The Zodiacs pulled in together to a small fishing-village harbour for lunch. The short wooden gangway was bordered by a row of red, corrugated-iron houses built on stilts over the water. Our boat was the last to come in so our guides Pål and Johann tied our Zodiac to the other two that were already secured to the gangway. We made our way over the other two boats with some difficulty – our mobility restricted by the many layers of clothing and the dry suits. I followed Angie up the ladder from the boat to the gangway, both of us collapsing on the wooden decking at the top to get our breath back.

We both laughed as we hauled our sumo-wrestler bodies upright and waddled up to the café.

I finally felt my blood slowly flow warm again as we sat at the table after eating and I cradled a hot paper cup of coffee gratefully in my hands.

"Tell me about your time in Africa, Angie," I said, thinking that talking about warmer climes might help warm us up some more.

And it worked. Between the coffee and Angie's African adventure tales, pretty soon I'd forgotten all about the cold.

"It sounds fantastic. It must have been amazing to have woken up in the Serengeti to see elephants right there in your camp."

"It sure was, honey," said Angie. "I'm having the time of my life on this world trip. Only a shame my Ron can't be here to share it with me – the ol' coot." She sighed and looked down into her coffee.

I touched her padded arm and she looked back up at me and smiled.

"I used to do a lot of travel myself," I said after a few seconds. "I just don't seem to do as much any more. In fact, this is my first trip away in almost two years."

"Why's that?" asked Angie.

"Oh, I don't know – lack of funds due to the money pit that is my new house, I guess. And lack of time because of family commitments and study. Not to mention the ongoing struggle at work to keep an overbearing boss happy."

"Jeez, honey, sounds more like a prescription than a

life!" Angie laughed and snorted. Then seeing my expression, she got serious. "Sorry, Mel, I didn't mean to joke – wanna talk about it?"

So I told her a little about the pressure I was under back at The Mill, and she listened to every word, asking me questions along the way, encouraging me to talk.

"It sounds like those folk in work have been tryin' to control ya, Mel. You gotta be careful that playin' the victim doesn't become your default position. Take that boss of yours, for example – he sounds just like a school-yard bully. And y'know what bullies do when they smell fear? They attack. Thing is, most bullies are just plain ol' cowards themselves." She sniffed. "I used to be married to a man like that – my first husband." She screwed up her nose. "He never struck me nor nothin' physical, but I sometimes think that what he did was worse – spent his time manipulatin' and controllin' everything I did, constantly criticisin' and puttin' me down. That son of a bitch had me bullied into submission over the years we were together, had me believin' that I was worth nothin'."

Angie's words made me grow cold all over again, and I surprised myself by saying, "I used to be with a man like that."

I said the words so quietly that I wasn't sure if she even heard me. She must have, though, because she looked at me so sympathetically that I almost burst into tears. But she said nothing, just turned her head slightly and kept looking straight at me, waiting for me to go on.

"Except that my fiancé did hurt me," I said finally. "Just once. And it nearly broke me – not as much as the way our relationship wore me down over the years, but the way it finally ended hurt – in so many ways."

Angie put her hand over mine on the table.

I took a deep breath in and straightened up. "Still, it was probably the best thing he could ever have done. It was the wake-up call I needed to finally get out."

And then I told her all about the last time Ian and I met.

It was yet another argument about my work. I'd been due at The Mill on Saturday night to host a group of potential sponsors for the performance of the Hungarian Symphony Orchestra. Ian had been expecting me to come with him and his family to his father's club for another of their family dinners – his brother's birthday or something. He wasn't happy when I told him I couldn't make it until later that night.

I didn't retaliate – not even after he shook me until I couldn't see straight, then shoved me so hard that I fell back over a kitchen chair, badly injuring my lower back. He threw me away like yesterday's rubbish, but I didn't hit back. Instead, I just struggled to the spare room in pain and shock, waited for him to go to work the next morning, then packed my bags and walked out of our rented apartment for the last time. I wrote a short note calling off the wedding and left it there for him with my engagement ring. I never saw or spoke to him again.

"Good for you honey," said Angie. "That wasn't easy. How were you afterwards?"

I took a deep breath in. I'd already surprised myself by telling Angie as much as I had about Ian. I'd never really told anyone the full story about the fateful row in the kitchen two weeks before our wedding date – not my family, not even Katy. At the time I think I was probably just too ashamed – I knew they'd never liked Ian, and I felt

I'd let them all down by letting it go so far. I just wanted the whole mess to go away, so I told everyone we'd had a row, that the wedding was off and we were finished as a couple, and they seemed to accept that without too many questions. Maybe they'd been expecting it all along.

"I was all right, I guess," I said to Angie eventually. "My family and friends were amazing – they really helped me get over the break-up." I took a deep breath in and sat up straight. "But anyway, tell me, Angie, what happened between you and your husband?" I'd already told her more than I'd told anyone about Ian, and I wanted to change the subject.

Angie sat back in her chair. "For me, it was my baby girl that changed everything – she was the only good thing to come out of our marriage. Amy gave me back somethin' I'd lost. I looked into her darlin' green eyes, and I knew I had a future again." She smiled and paused for a few seconds. "Soon after she was born, somethin' inside me cracked 'n' I said to myself: enough, no more – this creep is *not* going to destroy me, he is not going to steal my spirit, and no way is he going to get a chance to hurt my little girl. So I faced up to him, told him I was leavin' and takin' my baby with me. Course, he tried to stop me, so I pulled a shotgun on him."

I looked at her in shock.

"Oh now, don't go gettin' yourself all het up! I'm from Texas – we have our own way of dealin' with things. I wasn't ever gonna *actually* shoot him." She laughed. "Guess he didn't know that, though! Naw, I just wanted to shake the son of a bitch up a little – and y'know what? It worked – he ran off a-cryin' to his momma. Pretty much left us alone after that. A year later, I met my Ron at a rodeo. As soon as my divorce came through we got married, bought a plot of land, built the ranch, had a couple of strong sons and one more darlin' girl together – and the rest, as they say, is history." She patted my hand. "I guess what I'm tryin' to say, Mel, is that bullies are just spineless cowards underneath all the show. If you let them control you, they'll go right on doin' it until they crush your spirit and they win. But if you can somehow overcome your fear, find your strength within, and *woman-up* . . ." she gave me a soft punch in the arm and winked, "well, then you get to do somethin' real sweet – you get to watch them crumble before your very eyes. And boy oh boy, is that a happy sight! But hey, you know all this – you've been through it yourself."

I looked at her. Had I? I wasn't so sure.

"To be honest, Angie, I never saw my fiancé crumble," I said after a while. "In fact, I'm not sure he cared all that much when I left him. He made a couple of feeble attempts to contact me again but, other than that, nothing much." I closed my eyes as realisation dawned. "Oh God, I let that bully push me around for years. And I thought I was past all that, back in control of my life, but here I am getting pushed around again – only this time it's in work." I looked back at her. "Question is, Angie, how do I stop it? I don't want to have to leave my job as well as my fiancé. I love working at The Mill, even if my boss and others have made it very stressful over the last year or so."

"Can you use guns in Ireland?" Angie asked with a loud guffaw.

I tried to smile, but I felt so close to tears that it wasn't easy.

Angie squinted at me. "Aw, I'm sorry, kid, I shouldn't

joke. Y'know, in any bad situation you got three options: you can either accept it as it is, change it somehow, or get out of it altogether."

I thought about it for a second, then nodded. "I suppose that's true, Angie, but which should I do in this situation?"

"You'll find the way, Mel, don't worry. Sounds like you've taken a few knocks over the years. Made some poor choices of the heart along the way maybe?"

I nodded. "I guess."

"Well, y'know, honey, that's okay. Really it is. What's not okay is not to learn from those mistakes. See, I can tell you're a strong, courageous lady. Look at ya, comin' all the way out here to the Arctic Circle on your own, wantin' to spot them orcas. All ya need to do now is just dig down a little deeper inside yourself to understand what's been going on in your life, and to overcome whatever fears have been keeping you from leading the happy, fulfilling life you deserve. 'Cos that's all that ever holds us back, y'know? Fear. Once you overcome that, you'll find you can do just about anythin'."

I smiled. "Hopefully." Then I remembered the sign in the airport. "Y'know, on my journey I saw a saying written on the floor in Oslo Airport. It said: *If you cannot be where you are, Go to where you can be, and I will be there waiting for you.* You see, I think that's been my problem back home, Angie – with everything that was going on in my life I couldn't just *be*. I think I *needed* to come here to Norway, needed the beautiful surroundings and the peace to help me work it all out."

"It sure sounds like it," said Angie.

I put my hand on her arm. "Maybe the *I* that was

waiting for me was *you* – maybe I needed to meet a wise American woman to point me in the right direction!"

Angie let out another of her loud guffaws. "That's the first time I've ever been called *wise*, but I'll take it. Thanks, honey."

There was a bit of commotion just then over at the boat guides' table. Our guide Pål was standing up and talking loudly on his radio in Norwegian. He was nodding a lot, then he shouted over to Johann who was up ordering at the café counter.

The only word I recognised in all of the excited Norwegian ones that Pål shouted over our heads was: *orcas!*

"*Yee-haw!*" cried Angie. "This is it, honey. Let's go!"

Chapter 13

MELANIE

I stared at Pål as he waited for everyone to be loaded back as quickly as possible into the Zodiac. "We just got a radio call from a local fisherman," he said once he had everyone's attention. "He has told me that there is a large pod of orcas feeding over near Henningsvær in the Lofoten Islands."

I clutched on to Angie's arm, and we smiled at each other.

Pål went on. "We will try to take you there, but this means we will have to travel very fast. It will give us only a short time to see the whales in daylight. And we will be coming back in the dark, so the temperature will fall very low. If you are too cold now or don't want to come back in the dark, one boat can go back to the harbour and anyone who would like to return to the Inn can change to that boat now."

Some of the group rose to switch boats.

I turned to Angie. "To hell with the cold – I'm not moving. I haven't travelled this far to give up now."

"Me neither, honey," said Angie.

We sat tight and waited for the boats to get organised, and before long were racing against time through the fjords. The Universe seemed to be with us – the wind was in our favour, and having fewer people made the boat lighter. With just eleven of the original sixteen people left on board we coursed through the waves at such speed that there was still a good bit of daylight left by the time we got to the bay.

It had been a long day, but the destination was more than worth the journey. The bay of Henningsvær was surrounded on three sides by tall, jagged rocks and mountains and the sun was at a low angle above us, casting late-afternoon hues of pink, peach and red across them.

In the distance, I could see a small fishing boat. The sky above the fishing boat was awash with activity, alive with the noise of hundreds of gulls and even a couple of sea eagles squawking and battling for their share of the fisherman's catch.

Pål slowed the Zodiac down, and we moved slowly towards the scene.

And then I saw them – their tall, black triangular fins rising high above the water. We didn't have to hunt for orcas – they were everywhere – not just one or two, but about twenty or thirty in total, in small pods of between three and six each. I could hardly trust myself to breathe, afraid it was all a dream and I might wake up.

When we were about a hundred metres away from the fishing boat and the biggest pod of whales, Pål turned off the engine. There was a flurry of activity as people tried to get a good view of the whales. After a few minutes there was a loud cry from a passenger at the back of the boat, and I strained to see what was happening. A small pod of orcas had started to swim towards us. I tore off my gloves and quickly retrieved my camera from its waterproof bag under my seat. Then I stood up on the seat to get a good angle, but I stumbled as the boat lurched. There was a communal scream on board, and then laughter. One of the whales had swum under the Zodiac, giving it a nudge as he went by.

"They are investigating us, just being curious," shouted Pål. "No need to worry."

It was difficult to work out who was more curious about whom as the pod of three whales circled around our now seemingly very small boat. They swam directly underneath a few times and drowned out the noise of the gulls with the thrilling "*whoosh*" of their blow as they resurfaced. One minute they were there alongside us on the surface, revealing their true scale, the next they would disappear and we wouldn't know where they would emerge again until the large black dorsal fins rose dramatically back up out of the water.

I took photograph after photograph from where I stood on the seat.

"Amazing, isn't it?" I said down to Angie as the whales began to swim away.

"Sure is!" she said. "Did you hear Pål there? He said that we can get into the water in a couple of minutes – he's just waiting for the right moment. We'd best get ready, honey."

I took Angie's outstretched hand and got down from the seat. We put our cameras away and retrieved masks, snorkels and fins. I pulled up the hood of my dry suit.

Then I stopped for a moment and took a long, deep breath.

"We have to wait for them to come close again," Pål was saying. "There is no point in letting you into the cold water if they are not near. When Johann gives you the signal, enter the water as quietly as you can. Remember from the safety briefing this morning – float on the surface, keep your head down and look below." He paused. "Now please put on your masks and fins and sit on the side of the boat, but do not go until the signal."

The group of three orcas that had been circling earlier began to swim towards the boat again, their dorsal fins rising and falling in the water in front of us. I quickly put on my mask and fins and pulled myself up onto the boat's rim.

Angie was a bit ahead of me and helped me up. She squeezed my arm. "Good luck, Mel!"

I smiled back, but I was distracted. I hadn't wanted to take my eyes off the orcas for a single second, but when I'd put on my mask it had started to fog up. I quickly took it off, spat on the inside of the glass, cleaned it with my finger and dipped it in the bucket of sea water behind me that Pål had filled for us to clear our masks. It seemed to work – the fog cleared and I put the mask back on.

Then Pål said the word we had been waiting all day to hear: "*Now!*"

And with that we slipped as quietly as we could off the side of the boat into the water below, careful not to make a splash that might scare the orcas. Apart from the small exposed part of my face around my mouth, I couldn't feel anything. The dry suit and layers of clothing underneath mercifully kept out the cold and made us very buoyant – we floated effortlessly in the icy water.

My eyes level with the surface, I could see the orcas' dorsal fins coming towards us. Then they disappeared entirely. I put my head down into the water, and there was silence. All I could hear was my own quickened breath through my snorkel, and the trickling sound of the sea moving around me. I squinted to try to adjust to the murky darkness, and I wasn't sure if it was the poor visibility of the water or my mask fogging up again, but it became very difficult to see anything at all. I squeezed my eyes closed for a second to try to focus better.

When I opened them again I could see quite clearly, but I couldn't believe what I was seeing. I seemed to be suspended high above the water. There was no noise – nothing except the emptiness of pure silence. I could see the scene below me – the Zodiac bobbing in the waves, Pål at the wheel. Human black blobs, their arms and legs outstretched, were floating on the surface of the dark, choppy water. And amongst them was me – I was a little adrift from the others, and as I looked at my body below I instantly sensed its anguish. I felt all of its tension and tightness as it anxiously scanned the water for whales.

I closed my eyes and took a long, deep breath, feeling the clear ice-cold air seep down my snorkel and into every cavity of my body – gradually easing the tension, banishing the anxiety.

I slowly opened my eyes and I was back inside my body. It took a few seconds to adjust back to the cold, dark water but, as soon as I could focus, I saw her – a whale was swimming up towards me from the depths. This time both the water and my view were clear – I could make out the orca's every feature. But I wasn't scared; I was only afraid that she might swim away if I stirred so much as an inch. I watched spellbound as she swam closer and closer. Then just before she got to me, she turned abruptly and swam by on her side. I got a sense of her full size then; I could see the large white markings along the bulk of her body, and I was mesmerised by the almost mechanical movement of her tail as it moved up and down, propelling her through the water.

No sooner had she swum past than she doubled back and started to come towards me again on her other side, this time just a couple of feet below me. When her head was directly beneath me, she stopped and seemed almost to hover there. As we looked at each other an instant calmness washed over me, and I knew I was meant to be there. It was as if everywhere I'd ever been, everything I'd ever done, everything I'd ever seen had led me to this moment, this connection with another being, this communion of spirits. I looked into the eye of the whale, and she stared back at me so intensely that I felt she was trying to tell me something. But what? I felt so limited by my human intelligence. I wanted to reach out to her, but not physically – my arms stayed spread out on the surface of the water; I just wanted to understand, to be able to communicate with this creature that filled me with such awe and joy.

And then, just as quickly as she'd arrived, the orca gave a quick flick of her tail, turned and swam back down into the deep.

It was like coming out of a trance. I became aware again of where I was. I popped my head up above the surface and looked around. Pål was calling over to us to come back on board and I felt quite dazed as Johann helped me up the back steps of the Zodiac.

"Did you see them?" he asked.

I looked up at him. "Yes, yes, I did." I was almost surprised to hear my own voice.

"How was it?"

"It was possibly the most beautiful thing I've ever . . ." But I couldn't finish my sentence. Thankfully Johann didn't notice; he was already helping someone else behind me up the steps. I climbed up into the boat and sat down to take off my mask and gloves.

Angie collapsed beside me. "Did you see them, honey? Weren't they gorgeous?" She took off her mask and slumped back in the seat. "*Woweee* – those incredible expressive eyes – just beautiful."

I nodded.

"I can't believe we've just come eye to eye with wild orcas." Angie shook her head, then looked up to the sky. "Ron, honey, if you're lookin' down, I did it, sweetheart. That was for you, my love."

I felt my eyes mist up.

Angie looked around at me, tears in her own eyes. "It is a bit overwhelming, isn't it?"

Just then a few people on board let out a communal gasp as two orcas swam up to circle the boat. Unlike earlier, when we'd just arrived and everyone on board was squealing with delight and moving about the boat in excitement, this time there was a respectful silence and stillness on the Zodiac. We watched entranced as the orcas rolled through the rippling sea, before diving down into the dark water, then popping back up again.

"Am I dead?" I whispered to Angie.

"Haw?"

I looked from the shadow of the whales, up to the fiery

sky that was alive with the pink, red and orange hues cast by the disappearing sun. "I'm just wondering if I'm dead, and already in heaven," I said.

"It is out of this world, that's for sure," Angie said with a smile. "But you are still very much alive, Mel."

"Then something or someone is trying to get through to me," I said, as I struggled to fully take in the scale of the natural beauty all around me. "The whales, this place – it's just all too much to mean nothing."

Angie moved in closer and put her arm around me. "Maybe it's meant to give us courage, honey. Just think, any time you're feelin' worried or afraid in the future, you can remember this special moment, and take strength from the memory of these amazing creatures."

I smiled at her. "That's lovely, thanks, Angie. I'll do that."

We sat huddled together watching the orcas in silence for another ten minutes or so. I didn't ever want the day to end but, as the sun finally slipped down into the Norwegian Sea, all we could make out of the orcas were the black silhouettes of their fins as they swam away into the approaching night. I felt a little bereft when Pål put the engine back on and turned the boat around for home. We'd been in the bay for just over an hour, I'd probably been in the water only for about five to six minutes altogether. It was just a glimpse, a brief moment in time, but as we sped away through the starry night I knew that it was one I would never forget.

It was after nine o'clock by the time we got back after seeing the orcas, and there was a palpable sense of excitement throughout the Inn: the staff were smiling and joking with the guests, the guests were toasting the staff, everyone was in a good mood.

Angie disappeared for a few minutes after dinner and I was sitting by the fire in the bar chatting to Tanya, Bert, Johann, Pål and a few of the other guides when she got back.

"Care for a celebratory nightcap?" I asked her, about to get up and go to the bar.

"Sure, but just a second, honey. I wanted to give you this first." She handed me a DVD case as she sat down at the table beside me. It had the words *Orcas of Norway* written on the cover.

"What this?" I asked.

"That's the nature programme Ron copied for me not long before he died. It's just a documentary about the orcas here in Tysfjord. My Ron loved it – said he'd a liked to come see them whales for himself some day." She had tears in her eyes as she spoke. "I want you to have it now, honey."

"Oh Angie, I can't take this from you – it has sentimental value."

She sat up straighter. "I don't need it any more. I've seen the real thing now – for both me and Ron." She put both her hands over the DVD and pushed it towards me. "It's important, honey. Play it when you get home – I think you'll find it interesting."

"Okay, Angie. I'll do that. Thank you." I gave her a hug.

"Hey, Mel," said Johann, patting me on the shoulder. "How about an Irish song?"

I turned around to him. "What? Oh no, I couldn't!"

"Go on, honey," said Angie. "I'd love to hear you sing."

"You're supposed to be on my side!" I laughed. But I never could resist a sing-song. "Oh, all right then, but don't forget you asked for it." And with that I broke into a rousing chorus of *The Irish Rover* as the Norwegians, Americans and English clapped along.

Chapter 14

RICHARD

Takumi was due on night watch in a few hours – he was asleep in the cabin with the air conditioning turned off, snoring loudly, so I had to write my article in the campaign office. I stared at the calendar on the wall. It had been only nine days since I'd joined the *Illuminar*, but it felt like nine years. I couldn't get used to the constant swaying and the movement of the ship, or to walking diagonally through corridors with my shoulder pinned against the wall. I found the thirty-to-forty-degree temperatures of the Pacific overwhelming, and I was getting really sick of dodging flying objects whenever we hit a rogue wave – we'd already had more than our fair share that day. The campaign office was normally full of people, but they were all busy running around preparing for bad weather ahead. We'd been on typhoon warning all day, and even though Captain George had changed course to try to avoid it, we were warned to be prepared for a lively night ahead.

I may have been sick of living on board a ship, but my

respect for the crew had increased with each day on board the *Illuminar*. They worked hard against the elements, and seemed to take living at sea in their stride. I'd never seen such an energetic group of people – if they weren't cleaning, painting, or fixing a part of the ship, they were practising fire or man-overboard drills, taking Japanese lessons, or working out campaign manoeuvres. I helped out with the dishes after meals a couple of times, but other than that I pretty much left them to it. I just wanted to be back on dry land – back in my rightful job on the paper, back where I could get a decent pint, and back where there was the potential of meeting a woman without facial piercings or a wardrobe consisting solely of combat trousers and T-shirts covered in some variation of the *Save the Earth/Oceans/Whales* theme.

But despite all my misgivings about being at sea, and my concern about work back home, I did find myself getting more and more interested in Greenpeace's emerging publicity campaign.

I looked back at my computer screen. I'd tried to capture the story in my article about the imaginative multi-media campaign about the fifty humpbacks included in the hunt, and the impressive response from the public. After an online vote to name one of the humpback whales that Greenpeace had been tracking through its alternative humane whale-research programme, their online supporters had gone nuts voting for the name 'Mister Splashy Pants'. In response, the Greenpeace team had created a viral online campaign around the story, and 'Mister Splashy Pants' became the mascot for the public campaign to stop the hunt on the humpbacks. The Greenpeace machine went into overdrive: Mister Splashy

Pants was given his own social media page, video game, and range of T-shirts, mugs and button pins – all demanding we *Save Mister Splashy Pants*. It generated significant media interest, and in a short space of time Mister Splashy Pants went global – CBS, Sky News, you name it, they picked it up. I had to admit, it was genius stuff, and I watched it all unfold from inside the floating campaign office.

In fact, it'd be fair to say I got a bit caught up in the whole thing myself – even put a call in to Jangler for his help.

"So if you could ask the students there at Ashvale to sign the petition demanding an end to whaling, it'd really help the cause," I said, surprised he could make out what I was saying over the terrible ship-to-shore phone line.

"Yes, indeed, I'll get right onto it, Richard," Jangler said, seeming enthusiastic. "I'll try to get some of our other schools involved too. We'll see if we can't all get together to help you and Ray shake things up a bit out there. Keep up the good work."

"Will do. Thanks, Father, I knew we could count on you."

The momentum from the campaign seemed to have a positive influence on my writing too. I'd finished a first draft of my article within a couple of days of being on board – mainly focusing on the campaign within Japan, but it also had a piece about Jerry and Sinéad. Edith had been on to me by email, pushing me to send her something for the weekend supplement, and I was almost ready to submit when the Mister Splashy Pants campaign really took off. As events started to unfold I decided to hold off on sending my first draft – it seemed so lifeless and uninspiring compared to what was happening in real time. Then Edith sent a couple of uptight emails letting me know she was royally pissed off about the delay.

"She'll get over it when she reads this," I said aloud as I scanned my final draft on the screen. It was one thousand, two-hundred and eighty-four words of sheer genius about Greenpeace's humpback campaign. The crew – including Ray, Sinéad, and Takumi with the Japanese angle – formed the background to the story, but the main stars were Mister Splashy Pants, the humpbacks and their army of online supporters.

I smiled to myself as I finished reading the last few lines.

Definitely worth waiting for. It wasn't exactly unbiased journalism, but it was emotive, topical and bloody well-written, even if I did say so myself.

I hit the send button, then sat back to wait for it to go – but the quality of the lines on board was so bad, and the speed of the internet connection so slow, that it took forever to send an email.

I sighed as I sat back and waited for it to go through. The sea had already got quite rough, and we were starting to roll about a lot – I was glad the desks and chairs were nailed down, but had to secure my notes under a heavy stapler. I looked up at the clock – the article had taken me longer than expected to finish off. I'd been in the campaign office for the past two hours and it was now pitch dark outside. I was tired and just wanted to get to my bunk. I looked back at the screen – the damned connection was taking even longer than usual, probably due to the bad weather. The *sending* symbol just rotated round and round endlessly in front of me on the screen.

"Come on! Just send already, will you?" I shouted.

"Call for Richie on line two," Jules' voice came over the intercom system.

I picked up the receiver and pressed the flashing line – and just as I did the much-welcome *Sent* symbol appeared on screen.

"Hallelujah!"

"Richard?"

I recognised Jangler's voice. "Yes. Is that you, ol' fella? To what do I owe the pleasure?"

"Richard, I'm glad I could reach you," he said, sounding serious. "Where are you now?"

I looked out the window. I don't know why – it wasn't like the black horizon could answer the question. "We're in the Pacific Ocean – somewhere south of New Guinea at the moment, I think."

"Ah, still on the ship then." Jangler took a long pause. "Are you sitting down?"

"Yes. Is everything all right, Father?"

"No, Richard." He took a deep breath. "I'm afraid I have some upsetting news. There's no easy way to tell you this, but it's your mother – dear Rose passed away suddenly this morning. May God rest her soul. I'm so very sorry."

I slumped back in the chair.

"Richard, are you okay?" Jangler said.

"She's dead? My mother's dead?"

"Richard? Is there anybody there with you?"

I sat back up straight. "How did she die?"

"A heart attack. She collapsed a couple of hours ago at Mass in your local parish there in Richmond. They called an ambulance straight away, but it was too late. She died before they were able to get to her."

"Right," I said, still not quite able to register what he was saying.

"Your Aunt Sheila and Derek called and asked if I could try to track you down. They'll be going over to London, and . . ." he hesitated, "I've just spoken to Edward. I'd like to give him this number to call you on – would that be okay?"

I nodded slowly to myself. "Yes, of course – we'll need to make arrangements."

"That's good, Richard. I'm sure it will take a few days yet for the funeral. Edward tells me she wanted to be buried locally there in Richmond. When will you be able to get back?"

"I think we're due into port in a couple of days."

"Good. Well, speak to Edward, and let me know if you need me for anything – anything at all, Richard."

"Yes, Father. Thanks for the call. I appreciate it. I'll go now if that's okay?"

"Fine – if you're sure you'll be all right. You've had a bad shock."

"Yes, I'll be okay."

Jangler sighed. "She was a good woman. You'll miss her very much, I'm sure. Look after yourself now, son, and we'll talk soon."

"Thanks, Father." I hung up and sat staring at the wall ahead.

My mother is dead.

It just doesn't seem real.

She's gone.

I should speak to Ed.

I need air.

I zipped my laptop into its case and grabbed my notes,

then stood up and used my free hand to hold on to the fixed desks and the walls to steady myself against the swaying ship.

I walked out of the office down the narrow corridor and pushed the outer door open. A sharp blast of wind slapped me hard as soon as I stood out onto the deck. I put my laptop and notes under my fleece and pushed my way against the wind to get over to the lower deck. As I reached for the railing at the top of the steps, a huge spray of salty sea water splashed up right over me, soaking me through. I just kept going.

Takumi and Pierre, one of the other ship's mates, were at the bottom of the steps, about to come up. They stood aside to wait for me to come down first.

"Richie, you need to get inside!" Takumi shouted up at me.

I could only just about make out what he was saying over the howl of the wind.

"Use internal doors. Not allowed to be out on deck tonight unless have to be!"

"All right, thanks. I just needed air. I'm going to the cabin now." I struggled against the wind to walk down the stairs.

"You okay, Richie?" Takumi asked as I passed him at the bottom. "You look terrible. Seasick?"

I just nodded and kept walking.

"There are tablets in my drawer – take two!" he called after me. "And make sure to stow away anything you have loose in cabin. It's going to get a lot worse – we're passing close to the typhoon."

I didn't turn around, but held my hand up to show I'd heard.

The wind forced its way into the corridor behind me like an uninvited guest. The strength of the gust blew over the bin beside the inner wall. I pushed the door shut behind me, relieved to expel the noise, then I stepped over the loose rubbish to get to the door of the cabin. Inside, the room was alive. The iceberg photograph had fallen off the wall and shattered glass from the frame was scattered over the sink and floor. Some of my loose papers had fallen off the desk, and a couple of books had come down from the shelf above. Anything that wasn't fully secured was swaying from side to side – myself included.

The door flew open again as I started to gather up my papers and books, so I slammed it shut and this time locked it to keep it shut. Then I threw everything into the cupboard, before rummaging in my bag at the bottom of it for the emergency bottle of whiskey I'd bought in duty-free on the way over. I grabbed my plastic tumbler from where it had fallen into the sink bowl, and filled it to the top with whiskey. It slopped out the sides as I made my way over to Takumi's bottom bunk. I sat down and knocked back what remained in the tumbler in one go. Holding on to the bed frame to anchor me against the swaying, I poured myself another, then another.

After a few minutes the phone on the wall rang.

I looked at the flashing light for a few seconds. It kept ringing, so I knocked back the whiskey, eased myself up onto the chair and, holding on to the desk to steady myself, lifted the receiver.

"Richie, you're there – good." It was Jules. "The intercom system's just gone down, and the line's very bad. May be wind damage. Anyway, sorry, it's another call for you – urgent apparently. I'll put it right through."

"Thanks."

I waited.

"Richie, it's Ed."

I tried to sit up straighter. "Ed."

"You've heard?" he asked.

"Yes. Jangler rang."

"We need to sort out the funeral." Six months hadn't changed his voice – it was my brother all right, but he sounded so formal. This person was like a stranger. "I can organise it all from here," he was saying. "How soon can you get back?"

"I'm not sure. We get to Auckland in a few days, I think. I'm due to get off the ship there – so I'll get the first flight back."

"Good," he said. "It'll take us a few days to organise things this side anyway. We'll stretch it out until you can get back – I'll let you know the details once we have it all finalised. Better go make some calls."

"Have you been talking to Sheila?" I asked before he could go.

"Yeah, she's not good. Sh–" His voice started to crack. He stopped for a few seconds, then cleared his throat and continued. "She's taken it pretty bad. Nobody expected it, she always seemed so healthy. Derek's booking flights over for them today. I'm on my way up to their house now."

He was about to hang up but I didn't want him to go. "Ed?" I said.

"Yes?" He sounded impatient.

"Eh no. That's all fine. Cheers, thanks for sorting it, man." I felt so bloody nervous speaking to him.

What the hell was the matter with me? I knew we

hadn't spoken in months, knew I had hurt him . . . but this was still Ed, my brother Ed who I'd known all his life. I needed to stay calm, keep him talking.

"I'm really sorry I can't be there to help, Ed."

After a few seconds of a pause, he spoke again, "It's all right, Richie, there's nothing you can do."

"Are you okay yourself, man?" I asked.

"I don't know. It's all a bit surreal to be honest." He sounded a bit warmer. "I can't believe she's gone, Rich. There was so much I should have said to her, so much I still wanted to talk to her about."

"I know – me too, man."

"How . . . h-how are you doing?" he asked.

"Who, me?" He'd caught me off guard. "Ah yeah – I'm cool. No . . . like . . . well, sad really." The words tumbled awkwardly out of my mouth. It wasn't what I wanted to say – they didn't sound like my words at all in fact, but once I'd started, I couldn't stop. "Yeah, sad, I s'pose. Ah shit, I don't know, man. I just found out."

"Right." Ed's voice became sharp and distant again. "Well, I'm sorry you're out there on your own, Richie. Can't be easy. I'll let you know about the arrangements as soon as I can."

Click.

And he was gone.

I stared at the receiver.

Cool?

What the hell was I talking about – *cool*? I'm far from fucking cool! My mother is dead, I'm stuck on board a floating steel prison, and I can't even talk to my own brother about it.

I tried to get to the bed, to the whiskey bottle, but just

as I let go of the desk the ship lurched and I got flung up against the wall. As we continued to roll, I dragged myself up, and half-crawled, half-slid across the floor. I grabbed the bottle and the tumbler off the bottom bunk, and sat on the floor against the bed frame to pour the whiskey. I finished that in one go, then drank another. As the boat continued to lurch and sway violently, the liquid kept spilling over the sides of the plastic tumbler, so I threw the empty tumbler across the cabin and drank straight from the bottle.

I wanted to call Ed back, wanted to tell him that I didn't know how I felt about our mother dying, and I wanted to tell him that I had never felt so alone in all my pathetic life. I hung my head, and looked at the whiskey bottle in my hand. I turned it round and round, staring at the swirling auburn blur of liquid that was now almost gone.

I thought of the last time I saw my mother, those last few minutes by the front door. I thought of her wrapping my scarf around my neck, the uncharacteristic but welcome hug, her waving me off from the garden gate. I thought back to my Ashvale days, back to that great day when my team won the Leinster Cup – she was so happy then, so proud of me.

But the good memories disappeared when I recalled how crushed she'd been to see my father show up at the school with his new girlfriend that day.

"That fucking bastard!"

I threw the bottle across the cabin. It crashed against the wall, sending broken fragments of glass all over the floor. When I tried to stand to clear it up, I was flung back against the side of the bed. I tried to get up again, but I lost my footing and got thrown across the room, this time landing under the desk. I grabbed on to it and pulled myself up. Then just as I managed to stand up, I retched – violently, again and again until there was nothing left inside.

Then I heard a loud, pained scream. It was a few seconds before I realised it had come from me.

I fell to my knees, sinking down into my own vomit. The cabin around me went blurry, and I blacked out.

Chapter 15

RICHARD

I awoke to a hammering on the door.

"Get up, Richie, we've got humpbacks out here!"

I opened my eyes, then snapped them quickly shut again. I opened them very slowly then, and looked through narrow slits. I had no idea where I was, but everything ached. I pulled myself slowly up to a sitting position. I was on the hard floor. I could just make out an overturned chair, broken shards of glass and loose papers around me. I put my hand to my head, and felt the congealed vomit in my hair. And that's when I remembered exactly where I was: rock bottom.

The banging on the door started again, then the handle turned, but the door was still locked from the night before.

"Come on, Richie, open up." It was Ray. "We're launching an inflatable rib. Myself, Jules and Hilary are going out to get some footage for the campaign. We're taking the hydrophone too to get some humpback sound recordings. You don't want to miss this."

I got up and sat on the edge of Takumi's bunk for a second before slowly moving towards the door. I unlocked then opened it. Ray pushed it in, letting a blinding flood of light into the cabin. It was just the artificial light from the corridor, but it felt like someone was trying to burn my eyes out of their sockets.

I cupped my hand over my face. "Easy, man. *Easy*. What time is it?"

"Almost six." Ray took a step inside. "Jeez, the typhoon really made a mess of this place last night, didn't it? The rest of the ship is in chaos too. We'll have some job clearing up." He started to sniff the air then. "What's that smell? Some kind of alcohol?"

"Eh . . . yeah . . . it was a bottle of whiskey I bought in duty free on the way over." I rubbed the back of my head. "It got smashed." It was the truth – *more or less anyway*.

"Oh right." Ray had a good look at me then. "You look pretty rough yourself – did you get seasick?"

"Eh . . . yeah," I said.

"Don't worry, you weren't alone last night – it was a pretty wild one. Anyway, it's already threatening to be a beautiful day. The sun's about to come up . . . *and* . . . we've got humpbacks! A pod of four or five, including at least one mother and calf. We'll be heading out to film them in less than five. Get yourself together and we'll see you down at the launch deck." Ray went outside, then shouted back. "You won't need a dry suit – it's pretty warm already out there – just grab a jacket for the boat."

I stood up, and picked up the overturned chair. And that was when I remembered:

My mother is dead.

I sat back down on the side of the bunk.

I have to get home. I need to find out when we're due to reach Auckland. I need to book a flight.

My head was pounding, my stomach was in shreds, but I had to get it together. I grabbed my jacket and went outside to the launch deck. The crew were busy loading up the inflatable. Ray was passing his video camera to Jules who was already inside.

"Great. You made it, Richie," he said when he saw me. "Look! Out there. See?"

I looked over to where he was pointing. The sea was as flat as a sheet of glass, barely a ripple to be seen, and a few hundred metres away I could see fins moving just above the surface and wafts of water shooting up from the humpbacks' blow.

"Yes, very good," I said, turning back to Ray. "Listen, man, I need to talk to you for a minute."

"No time, Rich, we can talk later. We've got to move fast – no idea how long they're going to hang about. Come on, jump on board. I want to film your reaction – hardened news journalist meets humpback whales for the first time – it'll make a great piece."

I didn't feel one bit hardened, but I didn't have the energy to protest, so I just got into the boat after him.

"*Standby for launch!*" one of the crew shouted, and the boat, with us in it, was dropped the few feet into the water.

"This rib has a water-powered engine, so it's safer for the whales and better for the environment – clean fuel," Ray was saying.

"Right," I said, holding onto the rope on the side of the rib, almost in a daze, as we cut through the waves.

When we got within about a hundred metres or so of the whales Jules switched off the engine. Ray started to hoist his oversized video camera up onto his shoulder.

"We'll try to stay as quiet as possible now so as not to scare them off," he said to me. "Now we just watch, film and listen."

"Sorry, can I get in there, Richie?"

"Huh? Oh yeah, sure." I moved aside in my seat to let Hilary up to the side of the boat to lower the flex of the hydrophone into the water. It was just like a small microphone at the end of a long lead attached to a black recording box.

I looked out to sea.

The whales were close now. I could see two, then three of them at a time near the surface, then a fourth and fifth would pop up, blowing their streams of spray high in the air to signal their arrival. One of the biggest seemed to move a bit slower than the others.

"Watch this," said Ray from behind the lens.

The whale slowly disappeared beneath the surface, and as he did he flipped his tail clean out of the sea, sending water cascading down around the edges of the tail like a miniature waterfall. We watched as the other whales did the same, until they had all disappeared.

Hilary turned back to me. "That's how we identify them," she said. "Each whale has a unique pattern on the underside of its tail – or its fluke as it's called. We can tell a lot about their behaviour using photo-identification of the flukes. That's why Jules is helping me today." She nodded over at Jules, who had been taking photographs and was now changing the lens on her camera. "I'll send the photos to the research centre for cross-checking then.

If we can find a match, we could be able to find out more about the whales' migratory pattern, feeding and other habits. It all helps underline our assertion that we don't need to harm whales to learn more about them."

"Right – good stuff," I said, scanning the water, waiting for the whales to reappear, but there was no sign of them.

"When they tail-fluke like that they're diving deeper," Ray said. "They could be gone for anything up to fifteen minutes now." He leaned back to rest on the boat's side.

"Hey, Richie, want to hear what they sound like?" Hilary had a big pair of headphones on her head and a wide smile on her face.

I slid over in the seat to her.

"These are a chatty bunch," she said, handing me a second set of headphones.

I put them on.

The sounds were incredible. It was just like the campaign video we'd watched the first night on board the *Illuminar*, but more vivid. It sounded like something out of an old dinosaur movie – an eerie, groaning, moaning sound, interspersed with high-pitched cries and warbles and growls. It was surreal, haunting and thrilling all at the same time.

I looked up and caught Hilary's eye. I said nothing, just raised my eyebrows, smiled and slowly shook my head in disbelief.

She nodded, smiling. Neither of us had to say a word. It was pure magic.

Suddenly less than ten metres from the boat, a whale launched himself head-first right up out of the sea, causing the boat to sway and sending tall sprays of white, foamy water flying into the air. He jumped clean out of the ocean. His long head was covered in small white barnacles, and the fins and folds of his belly were a patchy white against his grey-blue body.

"Wow, look at him fly!" Hilary cried out. "Isn't that something?"

But I couldn't speak. I was transfixed. As I watched that huge whale leap for the sky, a powerful charge shot through my entire body, sending technicolour shockwaves through my black-and-white existence. He crashed back down sideways into the water with an almighty splash. The sound of the impact broke my trance and I jumped back from the edge of the inflatable. I quickly sat up again – just in time to watch his tail, like outstretched eagle's wings glide back down into the dark water below.

"Over here now!" Ray called out.

I pulled off the headphones just as a huge whale surfaced right beside us on the other side of the boat. We all moved to that side and leant over the edge – the whale was so close to the boat that we could see its double blowhole, like a pair of huge nostrils, rise up above the water. It made a loud whooshing noise and a massive spray showered over the boat, covering us in cold, smelly seawater. Hilary and Jules reacted quickly and dived to cover the equipment; Ray just wiped his lens and continued filming.

The whale disappeared down into the water and I stood up on a seat to watch him swim, just beneath the surface, around the back of the boat to the other side. I went over to that side and leant out over the edge to watch him. I could see him approaching very clearly through the water – his long, nobbly barnacled head, his scratched dark-blue and grey skin. As I watched, he flipped over so that he swam by me, this time on his back, just inches from the surface. Like a curious, friendly puppy, he was so close that I could almost have reached out and rubbed the folds of his white belly. Then he turned around and circled back for another go, this time swimming on his side. When he was right alongside me again, he peered up at me from just below the surface of the water and I looked right into his eye as he swam past.

"Did you see that?" I said to Ray who'd been filming the whole thing beside me. "He looked straight up at me."

"Yep, I got the whole thing," Ray said, pointing the camera at me. "So what's it like to see humpbacks up this close, Richie?"

"It's incredible, man! Unbelievable." I looked back for a moment to watch the whale swim off in front of the rib, then turned back to Ray and the camera. "I've seen some things in my time, but this tops it all. I just looked into the eye of that whale and it was pretty damned amazing." I rubbed the back of my head. "It's at times like this that it feels good just to be alive!" I laughed and turned back to face the sea.

"I'm using that," said Ray, putting his camera down.

The whales continued to swim around by the boat for another while. We watched as they circled, surfaced, then dived again in sequence, we even got treated to a full display of acrobatic tumbles and leaps. It was like being in another world entirely. I forgot who and where I was, and just enjoyed the spectacle.

After another fifteen minutes or so the whales left us to continue their own journey, and we turned to head back to base. As we sped back over the waves I held my hand over the edge of the boat to feel the water spray up from the sea below and, for the second time that day, I remembered that my mother had died. I felt guilty that I'd forgotten – ashamed that I'd been enjoying myself when my mother was dead.

I caught Ray's arm as we stepped back on board the *Illuminar* and told him my news.

"Oh no, Richie. I'm really sorry for your loss," he said. "You'll need to get home."

"Yes, thanks, man. Do you know when we dock?"

"No, not exactly, but I'll go check with George now."

He went straight up to the bridge while I sat out on deck waiting for him to return. I stared out at sea as I sat there searching the horizon for the whales, but they were gone.

A few of the crew who'd just heard my news came over to offer their sympathies, and it all started to seem real.

After about ten minutes, Ray came back and sat down beside me. "George says it'll be Wednesday morning at the latest before we dock in Auckland. He'll put the boot down now though and try and get there as quickly as possible." Ray put his hand on my back. "He asked me to give you his sympathies."

"Thanks, man."

"Is there anything else we can do? Do you need help sorting out flights and travel?"

"Nah, thanks, man. Best I do it myself. Good to keep busy." I stood up to leave, hesitated for a second, then turned back. "By the way, thanks for waking me this morning. Those whales are really something else, aren't they?"

Ray shaded his eyes against the sun and looked up at me. "Yes, they are. Worth fighting for."

I nodded my head slowly. "You're doing a good thing,

man – you know, being out here, fighting for what you believe in. I admire that."

"Thanks, Richie," said Ray. "Look after yourself, all right?"

I nodded, and headed down to the cabin. Thankfully Takumi wasn't about so I cleared the place up, then went for a shower and got into some clean clothes. I sat down at the desk then and looked up flights from Auckland to London, booking one for Wednesday evening. I was a bit worried it'd be too tight – if the *Illuminar* had any delays en route I could miss the flight. But I decided to risk it.

Once I'd sorted the flight, I called Ed, but his phone just went straight onto voicemail. I left a message. "Hey, Ed, it's Richie. I booked my flight. We're due in to Auckland on Wednesday and my flight gets in to Heathrow at . . ."

I tried to flick into the confirmation email on the laptop to check the times but the connection was so slow it wouldn't open quickly enough.

"Eh . . . the flight's at . . . *gah* . . . bloody email!" I slammed the laptop lid down. "Oh, look, forget that. Assuming all goes to plan, I'll get in to London on Thursday morning, your time. I'll be coming in on the Air Canada flight via Los Angeles. Give me a call if you can, or even drop me an email. Let me know how the arrangements are going, if there's anything you need me to do, anyone to contact, or whatever it is. I feel so damned useless out here. Just call, all right?" I hung up.

I tried Sheila's mobile number then, but it rang out. Then I tried my mother's home line, thinking they might all be there by then, but there was no answer there either.

I sat back in the chair and looked around the cabin. It

was lunch time; the crew would all be downstairs eating. I could have gone down to join them, but I didn't want to face more sympathies so I turned back to the laptop hoping that some of the lads might have been on.

I looked through my inbox. There were just four messages: two from Edith, one spam mail and one from British Airways confirming my flight details.

I opened the first mail from Edith:

Well, Richard, it seems like you are back on form – at last!

Superb first feature article, very well done. Not quite what I asked for, of course, but fortunately for you it's infinitely better. Mister Splashy Pants, eh? Who'd have thought it?

We're running it in the supplement next Saturday. Get Ray to send on some photographs to run alongside it, will you? I don't know where I've put all the ones he's sent me over the years.

Edith

At least she liked the feature. I opened her second mail, sent a few hours later:

Dear Richard,

I've just heard the news about your mother. I'm so sorry. This must be a terrible shock for you and your family. Make sure to get back home as soon as you can. Let me know your movements, and if there's anything I can do.

May dear Rose rest in peace. We will all miss her very much.

My deepest sympathies,
Edith

So the news was out. I looked back through my inbox. Strange that nobody else had got in touch. Not a word from any of the lads. I shouldn't have been surprised really. I hadn't been on to any of them in months. Still, it *was* my mother.

I sighed. Then I opened my British Airways confirmation and checked the details. All seemed in order. I reread Edith's two emails, and even read the spam mail, before finally turning off my laptop and going to find Ray to let him know my flight details.

I found him sitting with Jules in the media room. They were huddled around one computer screen.

"Ah, here he is now," said Ray.

Jules stood up, walked over to me, leant up on her toes and gave me a big hug. "I'm very sorry to hear about your mother, Richie," she said into my shoulder.

The human contact was almost a relief, and for that brief moment I clung on to her. But she pulled back all too quickly.

"Thanks, Jules," I said, nodding my appreciation for her kindness.

She gave me a sad smile, which I returned. Then she squeezed my arm gently, before going back over to sit down beside Ray at the computer.

I followed her over and gave Ray the flight details.

"Thanks, I'll let George know," he said, "but I don't think you'll have any problems making it. The forecast for the next few days is good. It should be smooth sailing."

"That's great, thanks, man." I turned to leave.

"Eh, Richie?"

He glanced at Jules beside him, who nodded.

"We've just been editing the video footage from this

morning," he said. "It's really very good – that sequence with the whale by the boat, and your impromptu piece to camera is particularly good – very genuine and emotional. We were hoping to release it to the media this afternoon, as part of the Mister Splashy Pants campaign – to help us to build support for the humpbacks. I realise it may not be the best timing for you to be seen on television – after your mother's death – but maybe you could take a look and see what you think." Ray turned the laptop screen around to me. "It's not finished yet. We need to top and tail it with some campaign footage, but have a look anyway and see what you think." He stood up to let me sit in his seat, then leaned over me and pressed play.

He was right, the video was good. The footage of the whales from that morning was brilliant – it brought it all back. Ray had really captured the thrill of seeing them so close and Hilary, Jules and myself could be seen clearly enjoying the experience. Right at the end came my piece to camera. I laughed when I first saw myself – I looked ridiculous: my overgrown hair standing on end on one side, bits of vomit stuck to it, the collar of my shirt sticking up from underneath my jacket, and my eyes completely bloodshot. But when I heard myself speak, none of that seemed to matter. The man I watched looked almost . . . *happy*? It was like looking at somebody else altogether, not me at all.

But I wanted it to be me. I wanted to go back to that moment on the screen, the moment when I'd forgotten that my mother was dead, forgotten that my brother hated me, forgotten that I'd let the MacDonaghs down. I wanted to go back to the place where my problems didn't seem to exist, to where I'd forgotten that there was hardly anyone in the world who cared enough about me to get in touch about my mother's death.

The clip ended with a close-up of the eye of the whale peering up at the screen. I felt the same sensation again when I looked into his eye – total awe and exhilaration.

"Well? What do you think? Would it be okay to use?" Ray asked. "If it's picked up, it may be seen by your friends and family . . . you might want to think about whether it's the best time?"

I stood up. "Use it. Do whatever you need to do, man – just stop them from hunting those whales."

Chapter 16

MELANIE

All good things must come to an end. It was past midnight by the time I finally got to Heathrow airport – the timing of my Oslo flight meant that it was too late to get a flight back to Dublin that night so I had to stop over in London. I was weak from exhaustion by the time I finally got into my bed at the airport hotel, or at least I thought it was from exhaustion – I tossed and turned all night and woke up the next morning with a pounding headache and a raging temperature.

I dragged myself out of bed and shuffled into the en-suite to turn on the shower, but it took all my energy. I had to cling to the basin for support while waiting for the running water in the shower to heat up. As I stood there, I glanced at the mirror: I was a sorry sight. My hair, wet with sweat, was stuck to my forehead, and I could barely recognise the pale reflection and sunken eyes that stared back at me.

I somehow managed to drag myself into the shower, then over to the airport and onto my flight home to Dublin.

Katy had been house-sitting while I was away – mainly to let in the builder who was working over the weekend to finish off the living-room renovations. She met me at the front door as I arrived home late Sunday morning. She was obviously about to leave. She had her jacket on and her gear bag slung over her shoulder.

"Hey there, welcome back!" she said. "Your living room looks great. I've got to dash to my yoga class now, but I'll call you later to hear all about the holiday."

"Okay, thanks for looking after the place, Katy." I walked passed her into the house.

"Hey, are you okay, hon?" she asked.

I dropped my bags inside the door. "Not really. I think I may have caught some kind of bug, I woke up this morning feeling lousy."

Katy put her hand up to my forehead. "Yes, you've a bit of a temperature all right. Will I take you to a doctor?"

"No, I think I'll be okay, thanks, Katy." I walked towards the stairs.

"I can stay for a while longer?" She let her gear bag slide down to the floor. "I don't need to go to yoga."

"No need, thanks, hon. You head on out. I'm just going to go straight on up to bed to sleep it off."

"All right then, if you're sure?" she said.

I nodded.

"Well, just shout if you need anything – anything at all. I'll call you later on. Feel better, hon." She closed the front door gently behind her and I went straight to bed.

I didn't wake up again until after three in the afternoon. I eased myself up in the bed. My limbs were very sore, my whole body was weak, and I felt more than a little sorry for myself.

I so wished I could just go back to Norway, back to the bay with the orcas.

As I recalled the memory of the moment with the orca, I started to feel a lump rising in my throat.

I just couldn't work it out – why was I feeling so strange and emotional about the whole thing? I knew that the orcas were beautiful, and the setting there was stunning, but was it more than that? What was it about those whales, that encounter, that had this effect on me?

That's when I remembered Angie's DVD.

Angie had left very early the day we were checking out – she was continuing her world tour by flying on to Iceland. She left me a lovely note wishing me well on my journey, but didn't leave any contact details. I tried to get them from the hotel, but they weren't able to give them to me. It was a shame – she was such a great lady I would have really liked to stay in touch. I rummaged in my suitcase for the DVD, finally found it, then grabbed my duvet and went downstairs. I made myself a cup of tea and some toast, and settled down to watch it.

I could immediately see what so inspired Angie's husband. The documentary really was very good. The photography and video footage of the orcas in particular was wonderful, and watching them swimming along in the dark-green arctic water was almost like being transported back to Norway. I couldn't have been any happier – snuggled warm under my duvet, reliving the magic of that moment when I had seen them with my own eyes.

At one point, the narrator was talking about the whale's ability to communicate. A whale swam right up to the screen, and the footage zoomed in to give us a close-up of its eye as it swam past. The film cut to an interview with an Australian artist and writer who'd apparently spent years travelling the world to paint wild dolphins and whales.

"*The therapeutic effects of close encounters with dolphins and whales have been well documented,*" he said, "*but the question is, why do they bring such healing? It is without doubt a very humbling and special experience to come so close to nature's largest mammals, but I would go further than that. When I'm with the whales I can feel my own presence with such intensity and such joy, that all thinking, all emotions, my entire physical body, as well as the whole world around me become insignificant. It might only last a moment, but when I look into the eye of a whale, I am looking through the window of my own soul. I am in a state of pure consciousness – my true self.*"

I sat bolt upright.

I searched around on the sofa for the remote, rewound a few minutes and pressed play. I sat transfixed to the screen, watching the eye of the whale pass by again, listening to the man's words . . . *when I look into the eye of a whale, I am looking through the window of my own soul . . . my true self.*

That's it! I sat forward. Being in Norway, being with the whales – it helped me to see into my own soul, to see me again – the real me.

And I will be here waiting for you.

I smiled as I realised exactly why Angie had given me the DVD.

The "I" wasn't Angie at all. The "I" was me. *I* was there waiting for me.

It's like the artist on the film said: when I was in Norway I was able to be myself again, my true self. For the first time in such a very long time, there was nothing to worry about – no work, no studying, no house refurbishments, no disastrous love life – it was just me – the real me, there enjoying the moment. I had to go to Norway to look into the window of my soul, to get back to myself again, to remember who I really was.

I sat back on the sofa.

The really big question was, now that I was back to being me, how could I make the most of it? And how was I going to make sure I didn't get lost again?

I didn't go in to work the next day. I probably could have managed it if I'd pushed myself a bit, but I still felt a little grotty, and the thought of having to deal with Marcus and the few days' inevitable backlog didn't appeal. So instead I took another day at home. Somehow work just didn't seem so important.

After a long lie-in, I got dressed in a comfortable pair of leggings, and the new red orca hoodie that I'd purchased in the gift shop at the Tysfjord Centre. It was a change from my usual head-to-toe black, and even though it had been a bit of an impulse buy, the hoodie was so baggy and comfortable that it felt great.

After I'd unpacked and put a wash on, I took out my laptop and spent several hours looking up photography courses and classes on the internet. I found an intensive course that I could do at night over two weeks. It started in January and even included an optional extra module on underwater photography. Before I had time to remember all of the events at The Mill that would make it difficult to get out on time for evening classes, I called the number and booked myself a place.

Then I looked up the details for my old tennis club in Greystones, vowing to get back to tennis in the spring. After all, Niamh Delaney needed a bit of competition. I smiled to myself. Then feeling empowered, I entered the words "**top scuba diving destinations**" into the search engine, and it wasn't long before I became engrossed in the underwater worlds of Egypt and the Great Barrier Reef. I couldn't decide where I wanted to go the following year, so I bookmarked a few pages to revisit over the coming days.

It felt like quite a productive morning, so after a quick lunch I decided to reward myself with a break and a bit of television. I brought my mug of tea into the living room, and searched the guide for some easy daytime viewing, spotting the Bing Crosby and Grace Kelly movie *High Society* due on at half past one.

Just what the doctor ordered: a nice spot of romance and cheesy musical tunes. What better way to recuperate for the afternoon?

I checked my watch – still ten minutes to go before the movie – so I turned on the channel and sat back to flick through the rest of the TV guide. The news was on, and I was only half aware of the reports in the background until I thought I heard the newscaster say something about whales.

I looked up, and turned up the volume on the remote.

What I saw next on screen was sickening – dramatic images flashed across the screen – whales being struck by harpoons from a towering ship above; dead whales being dragged up on to the rear of the ship, oceans red with blood. I flinched and closed my eyes, but I couldn't keep them closed. I was horrified. I thought whaling had stopped decades ago.

A voice came on in the background: "*Irishman Ray Kelly is a spokesperson for Greenpeace. He sent this film from on board the* Illuminar, *the Greenpeace ship that is following the whaling fleet to the Southern Ocean in a bid to increase international pressure on the Japanese government to stop the hunt.*"

The news report crossed to Ray Kelly, wearing a Greenpeace jacket and cap, standing by a ship's railing at sea. "*The whales are completely defenceless against the technology, money and power of this wealthy fleet,*" he said. "*We are out here to help them, and to try to make the Japanese government and other whaling nations see sense. The slaughter, under the guise of scientific research, cannot be allowed to continue.*"

"*Absolutely!*" I shouted at the television, sitting forward.

"*Just today we came across a pod of curious, energetic humpbacks,*" Ray's voice continued in the background as the images switched back to the whales.

I smiled as I watched their dorsal fins glide gracefully through the water.

"*It seems incredible that anyone would want to kill any of these gentle animals, but sadly they do.*"

The picture panned around then to another man who was watching the whales from the boat. He turned to face the screen.

Richard Blake, The Irish Chronicle, it said at the bottom of the picture.

No *way!*

I couldn't believe it. What on *earth* was Richie doing out there?

And I just had to laugh. The usually sharp-dressed Richie Blake was looking more than a bit dishevelled on the screen: his now longish hair was sticking up in a quiff on one side and even seemed to have something stuck in it in places. His eyes looked quite red and he had very dark stubble on his chin. And I wasn't sure if it was the camera, but he also seemed to have gained a bit of weight, even had a double chin I'd never noticed before.

But despite his rough appearance, the guy was beaming.

"*So what's it like to see humpbacks up this close, Richie?*" Ray Kelly was saying.

"*It's incredible, man! Unbelievable!*" He looked back at the whale, then turned back to the camera. "*I've seen some things in my time, but this tops it all. I just looked into the eye of that whale and it was pretty damned amazing.*" He was rubbing the back of his head. "*It's at times like this that it feels good just to be alive!*"

I couldn't help but smile when he laughed.

So Richie looked into the eye of a whale too?

I knew exactly what he meant – that feeling of pure joy and feeling good just to be alive.

Ray Kelly came back on screen. "*We don't know how long these and other whales in the Southern Ocean will stay alive. Time is running out for those that have been targeted in this year's hunt. We need people all around the world to come together now to get the Japanese government to call for a halt to this.*"

I slumped back on the sofa and muted the volume after the segment finished. I couldn't get the images of the blood-red sea and the shooting harpoons out of my head.

And then there was Richie . . . The last time I'd seen him was almost six months before when we'd literally bumped into each other in Dublin. What on earth was he doing on a Greenpeace ship in the middle of the Pacific? The guy was a business journalist for goodness' sake!

I smiled to myself.

It was nice to see him though.

He seemed different, very different. Funny, I'd never have figured him for the kind of guy who would be so affected by an encounter with a whale – I guess a moment like that would get to anyone though.

I stared at the silent, moving pictures on the television, then turned the volume back up and tried to settle back to tune in to Louis Armstrong who was singing his way through the opening number of the movie's title song.

But it was no good. I couldn't stop thinking about Richie, and about the whales being hunted.

I gave up, turned off the TV and sat staring at the blank screen.

Honestly, how could anyone hunt whales down? I thought. They were so awesome in size and power, and yet they could be such beautiful, gentle giants. They had to be among the smartest animals in the world – sure their brains were several times larger than ours – and they had their own complex languages and unique ways of communicating with each other over hundreds of ocean miles. I closed my eyes as I thought about the poor animals that had met their fate at the hands of the whalers on the news clip – no doubt some of them had been mothers, perhaps even young calves. Whales live their lives within the same close-knit family unit – they must suffer so much when one of their family is hunted and killed. Why on earth would you kill an animal for research purposes anyway? Surely it could tell us more about its behaviours alive than dead?

The more I thought about it all, the angrier I got. However they'd done it, the whales had helped me over there in Norway. I couldn't stand by and do nothing – it was my turn to try to help them.

I leapt up and went straight out to the kitchen, opened my laptop on the kitchen table and put **"Greenpeace and whales"** into the search engine. Bit by bit, I pieced together the details of their anti-whaling campaign. I read the expedition blog that the crew of the *Illuminar* had been updating every day. Their supporters had been leaving comments and messages of support on the posts, and the website was buzzing. It was a passionate, international online forum. I quickly moved about the keyboard, tapping away on pure adrenalin. Before long I'd signed up for all the campaign updates, put my name to the online petitions, and became an "International Whale Defender" – setting up my own profile page on the Greenpeace website and promising to raise money and awareness for the campaign.

Then I turned to the profile pages of the *Illuminar* crew. The final entry on the page was titled "Visitors", and sure enough, there he was – Richie's familiar face grinning out at me, looking more like the guy I met that first day at the lunch – he was wearing a collar and tie in the photo with no sign of the double chin. In his profile it said: *Irish Chronicle* journalist Richard Blake will be on board the *Illuminar* for the first leg of our Southern Ocean expedition. He will be writing about life on the ship and the progress of the campaign to save the whales.

And just underneath his profile was his email address.

I looked at it for a few seconds.

Oh what the heck, I thought. This is all too much of a coincidence not to see where it takes me.

And before I could change my mind, I started tapping away at the keys.

Chapter 17

RICHARD

My initial desire for my time on board the *Illuminar* to pass as quickly as possible was soon replaced by a feeling of dread at what lay ahead of me. As dry land came closer, the anticipation on board grew more intense. The talk over breakfast on Tuesday morning was all about what everyone would do, or would buy, when they reached Auckland: Jules was planning to buy some fresh pineapple, Takumi wanted an espresso, Ray was going to get a haircut, and Sinéad was just looking forward to walking more than fifty metres in one direction.

Me, I was going home to bury my mother.

I sighed as I stared out at the unending horizon after breakfast. Then I turned away from the railing and started to walk around the perimeter of the ship's deck. I'd found myself out on the deck of the *Illuminar* quite a lot over the few days since my mother's death. I'd walk around, or just stand by the railings for hours staring at the waves below, my mind racing with thoughts and memories.

What is it about death that gives it licence to uncover

all sorts of memories – good and bad?

The smells and sounds of the sea reminded me so much of my youth – hanging out with Ben at his family's house in Clifden in the West of Ireland. If I closed my eyes I could even have been sitting up in the tree-house there, Ben beside me, looking out across the bay, chatting, laughing and knocking back a few contraband beers from his family's hotel.

I smiled momentarily at the memory, but my smile quickly faded as the bad memories flooded back.

It happened about six months after we left school. We were all just beginning to settle into college life. I was in my first year of an arts degree at University College Dublin, studying three heavyweight subjects – Economics, English and Politics – so I had a big workload. I'd also started to play rugby for UCD, making the squad for the firsts with relatively little effort. There was a lot going on between my studies, rugby and a hectic social life, and I threw myself headfirst into it all.

Jonesy and Dec were with me at UCD, along with about ten or eleven old boys from our school. Ben had gone to Shannon in County Clare to study Hotel Management. I remember being surprised about that at the time – like me, Ben loved subjects like English and History in school. He always had his head stuck in a book, and was a brilliant debater. In fact I remember him saying several times that he was thinking of going on to study law, maybe take the Bar exams – he would have made an excellent barrister. He dropped the idea when we were in sixth year though, saying he was going to go into the family hotel business. I knew he wasn't looking forward to catering college, but I guess he didn't want to let his family down. That was Ben all over: a people-pleaser.

I didn't see so much of him after we left Ashvale. He wasn't able to come to Majorca in July – where twenty or so of us lads went for two weeks to recover from the Leaving Certificate exams. Ben had to stay at home for the summer to work at the family hotel in Clifden. He did come to Dublin a couple of times after we'd started college, staying in the flat the lads and I were renting. The last time I saw him was when he was up for a match in late November. He seemed to be in good form all weekend. I didn't notice anything different about him. Nothing at all. I'll never forget the last time I saw him.

"Superb weekend, Rich. Thanks for that," he said pulling on his coat in the hallway of our flat. "Don't forget to come down to Shannon soon, eh? Or maybe we can all hook up again here in Dublin for a few pints over Christmas?"

"Absolutely, my man, absolutely," I said, opening the front door. "I'll organise the lads for that." Myself and Ed would be spending the holidays in London with my mother, but I was sure we'd get to meet up at some stage before or after that. "I'll give you a buzz over the next week or so for sure."

"Excellent. Chat then, Rich. Good luck in the exams. I'll see you soon."

I watched him walk off down the road into town to catch his bus back to Shannon.

I was busy cramming for end-of-term exams over the next couple of weeks, then I got caught up in the round of parties and nights out that followed. Ben left a couple of messages on the answering machine in the flat. I called him back after one, but missed him. He returned my call, but we didn't manage to connect.

Then Ed and I went to London. It was a pretty dismal week. My mother was still withdrawn and morose after seeing my father and his new girlfriend Louisa together at Ashvale earlier that year. Ed was a bit subdued as a result – he spent most of the time playing guitar in his room, just filling in time until he could go back to Ashvale in January. I put up with it all as best I could, but I was in a big hurry to get back to Dublin. I was going out with Paula Hunt at the time. I'd met her at a rugby-club do in early November and had been trying in vain to get her into bed ever since. I was getting very frustrated with her unfailing ability to resist my charms, and was already considering ditching her for a girl of easier virtue. Before I did though, I'd decided to give it one last shot.

It was just after New Year and I was back in the flat in Dublin a few days earlier than normal having made up an excuse to my mother of having to get back for rugby training. None of the other lads were back so I had the flat to myself for the night. Paula was on her way over, having told her Dalkey folks that she was staying with her best friend for the night.

I was in good form as I put the finishing touches to the spaghetti bolognese dinner I was sure would be the final ingredient required to seduce Paula into bed. I tidied up a bit and cleared the sitting area by shoving discarded mucky rugby jerseys, empty beer cans and crisp packets under the sofa, or behind the curtains. When I was finished, I checked my watch and realised that Paula was over fifteen minutes late. Irritated, I turned on the television to watch the football.

When the phone rang I assumed it was Paula calling to let me know she was either cancelling or running late. I didn't want her to think I was too bothered so I let it ring for a while, then turned up the volume on the television and answered it.

"Y'ello," I said, as casually as I could.

"Rich? Is that you, man? I tried to get hold of you in London, but your mother said you were in Dublin for rugby training – I didn't know we had training this week."

It was Jonesy. He was talking so fast I could hardly make out what he was saying. I pressed the mute button on the television remote, and sat up straight.

"Hey, Jonesy. Slow down, man. What's up?"

And then he told me.

He told me that Ben, our friend of seven years, was dead. He'd taken a massive overdose of painkillers that morning on his arrival back to his digs in Shannon after Christmas.

There was no note. Nobody seemed to know why he'd done it. He was just gone.

I went through the next few hours in a daze. Paula arrived at the flat to find me slumped on the sofa still holding the receiver, the television on mute in the background, burnt bolognese sauce and spaghetti stuck to the pots in the kitchen. She got me over to Sheila's that night, but I don't remember seeing much of her after that.

The lads all came to the funeral in Clifden, every last guy from our year, and most of their families too. It was the first time we'd all been together in one place since leaving school, but not one of us had ever imagined we'd be meeting up again under those circumstances – to say goodbye to one of our own, to say goodbye to Ben.

The tall stone church on the hill overlooking Clifden town was overflowing with people, and many had to stand outside in the car park in the wind and rain to listen to the service on a loudspeaker. We all sat together a few rows behind the MacDonagh family at the front of the church. The lads were pretty cut up at the time. Most of them broke down at some stage during the funeral, or beforehand, or in the weeks that followed.

But I never cried.

I would look at Jonesy, who sobbed his big soft heart out in JC's pub the night before the funeral and all through the service, at Dec who I could hear sniffing quietly behind me as we carried the coffin on our shoulders out of the church to the strains of "Be Not Afraid", and at Jacko who stood supported on either side by his parents as he cried freely at the graveside.

And I would look at the MacDonaghs – at Ben's parents, and at Lucy. Tears flowed down Mr Mac's cheeks as Jangler threw a fist of clay on top of the coffin, and Mrs Mac had to lean on a pale-faced Lucy for support, their eyes bloodshot from days of tears. I almost envied them all. I wanted so badly to feel something too. I wanted to cry. I even tried to make myself do it by concentrating on Ben and the memories.

I tried to imagine the pain he must have been in to have taken his own life. It gutted me to think of him going through it all alone. I tortured myself regularly with 'what-ifs'. What if I had noticed he was unhappy? What if I had called him more often? What if I had told him to forget about the family hotel business, and go study what he wanted? What if I had made the time to meet him the week before he died? It was a never-ending circle of criticism and accusation, with me standing as judge, jury and the accused. And in every case, in every scenario, the verdict was the same: Guilty as charged.

My parents both stayed in London through it all. Even though my mother knew the MacDonaghs well, Mrs Mac in particular, she didn't come over for the funeral. She just about managed to call me the day after he died to see "how I was after poor Ben's passing". I said I was fine and told her not to worry. It was a strained conversation, though, and I didn't hear from her again for weeks after that. My father tried to call me a couple of times too, but I avoided his calls – he was the absolute last person I wanted to speak to.

Sheila and Derek wanted me to come back and stay with them after the funeral, but the lads and I all agreed that we wanted to be together – back in the flat. Ed even came to stay with me there until he had to go back to school. It was good to have them all around but we didn't really talk about Ben – we all just sat around, watched sport and videos, and drank too much cheap beer.

So as my best friend was buried at the premature age of nineteen, I tried to convince myself and everyone else that I was fine. I made jokes to disguise my dark thoughts and feelings, and even tried to cheer the other lads up when they were down in the weeks following the funeral. But despite the act that I put on, those weeks and months were very bad. When I was alone, I found myself engulfed in a dark place where all I could think of was Ben. I just wanted to turn back time, to go back six months to when everything was okay, when I knew I could turn around and see him just behind me on the pitch waiting to catch a pass.

As term went on, I drank more and more, and shagged about with more girls than names I could remember. I skipped most of my lectures and handed up assignments late, or not at all. I even started to miss rugby training, eventually getting myself kicked off the squad. I made out to the lads that I didn't care, that training was just curtailing my social life, but I was slowly and surely losing my grip on reality. All the while I was living a double life – pretending to the outside world that there was nothing wrong, behaving like the big man about college, making out to the lads and to everyone that I was living the dream, having a ball, when in reality I was just trying to escape from the black cloud that was my constant companion. The drink, parties and casual sex helped me to forget momentarily but, when I was alone, and there was no one to pretend to, I sank down deep into the numbing darkness.

The crunch finally came that summer. I was in America with Dec and Jonesy on a student working visa for the few months. It was a good trip, and I was enjoying surfing and hanging out on the beach during breaks from our work as waiters in the local restaurants of The Hamptons. I was still drinking and partying hard, but I'd started to feel a bit better. That is, until I got my exam results.

I'd managed to scrape a pass in English and Politics with a lot of luck and the minimum of last-minute studying of borrowed notes, but I failed Economics. I was completely floored – I'd always been in the top five in my year in most subjects at Ashvale, and I usually sailed through exams. I had certainly never failed anything in my life before – least of all Economics.

I had to call my mother to tell her my results and she wasted no time in letting me know how disappointed she was in me. Ed was a bit more sympathetic, but even he said he wasn't surprised, the way I'd been acting lately. He said that Dad had been on to him and was worried about me too. None of their intervention made any impact on me though, other than to make me feel worse, and to take me back into the dark place that I'd thought I'd been beginning to escape.

So I had to come home early from the States to repeat Economics. I wanted to go back to the flat in Dublin to study, but instead had to go and stay with Sheila and Derek. My mother insisted – she said I needed "some grounding and stability" and refused to pay the next year's rent on the flat if I didn't comply. I retaliated by staying in my room in Sheila and Derek's house in protest. I was not one bit happy at being back in Ireland for the summer while the lads were still off having a ball in the States. I couldn't summon up any enthusiasm to hit the books, and I would barely grunt to Sheila and Derek, despite their best efforts to shake me out of myself.

They must have called Jangler in desperation.

The first I knew he was coming over was when I was hauled down to the sitting room by Derek. Jangler had just returned from his own summer holiday visiting relatives in Boston, so he spent what seemed like forever regaling Sheila and Derek with his travel tales while I shuffled, bored and pissed-off, on the sofa opposite him.

After a time, Sheila and Derek left the room and Jangler turned his attention to me.

"So, Richard, I hear that things aren't going so well for you in college at the moment?"

I shrugged my shoulders.

"Your aunt tells me you've failed some exams, and have stopped playing the rugby?"

I said nothing, just looked away from him out the window.

"How do you feel about that, Richard?" he asked.

I turned around. "Fine, Father, thanks."

Jangler sighed. "I have to say I'm extremely disappointed to hear that, Richard. I had high hopes for you – both for your studies and for your rugby career."

I looked down at my feet, and said nothing.

"I can't say I'm surprised though. You've had a difficult time over the last few years since your parents split, haven't you?" he said softly.

I shrugged again, still looking at my feet.

Jangler paused for a few seconds. "And, you know, a lot of your friends have been struggling to come to terms with Ben's passing. They miss him a lot. We all do really. It was very unexpected, wasn't it?"

I nodded slowly.

Jangler went on. "I question myself that I wasn't there to help him, Richard. He was a fine young man."

I glanced up at him. "He was, Father."

"You two were very good friends, weren't you?"

"Yeah."

"I think he looked up to you, Richard – you know, being his team captain."

I nodded again. It was probably true and I didn't trust

myself to say too much more.

Jangler sighed, then got up and walked over to the window. He stood staring out for some time. I knew I wasn't helping him much and I felt bad about that because I liked Jangler, but right at that moment I just wanted to be left alone, to just go back up to my room.

After a few minutes of silence, he came over to sit beside me on the sofa. "So what do you imagine he'd think of you now then?"

I looked up at him. "Sorry, Father?"

"Sitting back here in Dublin feeling sorry for yourself, when you could still have been off having fun with your friends in America. I don't think Ben would be too impressed if he were here today, would he?"

I glared at him. I couldn't believe it – the nerve of him. Who was he to know what Ben would, or wouldn't, have thought about anything – let alone what he would have thought of me? I was supposed to be his best friend, and even I didn't know what he was thinking.

I sat up straight in my seat. "With the greatest of respect, Father, Ben's not here. He's like – *dead*, y'know? So it doesn't matter a God-damn whether he'd be impressed or not. He's not here to *be* anything." I stood up. "So now if we're finished here, I have to go and study."

"No, Richard. We have not finished. You'll get plenty of time to study, believe me. Sit down, please."

I knew better than to mess with Jangler when he used the stern tone I recognised so well. So I sat back down, folded my arms and stared at the wall ahead.

He continued in a softer tone. "Yes. Sadly it is true: Ben is gone, and that's very difficult to understand, and to accept. I know that, Richard, believe me I do. It's a sad waste of a young life, and of a good young man. But I want to help you to try to understand what happened."

He paused and I looked at him.

He had tears in his eyes. He wasn't just spinning me a line.

I started to really listen.

"Unfortunately though, we can't always make sense of what God sends our way, Richard, but we can try to learn, and to grow from it – the good, and especially the bad. Just as the waves beating against the rocks give the rugged cliffs their beauty, there is a sense to everything in this world. Our challenge is to try to understand what that sense is, and to grow from it."

I really wanted to understand, I desperately needed to find some sort of meaning to everything that had happened, but I was struggling.

"But, Father, what can I learn from Ben's death, other than that I let him down? I didn't even know he was in trouble. I didn't know, not a clue. I was too wrapped up in my own stupid, pathetic life to notice, or to care. What kind of friend is that? I didn't deserve to be his friend, Father. I don't deserve to be here, to be the one still alive."

It was too much.

I stood up and turned towards the door. "I can't do this, I'm sorry, Father," I said with my back to him. "I know you mean well, but I can't."

Jangler stood up himself, took my arm and turned me around to face him. "You've been through a lot, Richard. I don't know how you've been able to get this far, to be honest, but believe me you are getting there, son. You may not realise it, but even by talking to me here today you're taking a great step forward. It will get easier; please trust me on this. You'll learn to let go a little more, your harmful thoughts will start to release you and you'll find a way to finally be at peace with yourself."

I looked at him. I could see that he really meant what he was saying. Ben's death still didn't make any sense to me, but I trusted Jangler. He said it was going to get easier, and so, for the first time in months I started to think that it just might.

After Jangler's visit, I managed to pack away my guilt and my numb grief, almost as though I was packing away my old books into a box at the end of term. I crammed hard for my repeat exam and was relieved when I scraped through to second year.

Jangler called me a few times after his visit, but the calls stopped once the new school year started at Ashvale in the autumn. He advised me to open up more to my parents, to Sheila and Derek, and to the lads. And even though I promised him I would, I never had any intention of talking to my parents. I did think about maybe talking more to Jonesy or Dec, or to Sheila and Derek, but it was just too hard to start the conversation. Then when I seemed to be getting myself back on track at college, everyone stopped asking me how I was, so that pretty soon we were all just back to normal – whatever normal was.

I stared over the railing at the white, rippling, V-shaped trail in the sea behind the ship.

I desperately wanted to stop the incessant memories of Ben from haunting me.

I knew that if Ben had been alive, he would have been

seriously angry with me for the way I'd treated Lucy. And I would have no defence: he'd be right. I should never have got involved with his sister in the first place. Stupid. Bloody stupid.

And then there was my mother. I wanted to be able to feel now whatever it was I was supposed to be feeling when Ben died – that deep sense of loss, that crushing grief – whatever it was that everyone else felt. But it was the same now as it was then. I didn't feel anything. I just felt numb. There on board the *Illuminar*, I felt more alone than I had done anywhere else in my entire life, and the painful memories and dark thoughts just kept coming.

Chapter 18

RICHARD

I inhaled a long, deep breath of fresh sea air, then turned to head for the steps. Inside my cabin, I logged on to my laptop to try to work on my article. I'd been really struggling to find a fresh angle for my second piece but, with all that was on my mind, the ideas weren't exactly flowing.

Before I started, I opened up my email. There wasn't much in my inbox, but I started flicking through the few new messages anyway. There were the usual few press releases and emails from the paper, then one forwarded to me and the whole crew by Ray. It was from a fourteen-year-old boy from the West of Ireland. He said he'd watched the report on television that day.

Ray's piece to camera must have gone out.

I read through the email: **I'm really glad that you are stopping them hurting whales. It's mean, and we don't want them to do that any more. Thank you for helping to save them.**

Nice.

I smiled, and opened the second email from a Melanie McQuaid.

That name sounded familiar.

Wait a second. No, it couldn't be . . . Miss McQuaid?

I quickly scanned the mail.

To: Richard Blake
From: Melanie McQuaid
Subject: Look into the Eye
Date: 10 December 2007, 15:03 GMT

Well, hello again, Mister Blake! Imagine my surprise when I turned on the news today only to find The Mill's favourite (*ahem!*) journalist alive and well and spotting whales in the Pacific Ocean no less. How on earth did you end up out there? Things must be very quiet on the *Chronicle's* business desk these days!

I must say I was glad to see from the TV that the eye is all healed up now anyway, but perhaps the hair could do with a bit of attention? :-)

Jokes aside, Richie, I'd like to apologise for my rubbish attempt at chatting you up that night in Dublin – all for my friends' benefit. It was more than a bit childish and I'm pretty mortified about it to be honest. You were right to be annoyed with me. In fact, you were right about a few things – especially when you said I needed to work out exactly who I am. I wasn't in a great place then and, though I didn't like it that night (not one bit!), your words probably rang a little too true for my liking. But I think now that meeting you then – getting annoyed with you even – it all helped to push me out of my comfort zone. So, thank you for that, and sorry again.

The main reason I'm writing to you, though, is because of the whales. I was particularly struck by what you said on the news report about looking into the eye of the whale. It's so strange, and such a coincidence, but I had a very similar experience myself in Norway just last week. Yes, I heeded your advice from all those months ago: I brought the five-year plan forward and went to Norway to see the whales – and I looked into the eye of a wild orca. It was so amazing! I couldn't fully get my head around it at first, but the encounter has been having a big effect on me ever since.

It was only yesterday I heard it said that when you look into the eye of a whale you look through the window of your own soul. Okay, so I know it probably sounds a bit far-fetched, and it's only been a few days since it happened to me, but I really have felt so different ever since. It's almost as though, by looking into the eye of that whale, I was able to take a step back and really see myself and my life for what they are. Perhaps the whales appear just when we need them, to help teach us something like this? Something important? Whatever the case, I think I really needed to see those whales that day. In fact, I *know* I did.

How about you, Richie? D'you think you might have needed to see them too? Or has life been treating you better since last we met? I do hope so – and that you're where you want to be in life now.

Until I saw your report today I must admit that I hadn't realised whaling was still going on in the world – I was really gutted to hear it. So I've signed up with Greenpeace for updates on the anti-whaling campaign, and I'm trying to think of a way of fundraising so I can help support the expedition. So you'll be pleased to hear your journalistic skills are having some effect – on me at least! :-)

Anyway, best go. I've been sitting at this computer for far too long already. Look after yourself out there, and best of luck to all of the Greenpeace crew.

Mel

Well, well, well. That's a turn-up for the books, I thought. Mel McQuaid, eh? She's the last person I expected to hear from out here.

I sat back in my chair.

Jeez, but it was bloody good to hear from her. She had sounded good, very good in fact.

I sat back up and read through the email again from start to finish – this time slowly.

I laughed at the hair comment – then ran my fingers through my long, stringy tresses. She had a point – I really did need to get a haircut.

The rest of the email was very open on the whole, but then I remembered that about Mel: she was easy to talk to. I smiled when I read how embarrassed she was about the fake seduction attempt. Not right to tease a fella like that. I was pissed off about it at the time. Or was I disappointed? I wasn't quite sure.

It was good to hear she took a break from the five-year plan anyway – at least for long enough to get to Norway. She needed that – bit stressed out, that girl.

And funny that she had a similar whale encounter.

"Right, anyway, enough of all that," I said out loud. "Time to get some work done."

I pulled my chair in to my desk, then I shut down my

email and brought my article up on screen. I typed a couple of sentences, reread them, then changed a couple of the words. I wrote another line, read it back, then realised it wasn't working at all and deleted the whole lot.

I shuffled in my chair, looked back at the screen and sat with my fingers poised on the keyboard. But it was no good – I couldn't focus. I finally gave up and went to find out what was happening on the campaign front.

Ray was in the campaign office on his own. He looked up when I came in. "Hey, Rich, you got a second?"

"Yeah, sure. I was just coming in to see how it's all going." I went over to his desk.

"All good here," said Ray. "We wanted to give you something." He handed me a large white envelope.

"What's this? Payment to place a few more articles in the paper during the year?"

He smiled. "The crew all wanted to wish you well over the coming days."

I opened the envelope and took out a handmade card. On the front was a detailed pencil sketch of a group of small stick-insect figures in an inflatable speedboat in the middle of the ocean, and just in front of the boat a whale's fluke loomed large above the water.

"Sinéad drew it for you – not bad, eh?"

I nodded. "Not bad at all, man. Your wife is a woman of many talents."

"I know," said Ray with a proud smile. "Open it up."

Inside, every member of the crew had written me a message. There were words of sympathy about my mother, some more drawings, a couple of quotes, and even a short poem written by Takumi:

Rippling sea stands still
Teeming life continues below
See and let go

"It's a Japanese haiku," said Ray.

"Yeah, I know." I looked up at him. "This is really something. Thanks, man. I appreciate it." I was genuinely moved. "And thanks to the others too – now I know what Takumi gets up to when he's on night watch."

Ray got up and put his hand on my shoulder. "You gonna be okay, Rich?"

I nodded. "Yeah, I think so – thanks, man." I sat down on a chair to read through the card properly.

"I'll see you later so," he said. "I'm just going to help with the stock-take so we know what supplies we need to get tomorrow."

"Need a hand?" I asked.

He looked surprised – I guess it was the first time I'd offered to help with crew duties.

"Eh, yeah, sure," he said. "That'd be great, Rich, if you don't mind?"

"Course not – I should have helped out before now. Sorry I've been such a dead weight to you all." I nodded at the card. "And thanks again for this, man – means a lot."

I helped Ray, Sinéad and Pablo, one of the kitchen-hands, with the stock-take for a few hours. We had dinner soon after, so it was late in the evening by the time I got back to the cabin to work on my article again.

I needn't have bothered – I still couldn't make any progress. I wrote a few more sentences about developments on the humpback campaign, but it seemed so stale, so bloody dull. I selected the few sentences I'd just typed, and deleted the lot.

Takumi came in. "Hey, Rich, we're all down in the crew room." He grabbed a sweater from the cupboard. "You coming down?"

"Nah, I need to try to finish writing this article before we dock, thanks, man. And hey, thanks again for the haiku."

He smiled and gave a little bow, then looked over my shoulder at the blank screen. "You still working on that? You make heavy work of it. Maybe you need look at it in different way? But hey, what I know?" He laughed, and pulled the cabin door closed behind him.

I stared at the closed door for a few seconds, then I swivelled around in my chair – a full 360 degrees – the blank screen was still there taunting me when I got back round.

What if Takumi's right? I thought. What if I do need to try to look at this whole thing differently?

I sat up straight and flicked into email. I opened up the note from Mel and read the same few lines several times over: *When you look into the eye of a whale you look through the window of your own soul . . . Perhaps the whales appear just when we need them to, to help teach us something like this? Something important?*

Maybe they do . . .

But what?

I flopped back in my chair and heaved a long sigh. Then I just gave in, shoved the chair back and went outside.

I stood out on deck in my usual spot, looking over the side rail. It was a warm, sticky evening, but the sea below was very dark. The moon and stars were blocked out by a sky of black clouds, and the sound of the guys laughing drifted up from the crew room below. I took in a long, deep breath while Mel's words circled around my head: *through the window of your own soul . . . to help teach us something . . . something important.*

I stared down at the dark sea below.

If I had looked through the window of my own soul, when I looked into that whale's eye, what had I seen? What had I learnt?

It wasn't like this anyway, I thought. It wasn't dark then. In fact, for the short time I was with the whales, the darkness and the shadows disappeared. I could see everything clearly – the whales, the ocean, the people with me in the boat. I was alive. Right there, in the moment. It was exhilarating . . . uplifting . . . *bright.*

I stared out at the unending, black ocean. So why did everything turn dark again after the whales? Yes, my mother was dead, and I was struggling with that, but it was more than that. This darkness and negativity had been with me a long time.

I heaved a deep sigh.

There was a time when life had felt brighter. A time when I had felt fully alive, felt good about myself. I was captain of Ashvale's senior rugby team, best friend of Ben, brother of Ed, one of the lads. I belonged somewhere, had my whole future ahead of me.

I kicked at the railing. "Why the hell can't it be like the old days again? Why can't I go back to that time?" I shouted at the night air.

Then I froze, as there in the darkness, I suddenly started to see.

I realised that I could never go back there. Life had moved on, and I'd made a bloody great mess of it. I'd turned into a pathetic, miserable loser who'd alienated everyone I ever cared about.

I hit the rail with the palms of both my hands. And then the truth hit me: Where my soul, the real me, had once been, there now was an empty, black hole. I was completely lost.

I looked out at the horizon. It was impossible to tell where the sea ended and the sky began. All I could see was a black haze.

Just then, I heard a loud squawking above. I looked up to see a tern flying in the wake of the ship. It flew directly in the narrow beam of one of the deck lights so that it appeared a dazzling white against the dark sky above.

I watched it fly slowly along. It used the ship's bulk to shield it from the wind, to ease its flight path for a few minutes until eventually it flew back out to sea.

I sighed and looked back out at the dark horizon.

But I was tired of the dark.

Accepting that my life was a total mess was one thing, working out what to do about it was going to be a lot harder. Then I had an idea.

I swung around to face into the lights of the ship. I needed help with this – needed someone to talk to. Why not?

Before I could change my mind I went back inside to my cabin, looked up the internet for the telephone number of the Dublin Millennium Centre for the Arts and dialled the *Illuminar's* switchboard for an outside line.

Chapter 19

MELANIE

I was wading through my post-holiday email backlog on Tuesday morning when Grace rapped on the door.

She popped her head around. "Welcome back, boss. Are you feeling better?"

I glanced up. "Yes, thanks, a lot better today, Grace – that bug really knocked me out for a couple of days. Norway was brilliant though."

"Ah good," she said. "So did you see any whales?"

I turned around in my seat to face her. "Not only did I see them, Grace, I came eye to eye with an orca – it was so beautiful."

"Really? Gosh, weren't you scared it'd bite you, or eat you altogether?" she asked. "They're big, those whales, aren't they?"

I smiled. "Yes, they're quite big, but no, I wasn't scared – quite the opposite in fact. It was really special."

Grace raised her eyebrows. "You're a bit of dark horse, aren't you, Melanie?"

I smiled and turned back to my computer. "So how did

the last couple of days go? Anything exciting?"

She came in and pushed the door closed behind her. "Well, actually . . ."

I glanced up, then seeing her expression turned my chair around fully to face her again. "What is it?"

"Well, I don't want to be the one telling tales . . ."

I took a deep breath. "All right, let's have it."

"It's Shirley again," she said.

My heart sank at the mention of my chairwoman's niece – the biggest pain in the butt of my department over the last six months. In Shirley's wake there already trailed quite an impressive trail of destruction, and I had long since lost my patience with the situation.

"It's just that she double-booked some group seats for Saturday night's symphony," Grace was saying, "which wouldn't have been a major problem except that one of the groups was the potential sponsor for the dance festival."

I groaned.

"It gets worse, I'm afraid," said Grace. "Unfortunately the other group was Queen Fenella, King William and their regular court of cronies. It was just a couple of minutes before the performance started, when they came in to take their seats, that the mix-up was discovered. Thankfully front-of-house handled it very well – they sorted it all out and gave Fenella's crowd some of our house seats. The sponsor's group were apparently quite good-natured about the whole thing. Fenella was raging though, and the whole thing delayed the performance's start for about fifteen minutes. Shirley told Emma on front-of-house that you'd instructed her to give the dance-festival sponsor group Fenella's seats."

"Oh she did, did she?" I closed my eyes and took a long deep breath. "I asked Shirley to ensure that the corporate group had the best seats," I slowly opened my eyes again, "but I didn't say which ones, and I most certainly did *not* ask her to put them sitting on our chairwoman's lap!"

I could feel the old familiar tension and strain returning by the second. Damn it, is it all over now? I wondered. The feel-good Norway buzz? Was that all just a dream? Is this crap my reality?

"Yeah, I guessed what really happened," Grace said.

"We're just so close to closing this sponsorship deal – it could be absolutely huge for The Mill." I sighed. "I was hoping we'd get an answer from them this week, in fact. I'll have to give them a call now to apologise, reassure them that that's not how we do things here. Oh God, and Fenella? Of all people for it to happen to! Was Marcus there?"

Grace nodded. "'Fraid so. Not happy either – though nothing new there, eh?"

Great. It was just bloody marvellous. I couldn't even take a few days off without all hell breaking loose. I took a deep breath and sat up straight to try to ease the pressure on my back a bit. "All right, thanks for letting me know, Grace."

But she wasn't finished. She looked a little afraid to go on, but she did so regardless: "Sorry, Melanie, it's just that there were a few typos in Saturday night's programme too. Marcus was really unhappy about it – he was down here yesterday looking for you. Oh, and Father O'Mara was on – he asked if he could meet up with you when you have some time over the coming days?"

I put my head down, closed my eyes and rubbed the back of my neck.

"Are you okay, Melanie?"

But before I could answer her my office phone rang.

Grace, bless her, picked it up for me. "Melanie McQuaid's office," she said, then made a face and rested the phone on her shoulder. "It's Shirley. She's saying there's a call on line two for you. A Robert Burke she thinks, but she says she's not sure."

I looked at her. "Who's Robert Burke?"

Grace shrugged her shoulders. "Will I ask Shirley to find out what it's about?"

"No!" The less Shirley had to handle the better as far as I was concerned. "It's all right, I'll take it." I put my hand out for the receiver and dialled 2.

"Melanie McQuaid here."

"*Miss McQuaid!* Finally I'm through! Thank God! I thought I'd never get past that dozy mare – you really should consider sorting out your staffing situation."

It couldn't be.

"Richie?"

I couldn't believe it. I thought he was on a ship somewhere.

"Are you back in Dublin?" I asked.

"What? No, not yet. I'm phoning from somewhere in the South Pacific actually – the wonders of modern technology, eh? We're about a day away from Auckland right now."

What? This was nuts!

"Can you hold on a second, Richie?"

I put my hand over the receiver and looked around at Grace. "I need to take this. Can you go ahead and set that meeting up with Father O'Mara – whenever, wherever suits him, you have my diary. I'll have a think about the other situation and get on to Marcus shortly. And can you hold all other calls and visitors while I'm on this call, please?"

"Of course," she said, and slipped out.

I took a deep breath, then took my hand away from the receiver.

"So tell me now, Mister Blake – to what do I owe the honour of this high-tech phone call?"

"I got your email," he said. "I was going to write back, but then I thought what the heck? Give the girl a call. Make her day."

I laughed. "You are too kind, Mister Blake. Always thinking of others."

"So true, so true," he said.

I smiled.

"Seriously, though, Mel, thanks for the mail. It was great to hear from you – really great, in fact." His tone changed slightly then. "It . . . well . . . let's just say it came at a good time."

He sounded different, a little less cocky than normal.

"That's good, Richie." I waited to see if he'd go on, but when he didn't, I filled the gap: "I couldn't believe it when I saw you on the news, and with the whales. It was such a coincidence I had to write."

"I'm glad you did. And hey, what's all this about you looking into the eye of a whale as well? Are you trying to steal my thunder?"

I laughed. "Sorry about that! It was amazing, though, wasn't it?"

"Y'know, Mel, it was great. And I think it did have an

effect on me. I'm trying to work it all out at the moment – tell me, what was it about the whole thing that made such an impact on you?"

I thought about it for a few seconds. "I'm not sure, to be honest. Perhaps it was that the whales and that setting were just so beautiful, that being there in that moment I wasn't thinking about anything else. It seemed to almost lift me out of my own life, my own world. I'd just been so focused on the future for so long – on this bloomin' five-year plan – that I don't think I was really enjoying the present any more. Do you remember when we first met all those months ago, Richie?

"How could I forget? It was the bright spot of an otherwise . . . shall we say . . . stressful day."

I smiled. "You said to me then that I didn't seem to be enjoying life. Well, you were right, and at the time I naïvely thought that rolling down a hill would prove you wrong. Maybe for a short time that day it did. But after that, life pretty much went back to normal."

"Yeah, that night when I met you in Dublin, you seemed pretty confused about what you wanted, about who you are," Richie said. "I am really sorry though, I was quite hard on you, it wasn't fair of me."

"It's all right, Richie, you were right." I took a deep breath. "I guess since Norway, since seeing those whales, I've realised that I need to do a lot more than roll down a hill to get back to the person I really am, or at least the person I could be. I have some changes to make now."

"I see . . ." He sounded thoughtful and went quiet for a few seconds. "Good for you, Mel. I wish you well," he said eventually.

"Thanks Richie. And how about you? Have you felt

any different since you looked into the eye of that whale?"

"Honestly, Mel? I'm not sure. I mean, it was a great experience, and it did take me out of myself for a brief time like you say. But it hasn't really changed anything. In fact it's just made me realise more, just how much of a mess I've made of . . ."

His voice seemed to fade away. I wasn't sure if it was the line or something else.

"Are you still there?" I asked.

"Sorry, yes, I'm here."

"Richie, are you okay?"

"Not really." He sighed. "Maybe this wasn't such a good idea after all, Mel. I shouldn't be bothering you. You hardly know me."

"It's all right – you can talk to me, Richie. What is it?"

He said nothing.

So I waited, and finally he spoke again.

"It . . . it's my mother. She died a couple of days ago while I was out here at sea." His voice cracked as he said the last few words.

"Oh Richie, that's terrible, and here's me going on about myself and the whales. I'm so sorry. What happened? Do you want to talk about it?"

And so I listened as he told me about his mother's sudden death from a heart attack, about the awkward phone call with his brother, and about the marked absence of his friends throughout the whole thing. My heart really did go out to him – he seemed to be in a bad way.

"It's strange actually," he was saying, "but being out here at sea, it's almost as if it's not real – like my mother's not dead at all. I just can't quite process it – things were quite tense between us at the best of times so I'm struggling to feel the grief within me that everyone presumes I must be feeling."

"I'd imagine it must be very difficult being out there with nobody close to you around. I'm not surprised it doesn't seem real."

I thought for a moment before going on: "I wonder, Richie, if rather than focusing on what you think you should or shouldn't be feeling, what if you were to try to focus on just remembering the good times you had with your mother? Might that help?"

"I don't know really . . . Maybe. I guess I could try it anyway."

"Grief can be a strange thing," I went on. "People process it in different ways. Give yourself time."

"Thanks, Mel, I'll try. When did you get to be so wise about all of this?"

I took a deep breath, remembering the most difficult time our family had been through.

"My sister Nichola's husband died in a car crash three years ago," I told him. "I've been helping her and the kids get through it ever since."

"Ah, I'm really sorry to hear that," he said.

"Thanks, Richie. They still have good days and bad days, but mostly good of late thankfully."

"Your family is obviously important to you?"

"They're the most important thing in the world to me," I smiled to myself as I thought about our lot. "And I'm sure yours are to you too, Richie – that's probably why you're so confused about your mother's death, and still upset about falling out with your brother."

"Yes, I guess you're right. I'm really dreading the funeral, not to mention meeting Ed beforehand."

"I'm sure it will be fine," I said. "I remember how upset he was when you were being taken away in the ambulance that day – no doubt he'll be very nervous about meeting you too, Richie."

"Maybe he will, but I'll be honest, Mel – I've absolutely no clue how to sort things out with him. No doubt he hates me these days."

"I'm sure he doesn't hate you. How could anyone hate you, Mister Blake?"

I heard a faint laugh.

At least he was laughing again.

"I'd say the most important thing will be to show him you're genuinely sorry," I said. "Explanations and excuses are one thing, but those two words 'I'm sorry' said with genuine feeling can be very powerful. Whatever you've done, you're still brothers, and whether you realise it or not I suspect you both need each other at the moment."

"Yeah, might stop me calling up virtual strangers for free counselling sessions, eh?"

"*Pfff!* Strangers?" I said. "Who're you calling strangers? Surely a roll down the hill together, our first late-night squabble, and now a ship-to-shore phone call – all puts us firmly into the *friend* category?"

"Yes, it probably does that," said Richie. "Once you don't pretend to pick me up every time I meet you, Miss."

The ol' cheeky tone had returned.

"Don't, Richie!" I covered my eyes with my free hand. "I'm still embarrassed about that. For the record though, I did not attempt to *pick* you up, I attempted to *chat* you up – different thing entirely."

He laughed. "Whatever you say, Miss McQuaid."

"Anyway, now that we're officially friends, I solemnly

swear never to chat you up again."

"Eh . . . *riiiight* . . . not sure that was *quite* the result I was hoping for."

I laughed.

"But I'll take all the friends I can get at the moment," he said, sounding quite sad again.

"Ah Richie, your other friends will come round. If they're true friends they'll be there for you no matter what's gone on. Hang in there. Life may seem a bit bleak at the moment, but if you look at it another way you have a golden opportunity now to start putting things right, to get your life back on track."

"True," he said. "From the sound of things we both do – you mentioned you have some changes to make too? I'll give it a go if you will."

I nodded to myself, and sighed at the thought of what was ahead of me. "I will try, Richie, but it's not going to be easy. I just got back into work this morning – to the usual litany of problems. Let's just say the post-Norway glow is wearing off very fast."

"If I'm not mistaken I don't think there could be too many people who could get the better of you at the moment, Mel. Hang on to that post-Norway glow for as long as you can. Just get out there and kick some ass, girl!"

"Y'know what, Richie?" I sat up straighter. "You're absolutely right."

"Always, Miss McQuaid, Always."

I rolled my eyes and smiled.

"Right, I'd better push off if I'm to sort out this sorry life of mine," said Richie. "Good luck on your side, Mel, and hey, thanks, girl. Really – thank you. This has been just what I needed."

"Me too, Richie. Thanks, my friend."

We promised to try to meet up in the near future and hung up.

I put down the phone, took a long deep breath and smiled to myself. Then I got up and popped my head around my office door.

"Grace, could you call Marcus and try to schedule a meeting for later this morning. And could you hand me in the most recent box-office report, the dance-festival sponsor file and Shirley's employment contract, please?"

"I'm on it!" said Grace.

"Great thanks. Any word on Father O'Mara?"

"Yes, I just called him and he said he's actually in town tomorrow – he wondered how you would be fixed for lunch? I mentioned that you were just back from a few days off so would probably need to work through lunches for a few days – maybe a short meeting later in the week here at The Mill might be better?"

I smiled. "No, lunch with Father O'Mara tomorrow would be an absolute pleasure. I'll meet him wherever is handiest for him."

"Oh." Grace looked surprised. "Right then. I'll call him back and arrange it." She kept looking at me for a few seconds. "Melanie . . . I hope you don't mind me saying, but you seem different somehow? I can't quite put my finger on it."

"Thanks, Grace, I'm feeling good." I smiled to myself. "Oh and could you get me those potential sponsors on the phone? The company CEO, please."

Chapter 20

MELANIE

Marcus's office was the most impressive room in The Mill. Located on the top floor, at the front of the building, it was bright and spacious with a simple black-and-white decor. Abstract charcoal drawings depicting the various art forms of dance, drama and music adorned the walls, whilst framed posters of his previous productions left visitors in little doubt as to Marcus's artistic achievements.

He was sitting with his back to the door and his desk when I came in that afternoon. It was a bright winter's morning and he was looking out the window over the city's quays down onto the River Liffey while talking on the phone. He turned to look over his shoulder when he heard me come in but carried on speaking and just gestured for me to sit in the chair in front of his desk.

I was all revved up and ready for what lay ahead, but the phone conversation seemed to go on forever.

I stared at his back. Please, God, don't let me lose my nerve.

Finally Marcus hung up. He swivelled around in his chair and eyeballed me.

"I assume you've heard of the debacle by now?" he asked. "I can't begin to tell you how humiliating it was, Melanie. And for it all to happen in front of the chairwoman! What were you thinking, giving her seats away to a corporate group?"

I had to make sure to stay calm.

"I didn't give them away, Marcus," I said slowly. "I asked Shirley to organise our best tickets for the potential sponsors but –"

He held his hand up to stop me speaking. "If you don't mind? I haven't finished."

I drew a long, silent breath, and let him go on.

He rustled through some papers on his desk, pulled out a concert programme and threw it across the table at me. "There were serious print errors in the programme too. Fenella herself pointed them out to me during the interval. I'm sure I don't need to tell you how deeply embarrassing that was – on top of everything else."

I scanned the blocks of red-circled text, and then I really don't know what came over me, but I burst out laughing.

"You think it's funny?" Marcus looked furious.

I tried to contain myself. "I'm sorry, Marcus, but come on. It's not really the end of the world is it? A few typos in a programme? Sure how do we know that Mozart didn't prefer to spell his name 'Mozarz' anyway?"

Marcus squinted and leaned over the desk towards me. "The Millennium Centre has standards of excellence to maintain, Melanie. I have never before experienced such a sloppy approach from the marketing-and-development department. I think you might need to consider substantially upping your game, don't you? Just try to improve performance in future, and close the door on your way out, thank you." He picked up a memo from his desk and turned around in his chair to face the window again.

I stopped smiling and closed my eyes as I remembered my conversation with Richie.

Hang on to that post-Norway glow for as long as you can. Just get out there and kick some ass, girl!

I had to do what I went in there to do. Whether I was ready or not. As Angie would say: *The time has come, honey, to woman-up!*

"Have you finished?" I asked, my eyes still shut.

"Excuse me?" Marcus glanced over his shoulder.

I opened my eyes. "I asked if you had finished." I stood up. "Because, I have. In fact, I've had more than enough of this."

Marcus swung around a little more in his chair and frowned at me.

"But just before I go, I wanted you to see this." I threw one of the documents I was holding down on the desk in front of him.

He glanced down at it. "What's this?"

"That, Marcus, is the contract for the dance-festival sponsor that I just finalised over the phone an hour ago. They accepted in full the proposal I put forward. You see, I asked Emma on front of house to watch out for them on Saturday night. Of course, it was actually Shirley's job to do so, but I was worried she'd mess it up – as indeed she did. Thankfully the sponsor barely noticed the mistake with the tickets thanks to Emma's swift action and care.

And what's more they enjoyed their experience at the Millennium Centre on Saturday evening. How was it the CEO put it on the phone? Oh yes . . . they were so impressed by my proposal and by the Millennium Centre's professionalism that they agreed to sponsor the dance festival for five years, *and* for the full amount I pitched for." I pointed to the contract. "If you would like to flick to the back page there, you'll see the total amount of the deal."

Marcus looked down at the contract, then looked straight back up at me, his face a picture.

"Yes, that's right," I said, nodding. "Fifty thousand a year. So, let me see," I pretended to count on my fingers, "I reckon that comes to a quarter of a million euro over the five years. Not bad for a morning's work, would you say? Would that be classed as – how was it you put it again? Ah yes, *'substantially upping my game'*?"

Marcus was about to speak, but I held up my hand.

"If you don't mind?" I held up another of the documents that I'd brought in. "Just when you think it couldn't possibly get any better than signing the largest sponsorship deal in the Millennium Centre's history . . ."

I handed him the latest box-office report, and he flicked through it.

"A-are these figures correct?" he asked.

"Yes, indeed they are. Danish Symphony Orchestra sold out. *Messiah* – sold out. New Year Gala – sold out with a waiting list for tickets. In fact, the whole Christmas season is almost completely sold out, and our membership packages are flying out the door too. In fact, I think you'll notice an overall increase of fifteen per cent in revenue on the same period last year."

Marcus looked confused. "These are impressive

216

figures, very impressive in fact. I hadn't realised we had seen such an upsurge recently. What's caused it?"

He leant back in his chair then, and adopted his all-too-familiar smug look. "I suppose we do have a particularly good programme of events this Christmas."

I scrunched up my face. "*Myeh* – much the same as last year really. No – I think you'll find that the surge in ticket and membership sales coincides with the innovative new radio and press campaign we launched two weeks ago, not to mention the membership promotion and our public-relations activity over recent weeks."

"All right, Melanie. The situation is better than I thought."

"What's that, Marcus? Are you saying that my department may not be so sloppy after all?"

Marcus just coughed. "Well, all right, let's say no more. Good work. We'll just agree to move on from this now, shall we? We have to focus on the Phase Two development programme anyway. The next board meeting is just a couple of days away – we need to finalise the new presentation."

I smiled. "Ah, the board meeting! I'm so glad you mentioned it. I've actually finished the presentation." I handed him another document from my pile.

He picked it up and scanned through the pages. Then he looked up at me.

"I don't understand. This is the exact same presentation you gave at the last meeting."

"I know."

He stood up to look me in the eye. "Melanie, I don't know what's going on with you, but I don't have time for this."

"Let's sit down, shall we?" I said, and sat back into my

chair. I had to wait a couple of seconds before Marcus did likewise.

"Look, it's fine, Melanie," he said. "Just get the new slides over to me in the next couple of days. The meeting's not till Friday."

I nodded to the document on his desk. "Those *are* the slides I'm presenting. I may add another one or two to the end, but other than that, this is my final position on the issue." I leaned forward. "The Millennium Centre has become the most successful, highest-grossing arts venue in the country. We have the nation's top sponsors and corporates supporting us. We have a thriving membership programme and a box office working at full capacity. We can, and we should, expand. But we are not going to be able to do so within existing resources. You've seen what can start to happen as we push our staff and our resources to their limit." I pointed to the flawed concert programme on the desk. "I personally will not preside over a department with lapsed standards of excellence. We're on top now, and I am committed to ensuring we stay there." I sat back. "So here we are – fifteen million euro to raise." I reached out and picked up the presentation slides. "And this is the plan of how we're going to do it. We're not going to do it by halves, we are going to start as we mean to continue – professionally and strategically."

"But Fenella doesn't want us to hire a consultant. She wants us to do it all in-house."

"Marcus, with the greatest of respect, could you tell me exactly who is running this venue? I thought that we were the senior management team? The supposed experts?"

"Well, now, Melanie, Fenella is the chairwoman and a major donor, she –"

"She's an actress, Marcus! She doesn't have the first clue how to run an arts venue. *You* do. And I know how to promote and sell it. I've done the research. I've spoken at length to the experts, and to venues of similar size and structure as us in the UK, in the States, and Australia – and they all say this is the route to go down. You need to trust my judgement on this, Marcus." I stood up. "Otherwise there is absolutely no point in my being here."

I held my breath. Oh sweet Jesus, please, please don't let him call my bluff.

Marcus leant his elbows on his desk, tented his fingers together and looked up at me for a very long minute.

"I think you might be right actually," he said eventually. "Yes, I've been thinking all along that we need to hire in a professional consultancy firm. Do this thing properly. That's how they raised all that money recently at The Met."

I breathed out. All right then, I'll play along.

"And you were so right, Marcus," I said, nodding and sitting back down. But I couldn't let him fully away with it. I leaned in over the desk. "We're both right."

"Mmm," he said, looking at me for a few seconds. Then he sat back, and swung around in his chair. "I'm glad we had this conversation, Melanie. In fact, I've seen a whole new side to you today. Let's meet again tomorrow to work out how we're going to bring Fenella and the rest of the board along with my plan."

I coughed.

He looked at me. "The plan?"

I raised an eyebrow.

"Oh all right, all right – *our* plan." He looked away.

It was a start at least.

"One more thing," I said.

He groaned and looked back at me. "What now?"

I handed him the last document in my hand. "It's Shirley's contract. I want her gone – she's next to useless in the role and a liability to the department. We can't carry her any longer. The letter clipped to the top is your letter terminating her temporary contract. I'll be contacting the head-hunters and recruitment agents today to get the ball rolling on hiring our full-time sponsorship manager. We'll need to get an experienced professional to manage this new sponsorship deal."

"And you want *me* to sign this letter?" Marcus asked. He sounded as if he was about to burst into tears. "I don't know. It could have serious repercussions for me with Fenella – she's particularly close to young Shirley."

"You hired her, Marcus – you're the only one that can fire her." I stood up and handed him my pen.

He took it, and reluctantly squiggled his signature so it was barely legible.

"Many thanks." I whipped it up off the desk before he could change his mind. Then I took my pen out of his other hand, turned on my heel and walked towards the door.

"Melanie?"

I turned back. "Yes, Marcus."

He stood up. "Erm . . . congratulations on the dance-festival sponsor, and the box-office figures. They're really quite something. I, eh, I'm afraid I may have underestimated you."

I smiled. "Thank you, Marcus – all in a day's work."

I walked out of the office, turned the corner and almost broke the heel on my shoe when I landed after jumping up to punch the air.

Chapter 21

RICHARD

Takumi had already left the cabin by the time I awoke the next morning. After talking to Mel I slept through the night for the first time in weeks. In fact, I slept for almost ten hours in total – missing breakfast by a long shot. I didn't care, though – I felt better than I had done in a very long time.

Ally's voice came over the PA system just as I was getting dressed. "*Land ahoy, landlubbers! Less than an hour to port. All hands on deck, please!*"

I smiled to myself – I couldn't believe they really said that.

I threw my bag over by the door just as Takumi came in. "Hey, Richie, we've got land in sight up there." He threw me a cellophane-wrapped bread roll filled with egg salad and bacon. "I notice you sleep through breakfast. You were snoring your hair off."

I smiled. "Really? Sorry about that, man, must have been very annoying for you."

"Ah, it's okay – I was awake anyway," he said.

I devoured the sandwich in four hungry bites.

"Bring your bags up on deck when you finished," said Takumi. "You finally get to go home today, my friend."

I brushed the crumbs off my T-shirt, grabbed my bags, took one last look around the cabin and followed Takumi up on deck.

Ray was leaning over the railing with Sinéad. Jules was with them taking photographs. I put my bags down and went over to join them. I stood beside Ray and stared out at the welcome sight of approaching land.

"So will you have time for a few beers with us before you fly home?" he asked me.

"No, sorry, man. I'm heading straight to the airport. I should be okay for time, but I just want to get there to be sure."

He nodded and put his arm around my shoulder. "Well, best of luck, Richie. I'm gonna miss your grumpy mug about the ship."

I laughed. "Yeah, sorry about that, man – thanks for putting up with me for the last couple of weeks. I think I might actually have enjoyed it, y'know – despite myself."

Ray smiled. "Good to hear. We enjoyed having you anyway, and I'm looking forward to seeing your articles in print."

"You and me both, man. I still haven't finished the second one yet, but the first one should be published in this weekend's supplement. I'll email you a copy."

Just then Sinéad's pocket started buzzing. She took out her mobile phone. "I've got a signal – we must be back in range already." She called out to the crew who were either working to get the ship ready, or leaning on the railings like us watching land approach. "Hey, guys, we got mobile coverage!"

I couldn't remember where I'd put my own phone. I hadn't had coverage since we'd left Japan. I wandered over to my bag, opened the side pockets and finally found it tucked in under some dirty socks. I switched it on and, sure enough, within a couple of minutes it lit up to show it had a signal. Then it buzzed, and it went on buzzing. Five new messages, six, seven, eight. It went on until it displayed twenty-two new voice messages and eighteen new text messages.

I opened the first text: *Rich, just heard about your mother. Very sorry. In Galway now but hope to get over for the funeral. See you then.* It was from James, one of the lads I played rugby with in college.

And another: *Richard, so sorry about your mother. I remember her well, she was a great lady. We're so sorry for your loss. Love to Edward too. From Anne.* Anne was a neighbour of Sheila's, who we used to meet when we stayed there during school holidays.

And on and on – text after text from colleagues, friends and the Ashvale lads; obviously the message hadn't filtered through that I was out of range. I sat down on the deck beside the bags to listen to the voice messages. One of the first, dating back to the day my mother died, was from Jonesy.

"*Rich – Karen and I are very sorry to hear about your mother – sympathies, man. Where have you been though? I haven't heard from you in months. Jangler's saying you're on some hippy boat in Japan or somewhere – that true or has the ol' fella finally cracked? Give me a call, will you? And hey, sorry again about your old lady, man. I'll see you at the funeral anyway. Look after yourself, right?*"

I smiled to myself. It was bloody great to hear the familiar voice. Mel had been right about the lads – they had come through for me. It was a big relief.

"We should move on down to the lower deck to get ready to disembark now, Richie," Ray said, picking up one of my bags. "Are you ready to go?"

I put my phone in my pocket, stood up and grabbed my other bag. "You know what, man? I am. I think I'm finally ready to get my feet back on solid ground again."

It was harder to say goodbye to the crew than I expected it to be. They were good guys, and they had a tough few months ahead as they continued south to face down the whaling fleet. It was dangerous work, and even though I was very glad to be leaving, the *Illuminar* and its crew had got to me in a way I'd never expected. I knew I could follow the rest of the expedition on their blog but, before I left, I made Ray and Takumi vow to stay in touch, and Ray, Sinéad and I agreed to meet up back in Dublin when they were next home.

I arrived at the airport with over five hours to spare, glad to have the extra time to work on my feature article – I wanted to get it finished before I got back, before the funeral. It felt great to be back on dry land, and it wasn't long before I was sitting back in a comfortable leather recliner in the airport's executive lounge.

The lounge hostess came over as my laptop was powering up: "Would you like a drink, sir?"

I looked up at her.

Did I want a drink?

Yes, I did. A beer would have gone down very well.

But did I *need* it?

I looked back at my laptop screen. Probably not. In

224

fact, if I was going to write the article I wanted to write, I knew I had to be sober to do it; and if I was to get it right with Ed when I arrived in London, I needed to keep my wits about me.

"Sir? A drink?" the hostess asked again.

"Just a coffee, thanks."

I watched as she went back to the hostess's station, poured me out a coffee, and put it on a tray. One small cup for man, one giant leap for Richie Blake!

I smiled to myself. Then settled back to drink coffee and focus on my article.

Chapter 22

MELANIE

Father O'Mara was waiting for me in the foyer of the Gentlemen's Club on St Stephen's Green, overlooked by five ominous stags' heads hanging from the wall above him.

I felt a shiver as I walked in the door. I'm not sure if it was because of the poor ol' dead stags or because of the memories of the once-familiar foyer. When Grace told me where Father O'Mara had booked for lunch, I thought about asking her to contact him to change it. But realised then I was being stupid.

It had been years since I'd been there. It would all be fine.

"Ah, Melanie, thank you so much for coming." Father O'Mara stretched out both hands and took hold of mine. "You're looking well. Come on through, I've booked us a table."

"Thank you, Father, lovely to see you." I walked ahead of him, glad to leave the stags' stares behind.

The maître d' showed us to a window table in the main

dining room that overlooked the bustling streets around St Stephen's Green. I didn't remember him from before, but he and Father O'Mara clearly knew each other well, and they exchanged pleasantries as we settled in.

"It's very kind of you to meet me for lunch, Melanie," Father O'Mara said, as the waiter poured out two glasses of spring water and we looked over the menus. "I could have come to see you at the Millennium Centre, but I thought it might be better to chat away from there so you could have a break. No doubt you're very busy as always?"

"Yes, but it certainly is nice to get away for lunch – it's been quite a week already."

"Oh?" Father O'Mara said, arching one of his white, bushy eyebrows. But before I could go on one of the diners recognised him and stopped to say hello as she was leaving.

Her lunch companion went on ahead and Father O'Mara introduced the woman to me as Edith Maguire. He stood up, seeming to tower above the much shorter woman as they chatted a few steps away from the table. They were talking so quietly that I couldn't hear what they were saying, so I just helped myself to some bread and looked over the menu.

"Sorry about that, Melanie. Edith and I go back years – a fine woman," Father O'Mara said, sitting back down. "We just had a small private matter to discuss. Anyway, you were just about to tell me how you've been getting along at The Mill?"

"Yes, it's going great, actually, thanks, Father. I'm just back yesterday after my trip to Norway, so I've had a bit of catching up to do."

"Ah yes, Grace told me you'd been to Norway – how wonderful. Did you have a good time?"

"Yes, yes, I did, Father – the time of my life in fact." I felt the now familiar quiver of emotion in my voice.

Father O'Mara noticed it too. "That's wonderful Melanie," he said, squinting at me for a few seconds. "Tell me about it."

So I regaled him all through lunch with my story of the fjords and the orcas of Norway. He listened intently, then shared stories from his own travels over the years, and lunch went by very quickly.

After dessert Father O'Mara patted his mouth with his napkin, then put it down decisively on the table. "Well, that was most pleasant, and I'm very glad to hear you're enjoying life a little more these days, Melanie. But before I get altogether carried away by our conversation, I must admit that I had an ulterior motive in asking to meet you today."

"Well, I suppose there's no such thing as a free lunch?"

"No, indeed," Father O'Mara said, just as the waiter arrived with my coffee.

"Your tea is on its way, Father," he said.

"Thank you, Malcolm," said Father O'Mara, then turned back to me. "Melanie, I'd like to tell you about a small project that I've been thinking about for some years now."

I leaned in. "Oh yes?"

"For some time, I've been growing increasingly concerned about Ireland's young people. They have so much to contend with these days. I see it all the time – they run into difficulties, perhaps just ordinary day-to-day things like exam stress, problems with their parents or families, the pressure to look a certain way or to be on top form on the sports field – and many other more serious problems." He shook his head. "They just find it difficult to cope, and don't know where to turn for help. As a result too many are instead turning to drugs, alcohol or in the saddest of cases, taking their own lives. Ah –"

Malcolm arrived with the tea and Father O'Mara leaned back to let him pour it out.

"Thank you, Malcolm," he said as Malcolm withdrew, then he turned back to me. "I want to try to do something about this, Melanie, however small, so I had the idea of building a retreat centre for young people. Nothing too grand, just a place where young people could go to get away from it all. I've spoken to some of the members of my community, and we think the idea would get the financial support of the Order – but I think I'd like to keep the centre non-denominational if at all possible, open it up to as wide a group as possible. Which means I'll have to work that little bit harder to get it off the ground." He took a sip of his tea.

"It sounds very interesting, Father."

"Yes, thank you, Melanie. It is all still just a concept at the moment, but recently I have been given a small amount of seed capital to get it off the ground, so I feel it's a sign from Himself" – he looked up – "that it's time to get going. The thing is, I'm going to need a little bit of help to get the momentum going. So I thought to myself, who's the best person I know at building momentum?"

I smiled. As Father O'Mara was speaking I'd thought about my nieces and nephews. I'd have loved there to be a place like Father O'Mara described, where as teenagers they could go to get away from it all. After all, it was exactly what I needed myself recently – to get away from it all. I was able to go to Norway, but young people couldn't get away so easily.

"That sounds like a really wonderful idea, Father. I'd like to help. What can I do?"

He reached out and put his hand over mine. "I was hoping you'd say that, Melanie. You're such a marvellous organiser." He withdrew his hand, and sat back in his chair. "But I'm very conscious of your current work load and I don't want to overburden you. I know how hard Marcus works you all there at The Mill – he's not necessarily the easiest person to work for?"

"It's okay, Father, Marcus and I are good at the moment, and this is important. Some things we just have to make time for, don't we?"

"Yes, indeed. Well, thank you, Melanie. It shouldn't take too much time at the moment anyway, it's very early days. The first thing I need to do is convene a meeting. I'm gathering a group of people to get the discussions started – some potential funders and supporters. I'd love you to come along."

"Of course. When were you hoping to have it?"

Just then there was a loud crash.

"*You bloody idiot!*" a man's voice shouted out behind me.

Father O'Mara peered around me to look, but I didn't need to turn to see who it was – I'd have known that voice anywhere. How on earth hadn't I spotted him before now?

Father O'Mara looked back to me. "Poor Malcolm, he's a bit of a butterfingers at the best of times. He's just dropped some vegetables over that couple's table. The man is furious and Malcolm seems quite shaken. Justin, the maître d', has had to step in." He took a sip of tea. "Melanie, are you all right, my child? You've gone quite pale."

"Sorry? Oh yes, Father, I'm fine. Go on anyway, you were about to tell me when the meeting was taking place." I picked up my teacup but my hand was shaking so much I quickly put it back down without taking a sip.

Thankfully Father O'Mara didn't seem to notice.

"Ah well, that's just it," he said. "I want to move on this sooner rather than later, but with Christmas around the corner, time is tight. I managed to reserve a room upstairs here for three thirty next Friday afternoon. Would you be free to come along then?"

I fished my diary out of my bag and checked the date. "Yes, I'm free," I said, writing in the details with some difficulty given my shaking hand. "I'll be here."

"Wonderful," said Father O'Mara, but I wasn't entirely sure whether he was referring to me being able to attend the meeting or to the tempting petits fours that Malcolm had just placed down on the table in front of us, his hand almost as shaky as mine.

I stood up. "Father O'Mara, would you mind if we finish up now? I need to get back to the office." It wasn't entirely true, but I needed to get away from that voice as quick as my legs would carry me.

"Oh yes, of course, my dear," said Father O'Mara, nodding to Malcolm for the bill.

As I waited for Father O'Mara to get the coats I finally started to breathe properly again.

"Are you sure you're all right, Melanie?" asked Father O'Mara, handing me my coat and scarf.

I paused for a moment, then turned to him. "Actually, Father, yes, I'm fine, but there's something I really need to do. Would you mind if I leave you here? I'll see you next week." I gave him a quick hug and a peck on the cheek. "Thank you so much for lunch, and for asking me to get involved in the project – I'm looking forward to it."

"Not at all, thank you for –" Father O'Mara started to say, but I'd already started to walk back towards the dining room. I was afraid if I stopped for even a second I might lose my nerve.

Once inside the door I scanned the room and, sure enough, there he was.

I should really have known he would be there. Ian loved the Club – when we were together I rarely got him to eat out anywhere else. He hadn't changed much in four years, still the same Ian – tall and still strikingly good-looking. I couldn't help but feel pleased to see that his once full head of black hair was disappearing fast though – he already had a big bald patch at the back of his head. He was sitting with a stunning blonde woman, but they weren't speaking at all – in fact, she looked pretty miserable.

I remembered that feeling.

Malcolm came over. "Is everything okay, Miss?"

"Sorry? Oh yes, thank you, Malcolm, this won't take long. Would you mind holding these for a minute though?" I handed him my coat, scarf and bag and walked straight over to Ian's table.

He saw me as I approached. Clearly he hadn't noticed me earlier either – he looked like he was about to choke on his Brussels sprouts.

"Hello there, stranger, how's your lunch?" I asked, leaning my hand on the back of his chair.

"Melanie, eh, how have you been?" he asked, looking nervous.

"Absolutely wonderful! Thanks so much for asking, Ian." I turned to his dinner guest. At least she wasn't wearing my ring – hers was a lot bigger than mine had been. I held out my hand. "And this must be your fiancée, or is it wife now?"

"Fiancée," she said, giving me a limp handshake. "And you are?"

"Oh pardon me, where are my manners? I'm Melanie, Ian's last fiancée. You know – he must have told you about me: I'm the one he attempted to shake half to death, and then, when that didn't work, tossed across the kitchen like yesterday's rubbish." I turned around to face him, and smiled. "Good work, by the way, there, Ian – you'll be pleased to know you inflicted some nice long-term damage."

"Shut up, Melanie." His face had turned the familiar shade of red, his nostrils began to flare at the sides like they always did when he was angry. "Who the hell do you think you are, coming in here and ruining my lunch by throwing your vicious lies around?"

"*Lies*? Lies, is it?" I couldn't believe the nerve of him. I struggled hard to keep my voice low so as not to disturb the other diners. "I've had four years of recurring back pain, have been in and out of more physiotherapists and osteopaths than I can remember – but you know what?" I leaned right in to his face. "I'd go through it all ten times over rather than still be suffering in a relationship with you."

I stood back up straight and turned to the fiancée.

"My deepest sympathies. I know what you must be going through."

She just looked down into her plate.

"If you'd prefer Ian, we can continue this discussion outside? No need to drag your fiancée into it." I turned to her. "I really am sorry. I don't mean to ruin your lunch. It's just that we haven't spoken in almost four years – there are some things that just need to be said, y'know?"

She raised her eyebrows and looked at Ian.

"Whatever you have to say, you can say in front of Carla," he said. "Then just go get lost, Melanie."

I looked from my ex to my replacement. They each looked as miserable as the other.

And then, I surprised myself by what I said: "You know, Ian, I was going to give you a piece of my mind. Maybe give you a sense of just how miserable I was with you for those three years, how devastated I was by the way you treated me at the end. But, to be honest," I stood up straighter, "I can't actually be bothered now." I laughed as the realisation hit me. "I just don't care any more."

I'd swear I saw Carla smile a little.

Ian just rolled his eyes and shook his head slowly – he always was an arrogant sod. "Right, well, if you're quite finished making a fool of yourself, Melanie, perhaps you could trot along now and leave us to our lunch."

I nodded. "I will indeed. But just one thing, Ian. I think you owe Malcolm, your waiter, an apology for shouting at him earlier. This is a *gentlemen's* club after all – isn't it high time you started behaving like one?" I looked behind me and beckoned to Malcolm who started to walk over with my coat and bag. I turned back to Ian. "There's no time like the present."

"I think we're finished here,'" Ian said, ignoring

Malcolm and turning back to what I sincerely hoped was his cold lunch.

"Your things, Miss," said Malcolm, helping me on with my coat and scarf, then handing me my bag. "And you forgot these earlier." He handed me a small box. "Your petits fours," he said with a wink.

I smiled. "Why thank you, Malcolm. You're an absolute *gentleman.*" I emphasised the last word as I caught Ian's eye. Then I marched out of the dining room, walking just that little bit taller with each step away from my miserable past.

Chapter 23

RICHARD

All of my connections went as planned and by eleven o'clock on Thursday morning I was standing in the arrivals hall at Heathrow Airport. I was completely exhausted, but for once I didn't mind the luggage delays – anything that put off the moment when I would have to face Ed was okay by me. After almost thirty minutes staring at a stationary carousel, it started to move. My holdall was one of the first to come out – I watched it travel up the conveyor belt towards me and then go past. I let it go around twice more before finally picking it up and heading towards the exit.

I couldn't see him at first in the crowd of waiting drivers, tour guides and expectant families and friends at Arrivals, then I spotted him at the back. He was wearing his old duffle coat and Ashvale scarf.

Still the same old Ed then.

He saw me, nodded and started to walk slowly over.

"Good flight?" he asked when he got to me. He reached out to take my bag, barely looking at me.

"Wait," I said, keeping hold of the bag. "Ed, man?"

He looked up.

"I'm sorry, Ed. I'm really sorry."

He looked surprised, which made sense, I guess – I think it was the first time I'd ever said those words to him.

"Eh, okay. Thanks." He went to take the bag again.

"No, wait, Ed." I couldn't let the moment pass. I didn't want to pretend nothing had happened, to carry on through the rest of our lives never acknowledging, or even mentioning the pain I'd caused. Hard and all as it was, I knew that if I didn't do it right away, I might never get another chance.

"I messed up. I really messed up, Ed. I hurt you, and Lucy, and I let down both of our families." My voice started to crack, but I couldn't stop. "You didn't deserve it, man. I have no excuse – what I did was stupid and pathetic, and I have to live with that every day of my life. But I didn't mean it – I never meant to cause all that pain." I took a deep breath. "I'm sorry. I don't know what else to say, Ed, I'm just *so damned sorry*."

Ed continued to look at me without flinching, and then his whole body seemed to unstiffen. His face broke into a smile, and he grabbed me into a hug.

Finally – after six long months – I had a brother again. The relief was unbelievable. I started to well up, and before I knew what was happening I was crying like a baby.

I patted his back and Ed pulled back, which was when I noticed that he was crying as well.

"What are we like?" I laughed and wiped my face.

But Ed looked serious. "I'm sorry too Rich – for hitting you like that, and then for leaving the house without telling you. I needed to do it, though, y'know? Needed to get away."

But I didn't need to hear any more. It was all over as far as I was concerned. "Yeah, I know, man. I'd have done the same." I put my arm around his shoulder and handed him my laptop bag. "Here, as you insist. I take it you've got a car?"

"When did you last talk to her?" I asked Ed as he drove us out of the airport in the hire car.

He pulled into the slow lane, and drove at twenty miles under the speed limit. I didn't even comment.

"Mum? I came over to see her about a month ago."

"Really? She never mentioned that to me. I saw her the night before I flew to Japan, a couple of weeks ago."

Ed just nodded.

"How did she seem to you when you saw her?" I asked.

"Okay. Probably a bit on edge, But no more than usual." He glanced at me. "She asked me about you."

"Really?"

"Yeah. I told her I hadn't seen you though. We had a nice couple of days together actually."

I nodded. "Well that's good. So how have you been keeping yourself? Where have you been living?"

Ed shifted in the driving seat, eyes straight ahead on the road.

"Don't worry – you don't have to tell me if you don't want to," I said.

"No, it's not that." He paused for a second then glanced at me. "After I moved out of your place I called Jangler and, to cut a long story short, I ended up going down to Ashvale to stay. It was just supposed to be for a few days until I worked out what I wanted to do next – like a retreat almost. But I found that I settled in really well there. I'd been really loving the teacher training as you know, and it was great to get so fully immersed in the school environment. I ended up staying on and helping out with the exams in June, then I worked over the summer with Father Hynes to put the school timetable together for next year. It's quite a complex job actually, Rich, you wouldn't believe all the dynamics you have to consider – making sure each year has a quota of good and . . . well . . . not-so-good teachers, giving each teacher enough free periods . . ."

And he went on and on . . .

I'd rarely seen my brother so animated on a topic. It was good to see. But living at Ashvale? I needed to make sure he wasn't hiding out there, wasn't avoiding the real world.

"So are you still there now then?" I asked, interrupting his step-by-step guide on how to construct a school timetable. "Are you still living at Ashvale?"

"Hmm?" He looked at me, then turned back to the road. "Oh yes, sorry, didn't I say? I'm going to be living there for the next school year. They've taken me on as one of the night housemasters while I finish my final year in teacher-training college. I have quarters in one of the dormitories and I'm housemaster for fifth years. I'm actually living in St Francis Dormitory now."

"No way! 'Frankie's'?" I had some great memories of my year in that dorm. "Still as cold and damp as ever, I suppose?"

Ed shook his head. "Not any more – they did it up last

year and it's practically palatial now. Those kids don't know how good they have it." He smiled. "Ah, they're great lads though."

I took a good look at my brother. He seemed happy, but I had to be sure. "Ed . . . is this my fault? Did you end up having to stay at Ashvale because you had nowhere else to go? Did I push you into it . . . because of what happened with Sonya?"

Ed laughed. "Even the mighty Richard Blake isn't that powerful." He glanced at me for a second again. "No Rich, I'd been planning to break up with Sonya for some time before all that happened back in May. I hadn't been happy with her for a long time. I mean it was fun for a while at the start but we weren't ever suited really. And she was right when she said it was my fault. You see, I wanted more – something deeper. I suppose you could say the argument that day was the turning point. I mean, it was tough. I couldn't believe you and Sonya would do something like that."

"I'm sorry, man. I didn't mean –"

"It's all right. To be honest, Rich, you did me a favour. I mean I'll admit, for the first few weeks – perhaps months – afterwards I hated you. I was miserable and it was easy to blame it all on my evil brother. I felt like I'd always lived in your shadow – at home, at school, on the rugby pitch. Travelling around Africa a few years ago was brilliant, but when I got back to Ireland I just more or less fell back into my old routine of trailing around in the wake of my big, popular brother."

"I didn't realise . . ."

"It's not your fault, Rich. Once a bit of time had passed after that lunch, I finally realised that it wasn't about you, or about Sonya, or about anyone or anything else for that matter. It was about me, and about the young people I want to teach. So I went to talk to Jangler and he helped me to work through my anger, to forgive you and Sonya – and eventually to do what I felt was right for me."

"Sounds like he brainwashed you into moving down to Ashvale!"

Ed laughed. "No, nothing like that – it was all my idea. When I qualify next year, my plan is to go to Zambia. I want to teach out there for a few years at least, work in the small missionary school I volunteered in when I was travelling a few years ago. There's a whole world out there, Rich, and I want to do my bit towards making it a little bit better. Okay, so I'm only a rookie teacher, but if I can make a difference to the lives of a few children who really need an education, well hey – I'm a happy man."

I listened to my brother talk about his plans for the future. I could hear the enthusiasm in his words, could see the spark in his eyes. It was almost like a whole new person had emerged from inside the shell of the man I'd known just six months ago. It was clear he was happy – happier than I'd probably ever known him. I found myself almost impressed by him. Nah . . . definitely impressed by him. Perhaps even a bit envious too if I was being honest – he seemed to have it all worked out.

We pulled up into the driveway of the house in Richmond and Ed turned off the engine. "So there you have it. Now you know everything."

"Yes, now I know." I undid my seatbelt, then turned to look at him. "I hope it doesn't sound patronising, Ed, but I'm proud of you, man."

Ed looked down and nodded his head a few times. He

had tears in his eyes when he looked back up at me. "Thanks, Rich, that means a lot." He opened the car door, but I stayed seated and looked ahead up at the house.

"It's going to be strange going in." I looked round at him. "You know – without her being there."

Ed sat back in his seat. "I know. It is strange. Sheila and Derek are here though, and they're looking forward to seeing you. Come on, we've got a lot more to talk about. Let's go in."

Sheila was sitting in my mother's armchair by the electric fire when we got in. For a split second I thought it was my mother sitting there.

"Welcome home, love," she said, jumping up and giving me a quick hug. "Was the flight on time?" she asked Ed.

"Bang on," said Ed, sitting down.

Derek got up from his own seat and shook my hand.

"How are you both holding up?" I asked as I took my coat off.

Sheila just nodded a few times, and blew her nose. She looked tired.

"We're grand, son," said Derek as Sheila took my coat from me and went to hang it up in the hall.

"Sit down there now." Derek pointed to my mother's chair.

I sat down, but in the armchair opposite my mother's.

"You'll have something to eat?" said Sheila, coming back in.

"No, I'm all right, Sheila, don't worry. Why don't you sit back down?" I just wanted to talk to my aunt, see how she really was.

"Ah now, don't be silly!" she said, moving towards the kitchen. "You've come all the way from Australia, you must be starving."

"New Zealand. And they do feed you every now and then, Sheila. Even on airplanes." I smiled over at Derek who winked back at me.

She turned back to me. "Airplane food? Sure that wouldn't fill a big man like yourself. I have a roast to cook for dinner later on, but you'll have a cup of tea and a sandwich at least now, Richard? You will," she answered her own question, then disappeared into the kitchen before I could change her mind.

"Everything okay with you boys?" Derek asked after she'd gone.

I nodded, and looked over at Ed who nodded too.

"Did you tell him about you moving down to Ashvale? And about Africa?" Derek asked.

"I did," said Ed, pulling up a chair beside me.

"What do you make of it all then?" Derek asked me.

"I think it's great." I looked at Ed. "I'm sure you're a big hit down at Ashvale, bro, and at least you won't be moving back in with me any time soon! Who knows, I might even come out to visit you in Zambia next year – I've never been there."

Derek smiled, then picked up a large brown envelope from the floor beside him.

"Ah, the will," said Ed. "I haven't had a chance to tell him about it yet."

Derek handed me the envelope. "Have a look at that, lad."

I took out a bundle of legal papers, and quickly scanned through them. Then I looked back up at Derek.

"*Two* houses?"

Derek nodded. "Yes – she's left you and Edward this place, and the family home in Wicklow."

"What family home in Wicklow?" I asked Ed. He just nodded me back to Derek.

"It's the house where your mother and Sheila grew up," Derek said. "It's on the coast road, not far out of Wicklow town. Their father, your grandfather, inherited it from his own parents. It's been in your family for generations."

I'd never heard my mother speak about her childhood home, or about her father for that matter. I knew he was a solicitor, that they were from Wicklow, and that her own mother had died when she and Sheila were young, but that was about it.

"I'd say the house and the grounds are in a pretty bad state now," Derek went on. "Nobody's lived there since your grandfather died just before you were born, Richard. Your mother inherited it in his will, but she never did anything with it."

"That's crazy – she should have sold it," I said. "She could have done with the money – they weren't exactly rolling in it back then."

"Yes, why didn't she ever sell it, Derek?" Ed asked.

"I think because it brought back bad memories? She probably just wanted to forget the place even existed." Derek pulled his chair a bit closer to the fire. "Sheila and your mother suffered a lot at their father's hands, lads. He got very depressed after their mother died – he drank a lot, and I think he raised his hand in anger to them on more than one occasion. It wasn't easy. Sheila left when she was eighteen to marry me, and on the very next day your mother packed her bags and left for Dublin. I think she'd only stayed so long in Wicklow to keep an eye on her younger sister. She met your father soon after. Anyway, I don't think she ever set foot in the place again – almost denied that part of her life had ever happened."

"How come we never knew any of this?" I looked at Ed.

"Well, I knew she'd had a rough childhood," he said. "She told me once after Dad left, but I didn't realise how bad – she never talked about it again after that."

The mention of my father brought up all of the old familiar feelings of anger and resentment. I turned to Derek. "He really messed her around, didn't he?"

"Who?" Derek asked, "Your father?"

"Yeah, who else? She could have done without marrying him, after such a crap childhood."

"No, Richard. Your father's not to blame." Derek glanced over at the kitchen from where we could hear Sheila moving about preparing the food. "Close the door over there, Edward."

Ed went and shut the door, then sat back down.

"I love your aunt, lads, but she's not always, eh –" He glanced back at the door, then looked at Ed. "Definitely shut?"

Ed nodded. "Shut tight."

Derek went on. "Your mother and Sheila had to be tough to get through their childhood, and I think perhaps that made them quite hard. Over the years I've managed to break down some of your aunt's defences, but it hasn't been easy. Most of the time, I just let her have her way, but I've had to stand up for myself on more than one occasion. I get by, but I can't say I haven't thought about leaving myself a few times."

Ed and I looked at each other in shock.

"Don't worry," Derek said. "I'm not going anywhere. Not now. We've found our own way of being together – Sheila and I – we're happy enough now. In our own way."

Thank God, I thought. I definitely could not handle another family break-up.

"I don't think your father found it at all easy though," Derek was saying. "Let's just say your mother wasn't the easiest of women to live with."

I snorted. "Understatement!"

"Stop, Richie, this is important," Ed said. "Go on, Derek."

"She loved you two boys," Derek said, "but she found it very hard to show it. God bless her, she hadn't been shown much love in her own childhood – certainly not since her mother died. When she married your father and had you two I think that was the happiest she'd ever been in life. She loved you two boys and your father very much. But as time went on, after you moved over to London and your father's building business picked up, he had to spend more and more time working. You were still both young, and I think the pressure of raising two children almost on her own eventually got to your mother. She lost a child around then too – a girl. I think that was the final straw – it broke her heart."

"I never knew that," said Ed.

Neither did I, but it explained a lot. How the hell could my father leave her after something like that?

"All the more reason for Dad to stand by her," I said.

Derek shook his head. "She completely shut your father out after she lost the baby. He was grieving himself, but they didn't give each other any comfort. In those days we didn't really talk about these things so much – we were just expected to get on with it. Sheila and I know only too well, we've had our own difficulties in that area over the years." He looked into the distance for a moment.

"I'm sorry Derek," I said. "I didn't realise." Of course I knew Sheila and Derek couldn't have children of their own, but I hadn't really thought much about it before, never considered how hard it must have been for them.

"Thanks, lad," said Derek. "Anyway, your father turned to the drink as a result of everything. It was a very bad time for them both."

I had a flashback to the late-night rows when we were back in London from Ashvale for the Christmas holidays the year before they split. My father would come home drunk most nights and sleep on the sofa, while my mother would cry herself to sleep. They hadn't been getting on well in some years, but I remember the year before they split as being particularly bad – I couldn't wait to get back to Ashvale after the Christmas holidays.

"Louisa saved him really," said Derek.

"What do you mean?" asked Ed.

"She was his secretary, and over time I think they just fell in love. That's what it was."

"Bullshit!" I stood up. "There's no excuse for abandoning your wife and kids. No matter how bad things are, or what slapper bats her eyelids at you!"

Derek shook his head. "It wasn't like that, Richard. I met your father in Dublin shortly after he left your mother. I had to tell Sheila I was going to the dog races – she'd have had a fit if she'd known where I was really going. Your father was a broken man at the time."

I sat back down.

"He admitted that he and a woman at work had feelings for each other," Derek went on, "but at that stage nothing had happened between them. He'd clearly fallen for her, but he couldn't bring himself to be with her. He was crushed knowing that he'd hurt you boys and your mother, you see? He felt so guilty about leaving you, and he missed you all. But, as he said, he had to do it – he was miserable with your mother, and if he'd carried on like that he'd probably have drunk himself into an early grave. He hasn't touched a drop of the drink since he and Louisa got together."

"So he wasn't with her before they split up? Before he left us?" Ed asked.

"No," said Derek. "They were friends, and she helped him through that time, but it was another year or so before they got together. I knew about it at the time, but I didn't tell Sheila or your mother. I regret that now. I should have found a way to tell them so it didn't come as such a shock the following year when your mother did find out – that day when they showed up together at your school."

Ed stood up and put his hand on Derek's shoulder. "It's all right, Derek. You weren't to know how hard she'd take it." He looked at me. "Hey, are you okay, Richie?"

But I wasn't at all okay. In the last few minutes, Derek's words had turned everything I'd believed to be true about my parents upside down. For the first time in my life I started to see them as real people – people who had struggled, suffered, and made mistakes – just like me.

"Why didn't you tell us all this before?" I asked Derek, struggling to keep the anger out of my voice. "Or more to the point, why didn't our mother tell us? Why all the secrets?"

"I'm sorry, Richard. I did try to talk to you about it a few times," he said, his own voice starting to quiver.

"Leave it, Rich, it's not Derek's fault – he said he tried," said Ed.

"Well, he should have bloody well tried harder!"

"You're right, of course," said Derek, "but it wasn't easy to bring up. Especially after your friend Ben died – it was very hard to get through to you at all after that, Richard." He looked very upset.

But I couldn't handle any more. "I need to get some sleep," I said, standing up.

Just as I did, Sheila opened the kitchen door and came through with a huge plate of sandwiches. "Sit up at the table now, all of you."

"Sorry, Sheila," I said. "I'm going to sleep for a few hours. I'll look forward to that roast later though."

"What? No, no, no. Sit up there at the table and have something small to eat now. Come on!" She waved me over to the table.

"Leave the lad go, Sheila," said Derek. "He's been travelling for over a day, he needs to sleep."

"No, he'll be hungry," she said.

Ed went over, sat down and picked up a sandwich, followed closely by Derek who also reached for a sandwich.

"Sure can't he sleep all day tomorrow?" said Sheila. "The funeral isn't till Saturday. Come on now, Richard, sit up at the table –"

"*Leave him!*" Derek spat out breadcrumbs as he spoke. He swallowed his bite, then glared up at his wife from the table.

Sheila just stared back at him, holding firm. It was a battle of wills.

Eventually Sheila pursed her lips and frowned, then went back into the kitchen without another word.

I think it was the first time I'd ever witnessed Derek stand up to his wife – he looked drained by the exchange.

I put my hand on his shoulder. "I know you did your best, Derek, thanks."

He smiled sadly at me.

I glanced over at Ed, who nodded.

Then I went upstairs and slept for the rest of the day, and the whole night.

Chapter 24

RICHARD

"Richard, the car's here!" Sheila shouted up the stairs.

I was sitting on the single bed in my old bedroom, staring at the tightly rolled black tie in my hand.

This is really it, I thought. We're about to bury my mother.

I was still exhausted from the travel and emotionally drained from everything I'd learned over the previous days, but right at that moment the main thing I felt was a rising wave of nausea. I made it to the bathroom just in time to be sick.

A few seconds later there was a light knock on the bathroom door. "Richard, are you okay?" Sheila asked.

I washed my mouth with some water from the bathroom tap, and opened the door. "Yes, sorry. Let's go. Is Ed down there?"

"He's already in the car with Derek. Come on."

Sheila went ahead of me down the stairs. When we got to the bottom, she reached out and took the tie out of my hand. It was the exact same spot where I had last spoken to my mother, where she'd wrapped my scarf around my neck.

"There now." Sheila said, tucking my tie into my jacket after she'd finished doing it up.

"Thanks."

"Not at all." She looked thoughtful for a moment, then said, "You know she loved you very much, Richard, don't you? She may not always have been able to show it. But she did love you two boys, and she was very proud of you – both of you." She paused. "And I am too."

I nodded, willing myself to believe it all.

I was surprised that so many people had travelled over from Ireland for the funeral. There was a big crowd from the paper – Edith, her husband and most of my own team from the economics-and-business desk were there. The Ashvale crowd were also over in good numbers. It was good to see the familiar faces in the crowd as we drove into the church grounds.

I noticed my father standing alone towards the back of a group of people as we lined up to carry the coffin into the church. It had been so many years since I'd seen him that I was surprised by how old he looked. He still stood taller than anyone around him, but he had aged – his hair had gone completely grey, he seemed a bit stooped over and his face was well wrinkled.

At least he'd had the good grace to come alone.

"Gentlemen, are you ready?" said the undertaker. "One, two, three!" And with that we heaved the coffin onto our shoulders and carried my mother on the last leg of her journey.

I found myself thinking about my father as Jangler

spoke about family during my mother's homily. I still wasn't sure what I felt about him, but I realised as I listened to Jangler, that the anger had started to fade.

It was a start.

"It was a beautiful service, Richard," Edith said. "You did Rose proud."

We were standing by the fire in the room Ed had hired for the reception at the Richmond Arms Hotel. The cemetery had been freezing, and the heat from the blazing grate was very welcome.

"Thanks, Edith, but I had very little to do with it, to be honest," I said. "Ed and Sheila organised everything – me being stuck out in the middle of the Pacific Ocean 'n all."

"Ah yes, sorry about that," she said. "Did you at least get to see your first feature in today's supplement?"

"No, not yet. One of the lads mentioned it to me earlier though. Did it turn out okay?"

"It was really great, Richard – you did a very good job – and I have to say the second feature is even better. It's really something, in fact – very honest. You clearly did a lot of thinking out there. We're going to run it next week if you're okay with that?"

"Sure. Thanks, Edith." I took a sip of my coffee. "Funny – I really hated the whole idea of going over there."

Edith laughed. "You don't say? I was watching my back before you left!"

I smiled. "You know, though? It turned out to be one of the best things I've ever done – really opened my eyes."

"Yes, I can see that from your writing, Richard," Edith said. "Those whales seem to have had a big effect on you."

I thought about my conversation with Mel then. "Maybe it was just a coincidence? Good timing, y'know?"

"Well, about that, I actually have a bit of a confession to make." Edith looked pensive. "I wasn't sure whether to tell you today of all days, Richard, but on reflection I think you should probably know."

I tilted my head to the side. "Edith Maguire, what have you done?"

"No, it's nothing I've done as such. Well, not really." She took a step closer to me and put her hand on my elbow. "It's about Rose."

"My mother? What about her?"

"She called me that week, Richie – before I sent you to Japan. She was worried about you. She knew you were drinking too much, had fallen out with Edward, and well . . . you know how it was."

I stepped away from the fire. "Please tell me you are joking? My mother? Called you? My boss? She actually called you to . . . to . . . Why exactly *did* she call you, Edith?"

"It's not as bad as it sounds, Richie, we often spoke on the phone . . ."

She was delaying.

"Bullshit – my mother rarely used the telephone unless she absolutely had to. Come on, Edith – why did she call you?"

She coughed and avoided my eye. "Well we talked about all of our boys," she said eventually, "but I suppose about you in particular, Richard – you seemed to be spiralling out of control. She asked me if there was anything I could do to help."

"She did *what*?"

Edith just went on. "So that was when we came up with the idea of sending you away on assignment – somewhere far away to clear your head. My nephew Ray had been on and on at me for weeks to cover the anti-whaling expedition, and I suppose it just all sort of fell into place from there. Rose wasn't sure the Greenpeace assignment was a good idea at first – she was worried it might be dangerous – but we both agreed it was the lesser of two evils – the way you were going, you were a lot less likely to get into trouble on board a ship than you were at home."

I couldn't believe it. My mother had cooked up the idea of the Greenpeace gig with my boss? The bloody humiliation of it! But then my mind flashed back to what Sheila had said that morning. My mother must have really cared about me, and she must have been really worried about me to have made that phone call to Edith, to have agreed to send me halfway across the world to let me work out for myself what an idiot I was being. Maybe my mother had actually known me better than I knew myself.

I put down my coffee cup, and grabbed Edith by both arms. Then I gave her a kiss. The look of surprise on her face was priceless.

"Edith, you're a legend. You may have done me the biggest favour of my life." I shook my head slowly. "I can't believe my mother was behind the Japan thing all the time. She really did care, didn't she?"

Edith smiled and put her hand on my shoulder. "Of course she cared, Richard. I just thank God it worked out so well for you."

"Thanks, Edith. You know, the best thing about the

trip was that I got a chance to see her on my way over to Japan. I didn't realise just how important that visit would turn out to be, that it would be the last time I'd ever see her."

Edith smiled sadly. "I'm glad you got that chance, Richard."

I smiled too. "But no more rogue foreign assignments for a while, okay, Edith?"

She laughed. "It's a deal. Anyway, I need you back on the business desk as soon as possible. Jeff is making a right mess of it!"

"Hey, how you doin' there, Rich?" Jonesy interrupted us.

Edith moved off to join Jangler who was talking to Ed.

Jonesy held out a fresh pint of Guinness for me. I gazed at it. I'd been off the booze for a few days by that stage, and it wasn't proving easy. I'd been having headaches and was feeling tired all the time. But I was determined to tough it out, determined to get my life back on track – no matter what it took.

I shook my head at Jonesy's offer. "You have it, man. I'm off the booze for a while."

He put the pint down on the mantelpiece while he finished the one he was drinking.

"Thanks for coming, man." I picked my coffee cup back up. "It's bloody great to see you and all the lads here – been too long."

"Not at all, Rich," said Jonesy. "Sure where else would we be? Are you bearing up okay?"

"Yeah, thanks, Jonesy. I'm actually doing very well."

"Good stuff, good stuff." He took a sip of the pint, then licked the creamy foam from his upper lip. "Listen,

Rich, sorry we haven't been in touch much over the last few months."

"It's okay, no need to explain. I acted like an idiot earlier this year. You and the lads had every right to avoid me for a while."

"No, it wasn't that, man," said Jonesy. "I mean, yeah, you were an idiot, but that's your business. No, there's been a lot going on. I just heard that Dec's been having trouble with his eldest Tara. She's been taking drugs and got kicked out of school – they really don't know what's going on with her."

"Shit, sorry to hear that."

"And me and Karen, well, we've been having a few problems ourselves. It's all sorted now, though – we're actually expecting another baby – very early days so we haven't told too many people."

"Wow, that's great, Jonesy. Congratulations, man!" I slapped him on the shoulder, just as Dec and Ed joined us.

"Here, Dec," said Jonesy, "what do you think of our Moby Dick here?" He threw an arm around my shoulder. "Get it? Richard – Dick?"

I nodded. "Mmm, I get it – inspired, man. You're an absolute genius."

"Great article today, Rich," said Dec. "So have you saved all the whales yet? Mister Splashy Pants, how are ya!"

He and Jonesy burst into laughter.

I'd missed the lads – it was good to see them, and from the sounds of things they needed to relax and have a laugh themselves.

"Jangler's about to go, Rich," Ed said to me. "He's got to catch an early evening flight back."

"Oh right, thanks." I put my hand on Ed's shoulder and looked at the lads. "I'm leaving the defence of the Blake family name in my brother's hands."

I went over to where Jangler was putting on his coat by the door.

"Father, thanks for everything today, and over the last week. You've been brilliant as always." I reached out to shake his hand. "The Mass was pretty special – it meant a lot to all of us to have you here."

"Not at all, Richard, not at all," Jangler said, shaking my hand. "Rose was a good friend to me, and to the whole Ashvale community. You'll miss her."

I nodded. "Yes, Father. I'm probably only now beginning to realise just how much."

Jangler nodded, then turned and looked behind him. "I see your father's here. Have you spoken to him yet?"

I looked across the room to where my father was sitting talking to one of my mother's old neighbours. "No, not yet, I'll go over in a minute." I hesitated. "Just . . . it's been a while."

"I understand." Jangler put on his scarf over his coat. "That said, all you have to do is just say hello."

It reminded me of the advice from Mel when we spoke on the phone – about just saying sorry to Ed. It worked then. Maybe it could work now?

"Thanks, Father. I'll see."

"You've heard about your brother then?" Jangler said, nodding at Ed as he fixed his scarf.

"Yes, he told me a couple of days ago. You kept that quiet, Father – I had no idea you were harbouring a Blake down at Ashvale."

Jangler nodded. "Yes, I'm sorry I couldn't tell you,

Richard. I think Edward just needed some time to decide what he wanted, to settle in. He's been a great asset to the team at Ashvale. He's got a book club going, and he's even teaching some of the students guitar – he's very popular with them."

"Yes, I heard you signed him up as a housemaster – that's great – once you don't persuade him to join the Order next!"

"Well, there is always room for one more at Ashvale, Richard. Edward doesn't seem keen on the priesthood, he's more determined to go out to Africa to teach, but maybe you'd like to have a chat with me about a vocation yourself? We could actually do with a good rugby coach." He grinned, and raised a bushy eyebrow.

I laughed. "I think your founding fathers would turn over in their graves if the likes of me discovered I had a vocation."

"Ah sure, some of them were no saints themselves in their early years." Jangler chuckled at his own joke.

"Nonetheless, I think you'd be waiting a long time to convert me."

Jangler nodded. "You may be right, Richard. But now, all jokes aside, I do have a small favour to ask of you if I may?"

"You name it, Father – whatever I can do. Well – short of taking a vow of celibacy, that is!"

When I'd finished talking to Jangler, I took a deep breath, then crossed the room over to where my father was sitting. He stood up when he saw me approach and edged his way out from the seats to reach me.

I held out my hand. "Hello, Dad."

He shook my hand firmly in both of his, but he seemed very nervous. "Hello, son," he said. "I saw you there earlier. You spoke very well after the meal."

"Thanks," I said. He let go of my hand, and a moment of awkward silence passed before I said, "Did Ed tell you he's teaching down at Ashvale now?"

My father looked relieved I had said anything. "Yes, yes, indeed. Although I only heard about it today."

"I only found out a couple of days ago myself." I looked over to where Ed was standing talking to Jangler. "He seems good though. Maybe he's found what he was looking for?"

My father nodded slowly. "Maybe indeed." He looked right at me then. "And what about you, Richard? How are you?"

"Ah, I'm okay. Getting there, I guess."

"I read your article this morning. It was very good – great writing, son. You get that from your mother. She had a way with words too. God rest her soul." He bowed his head.

It seemed strange to hear my father talk about my mother. For so many years I had seen them as such separate entities it was hard to remember that they had ever even known each other, let alone been married for seventeen years and had two sons together.

"Do you think that maybe in a few weeks we might be able to . . . I don't know . . . maybe meet for a pint or something?" my father said, interrupting my thoughts.

"I'm actually off the booze for a while."

"Oh I see, yes, not a bother, I understand," he said, lowering his eyes. Then he coughed and looked up again. "Well, maybe you and Edward could come over to the house for a visit soon? See Louisa, and the twins – they'll be eighteen in a few weeks – they'd all love to meet you."

He looked so hopeful that I didn't have the heart to say no straight out.

"Yeah, we'll see," I said. "Maybe." Then I looked at the old man in front of me for a couple more seconds, before taking out my wallet and handing him my business card.

It was a start at least.

Chapter 25

MELANIE

I loved nothing better on a Saturday afternoon than settling down with the newspaper and a cuppa after taking my sister Nichola's kids swimming. The kids were always good fun – but the constant chatter and activity made me appreciate my peaceful adult time all the more.

I'd just got inside my house and put the kettle on when the doorbell rang.

"Drat, who can that be?" I put the paper down on the kitchen table and went to answer the door.

It was Katy.

"Hey, come on in, Katykins," I said, leading her into the kitchen. "To what do I owe this pleasure?"

Katy almost bounced into the kitchen. She was beaming from ear to ear. "Ta-*daaah!*" She wiggled her fingers in front of me – showing off a stunning sparkling solitaire on her left hand.

"Oh my God, you got engaged? No way!" I grabbed her and gave her a huge hug. "Show me, show me!" I took her hand and examined the ring.

She laughed. "I've been trying so hard to keep it a secret for the last week or so. We wanted to pick out the ring before telling anyone. Then it had to be resized – I thought I was going to burst with the news. Do you love it?"

"Yes, I most certainly do. It's such a beautiful ring. Congratulations!" I finally let her take back her hand.

"Thanks, Mel. I just can't believe it. You're the first person I've told after Mum and Dad."

"Ah, that's brilliant, hon. I hope Frank knows what a lucky man he is?"

"He knows, but feel free to remind him any time!" She laughed. "Oh, Mel, I'm the happiest girl in the world."

And she looked it. My best friend was positively glowing with happiness. And it was infectious – I loved seeing her so happy.

"I want to know all the details," I said. "What he said, how he said it. Did he go down on one knee?"

She giggled. "Yes, he did, actually, only with his dodgy knees he could hardly get back up again. When I said yes, I had to hunch down to kiss him!"

I laughed. "Poor ol' Frank!"

"Of course you have to be my bridesmaid!"

"Ooh, yes, I would absolutely love to! Yay!" I threw my arms around her again. "Sit down there now," I said after giving her a big hug. "I'll make the tea and you can tell me all about the wedding plans."

She sat down at the table while I flicked the kettle back on. "I'm so relieved you're happy for me, Mel," she said.

I looked around. "What do you mean? Of course I'm happy for you."

"I was just a bit nervous telling you. Y'know, after everything with Ian? And because of how you feel about relationships and marriage, and all that?"

I gave her a smile. "That's all in the past, Katy. Let's just say I've mellowed in recent weeks. I'm moving on. Norway and the whales were amazing, and a couple of interesting things happened during the week – I'll tell you about it all another day though." I pushed the papers aside to put the mugs and milk jug down on the table – which was when I noticed Richie's face staring out at me from the front cover of the newspaper supplement.

"No way!"

I sat down on the chair opposite Katy and pulled over the supplement.

Richard Blake Reports from Greenpeace's Campaign to Save Mister Splashy Pants, said the title.

I quickly flicked through the pages to the article, and there it was – a four-page spread written by Richie.

"What is it, Mel?" asked Katy.

"It's that journalist, Richie Blake. You might remember him from the fundraising lunch in Wicklow last May?"

"The guy who got punched out by Frank's friend? His own brother?"

I nodded. "We've been in touch a bit since then."

"Oh Mel! Not another of these guys? Ed's a nice fella, but his brother sounds like bad news!"

"He's not that bad, Katy – just has some issues, that's all. There's nothing going on with us anyway, so don't worry."

I quickly scanned through the article to the end: **And so the fate of Mister Splashy Pants, his fifty fellow-humpbacks, six hundred fin and four hundred minke whales hangs in the balance. It is difficult to predict how the international wave of protest will play out over the** coming weeks, but one thing I do know is that if I was Mister Splashy Pants I'd want Greenpeace, Ray Kelly, Takumi Yoshito and the crew of the *Illuminar* on my side.

I sat back, smiling.

"I haven't read it properly yet, but it looks like a good piece," I said, looking at his picture. "Good for Richie."

I wondered how his mother's funeral was going . . . And how it went for him meeting Ed . . . Then it struck me: "I'm surprised he didn't mention anything about looking into the eye of the whale," I said, looking back at the article.

That was when I noticed the footer: **This is the first of two features from Richard Blake on board the *Illuminar*; the second will appear over the coming weeks as his journey progresses.**

"Ah, good."

"Mel, what's going on between you and this guy?" asked Katy.

I looked up at her. "Sorry – now let me get the tea and you can tell me all about the proposal and the wedding plans."

"No way!" said Katy. "There's something going on with this journalist guy and I want to know everything. Now spill!"

"All right, I'll tell you about it, Katy, but there really is nothing much to tell. We're just friends – barely even that really."

We were all seated and chatting by the time Fenella finally arrived into the boardroom to convene the meeting on Monday morning. She flew in the door, looking quite flustered.

She glared over at Marcus as she sat down. "Oh, here you all are. I expected to meet you down at reception as usual, Marcus. Especially now that poor Shirley is no longer here to greet me."

"Ah, apologies, Madam Chairwoman, I came in ahead today," said Marcus, unable to look straight at her.

"No problem," she said with a frown. She seemed to collect herself then and flashed a fake toothy smile at everyone sitting around the table. "We'd better press on. Lots to get through today."

The meeting went well on the whole – the board were all delighted with the huge jump in box-office figures and membership numbers, not to mention the new dance-festival sponsorship.

"You've made very impressive progress in such a short space of time, Melanie," said Hugh McWilliams. "Congratulations to you and your team. I don't suppose we could tempt you away from the Millennium Centre and over to my music school any day soon?"

I just smiled, especially as I noticed Marcus looking uncomfortable at the suggestion.

"All right then. Shall we move on to the next item on the agenda?" Fenella asked. "The new development campaign. Melanie dear, it's back to you again. You were to present to us on some new ideas for operating the new campaign?" She sat back.

"Thank you, Fenella, *dear*." I coughed. "Yes, indeed. If I could get the lights turned down a little?" I looked over at Marcus's assistant Margaret, who made a face, sighed loudly, then got up and did it.

"Thank you, Margaret."

I went through the first few new slides I'd added which

gave a summary of my findings from the British and American arts venues I'd surveyed. Each subsequent slide built my case, and led to my final set of slides: the same proposed campaign-operation plan I'd presented at the last meeting.

"And so," I concluded, "I hope you will agree that the most sensible option for us to pursue at this time is to adopt a professional, strategic approach from the outset of this campaign, in order to ensure that this new activity does not jeopardise existing successful operations. And we need to bring in the expertise required to ensure that we can successfully meet the private funding target to build Phase Two of the Millennium Centre within our very challenging three-year time period."

"I agree!" shouted out a voice almost before I'd finished.

It was Father O'Mara.

"This is a most excellent piece of research, Melanie," he said, "and a very sensibly thought-out plan. I say we agree it this time, and get moving on it straight away."

There were several loud murmurs of approval.

"Just a minute." Fenella half stood in her seat to regain control. She settled back down again as she got the floor. "Melanie, dear. You were *meant* to be presenting today on the other options available to us, as recorded in the minutes of our last meeting. This –" she pointed dismissively to the screen, "is simply the same rehashed plan from last month with just a few extra pointers thrown in in an attempt to sway us. And as you know, I'm not in favour of this approach at all. It's completely unnecessary, given the Millennium Centre's standing. Marcus, wouldn't you agree?"

Marcus, who'd stayed very quiet until then, sat forward. He put his fingers through his few hairs, patted the top of his scalp, then took a deep breath.

"I'm afraid I would not, Madam Chairwoman," he said.

I looked around the table. The other board members looked stunned. Fenella's face had started to change colour, but she continued to smile so widely that every single one of her teeth was visible.

"I have looked at the research results Melanie has provided," Marcus continued, "and I find them to be very sound. Furthermore, I spoke to several of my own counterparts in the UK, Europe and in the States this week, and they are all agreed that a campaign on this scale, were it not to be given the appropriate, professional resources to ensure the best chance of success, could have the potential to seriously damage the reputation and financial viability of the venue. I therefore stand behind my director in this regard, and I recommend the board fully endorse and action our plan." He coughed, turned around slightly towards me and smiled. "Without delay. We have no time to lose."

"Here, here!" said Father O'Mara, who was joined in his approval by Hugh McWilliams, and in turn by each of the other board members.

"That's fine then," said Fenella.

I'd swear I even heard her teeth gritting, but she kept on smiling.

"Whatever you want," she said. "We've spent far too much time on this issue already. Let's move on."

I closed down my presentation and sat down. I've no idea what else was said in that meeting as I sat through the rest of it in a completely blissed-out state.

Chapter 26

MELANIE

I was already starting to get into the Christmas spirit and had taken a half day off on Friday afternoon to get my hair cut before Father O'Mara's meeting. I caught sight of myself in a shop window as I strolled up Grafton Street. I was delighted with my new shorter, choppier look, and my long fringe – Ian had always liked me to wear my hair long and straight, and over the years I guess I'd just got used to it that way.

I smiled to myself as I bounced up the granite steps leading to the entrance of the Gentleman's Club. It was the Friday before Christmas and I just had the meeting to get through before enjoying an evening's late-night shopping and a bite to eat afterwards with my mum and sisters.

Father O'Mara was just inside the foyer, standing next to a large Christmas tree which thankfully was obscuring my view of the poor ol' stags' heads.

"Ah, Melanie, wonderful to see you. You're looking very well," he said. "Come on up – you're the first to arrive."

I followed him up the old, marble staircase into a reception room on the first floor. An open fire was burning in the grate and the room inside was lovely and cosy.

"Come, let's sit here by the fire. We've a few minutes before the others start to arrive." Father O'Mara settled into an armchair. "Tell me now, how has life been treating you since last we spoke, Melanie?"

"Very well, thank you, Father. Marcus allocated my department a couple of extra administration staff which has really helped to take some of the pressure off. The Christmas season is in full swing and we're getting close to signing up a new sponsorship manager that we headhunted from a major international film festival. *And* . . . Marcus signed off the tender document for the new fundraising consultancy this afternoon too. I may have to watch my back when a certain chairwoman is around, but other than that, work is going great."

Father O'Mara laughed. "That's very good to hear. Thank you for coming today anyway, Melanie dear."

"Gosh, not at all. I really wanted to come. I want to do whatever I can to help you get this initiative off the ground."

"Wonderful, wonderful," said Father O'Mara.

A couple of men arrived then for the meeting. They greeted Father O'Mara warmly. He introduced us and left me with them while he went to greet the next arrivals. The two men I spoke to had gone to school together and much of the conversation was about schools rugby. I hadn't a clue what they were talking about really, so I winged it and think I just about got away with it.

"I think we'll get started." Father O'Mara announced

to the room after another few minutes. "We have a few more to arrive, but I'm conscious of the week that's in it – no doubt you all have exciting Christmas parties and events to dash off to."

I glanced around at the people taking their seats around the long table, and for the first time realised that I was the only woman there. I thought it strange, but reasoned that there might be another few women yet to come. At that point there were about eleven men and me. A couple of the men looked familiar, but I couldn't quite place them.

Father O'Mara began the meeting by leading us in a short prayer. The men all seemed to know the words, but I could only just about mumble along, pretending to know it.

"So," Father O'Mara said, after blessing himself, "before I outline the details of the project perhaps we might go around the table and introduce ourselves. Most of us know each other already but there are a couple of new –" he looked at me, "and most welcome faces. Right so. I'll start. My name is Brendan O'Mara. As most of you know, I'm a retired teacher, and former rector, of Ashvale College in Wicklow."

He sat down after his introduction and, as I was sitting to his right, I went next.

"My name is Melanie McQuaid. I'm director of marketing and development for the Dublin Millennium Centre for the Arts." I looked around the roomful of men. "I must admit, I'm feeling a little outnumbered here today."

There was a murmur of laughter.

"Ah yes, sorry about that, Melanie," said Father

O'Mara. "I should have said it would be just us men, but I had to make sure you'd come. Melanie has a great way of getting things done, gentlemen. I'm hoping she'll help me put manners on you lot. God knows, I failed abysmally when you were my pupils."

"You taught us everything we know, Father," said one man, elbowing his neighbour for a reaction.

"Did I indeed?" said Father O'Mara, peering over his glasses, pretending to look stern. He had the look down very well. I'd forgotten that Father O'Mara used to be a teacher – it was a side of him I'd never really seen. The two men stopped smiling for an instant and sat up straighter. It was an amusing dynamic to watch.

Father O'Mara nodded then to the man sitting to my right.

"My name is Ed Blake," he said.

I swung around. I knew his face had looked familiar. It was Richie's brother.

"I'm training to be a teacher," he was saying. "And working down at Ashvale now as a night housemaster."

Father O'Mara looked down the table at Ed and smiled. "On a serious note, gentlemen – and lady," he nodded to me, "I would like to extend my special thanks to Edward and to his brother –" He looked around the room. "Where is Richard?"

Oh my God, so Richie was coming too?

Just at that moment the door flew open. "Sorry, Jangler – I mean, Father. Sorry, lads. Damn carparks are all full. I'm parked halfway to bloody Ranelagh – the world and its dog seem to be in town this afternoon."

That can't be him? I thought. I watched him move around the table to a seat opposite me. He looked so much more together than he had done on TV. Hair cut short, clean-shaven, full of life. He looked . . . well, he looked really good it had to be said.

"Good to see you, Richard," said Father O'Mara. "I was just thanking you and Edward for coming along today, so soon after your mother's passing. I know I speak for us all when I offer our most sincere sympathies."

"Here here!" said one of the men, and the rest murmured along.

"Thank you, Father. Thanks, lads," Richie said. "And apologies again for being late."

"Not at all, Richard. We'd only just started to do the introductions. This is Melanie McQuaid."

I looked right at Richie, and promptly felt my cheeks start to glow.

"Melanie is joining us from the Dublin Millennium Centre for the Arts where she works as –"

"Director of marketing and development," Richie looked at me, and a wide grin spread across his annoyingly handsome face. "Miss McQuaid, is it yourself?"

"It is indeed, Mister Blake." I smiled, my cheeks growing warmer by the second.

"Fancy meeting you here," he said, still grinning. "Good to see you again, Mel, very good indeed."

"You too, Richie," I put my head down to write the date on my notepad. Anything to deflect the attention from my rosy face.

"Ah, so you know each other then?" said Father O'Mara.

"You could say that," said Richie, which made me blush again.

"Very good," said Father O'Mara. "Okay then, let's

push on, lots to get through. Bill, would you like to continue?"

I tried to pay attention, but I was so conscious of Richie sitting across from me that I didn't hear one word. As the introductions went on, I stole another glance over at him. Same playful grin, same smiling eyes. He caught me looking over and gave me a wink. I smiled, then quickly turned back to look at Father O'Mara.

Once the introductions were over, Father O'Mara outlined his concept for the new youth centre, then opened the meeting up to the floor for discussion.

"Is this the best use of resources to help young people?" he asked. "Have you any further thoughts on how the concept could be conceived? Is it the right thing to do?"

"Through the Chair?"

Father O'Mara nodded to the man sitting beside Richie. I hadn't caught his name.

"I think that it is exactly the right thing to do," the man said, looking quite serious. "We need to do something to help our kids. I'm having a lot of problems with one of my teenagers at the moment, in fact." His voice started to crack a little. "I think a centre like you describe, Father, could be a big help to her, and to other kids like her." He coughed to clear his throat. "It could be just what they need to help them to get through whatever the hell it is they're going through. Because, I can tell you, we as parents haven't got a bloody clue what more to do for them. The system of support for young people in this country is atrocious."

Richie put his hand on the man's shoulder, who nodded his thanks for the support.

"Through the Chair?" said Richie.

Father O'Mara nodded.

"To follow on from what Dec is saying," Richie said, "I agree that young people need help finding their way in life. Maybe with this centre we can help them to realise that it's okay to be who you are, that it's okay to be different and to follow your own path." He glanced over at me, but this time he didn't grin or smile – in fact, he looked quite serious. "Who knows, if we'd had a place like this when we were kids, then maybe Ben MacDonagh would be here today, and there might be one less empty chair at our gatherings."

It was a deeper, more serious side to Richie than I'd ever seen.

Who was this guy Ben? And what happened to him? He was obviously very important to Richie anyway, judging by the look on his face and the way his voice trembled when he mentioned his name.

"Yes, indeed, Richard. Very true, very true indeed. Thank you." Father O'Mara pushed his glasses up on his nose as he looked around the table. "Melanie, what do you think?"

He'd caught me off guard. I looked at Richie, then at his friend Dec beside him – the poor guy looked broken.

"I think Richie is absolutely right," I said, straightening up in my seat. "Young people should be given every encouragement to find their own path in life – the retreat centre is a great idea. We absolutely must make it happen. I just wonder also, Father, if it should be built somewhere that is naturally beautiful? Somewhere with lots of space for games and sports, and perhaps even a view of the sea. Actually no – *definitely* a view of the sea."

I glanced over at Richie. "It's good for the soul."

All of the heads nodded.

Richie smiled. His expression changed then and he raised his hand. "Through the Chair?"

Father O'Mara nodded.

"I agree that we need to give these kids somewhere to go," he said. "But once they're there, once they start to unwind and relax a bit, that's when they're going to need someone to talk to." He put his hand on his friend's shoulder again. "No offence, Dec, but it's not always easy opening up and talking through your stuff with the people closest to you, even your parents."

"Especially your parents," said Ed beside me.

Dec nodded. "You're right, lads – we can't get anything out of our Tara these days. I honestly have no idea what's going on inside her head."

"I don't have kids myself, but I do remember being one," said Richie. "Young people are like the rest of us – they just need someone to talk to, someone to listen to them. It might be their parents or a caring teacher," he looked at Father O'Mara. "But it could just as easily be someone else entirely – perhaps a stranger who just gets it. Someone who gets them." He looked straight at me then and smiled.

I smiled back, and this time I didn't blush.

"In fact, what might work well," he went on, "would be if we could get someone experienced on board from the outset – a professional counsellor or therapist or whatever – someone to advise us, maybe even run the place when it opens."

"A great idea, Richard. Splendid," said Father O'Mara.

"I know someone who would be perfect," I said. "A good friend of mine, Katy Butler – she's a qualified psychologist, and actually specialises in children and young people. I can ask her if she could help?"

"That would be wonderful, Melanie. Thank you." Father O'Mara rubbed his hands together and sat back in his chair, seeming very pleased with the way things were going. "Very good, very good indeed. Anyone else?"

Richie smiled over at me again as someone else started to talk about the benefits of animal therapy. I smiled back, then pretended to listen to the discussion, but I honestly didn't hear a word of it. I couldn't wait for the meeting to be over, so I could talk to Richie.

Chapter 27

RICHARD

As soon as Jangler mentioned to me at my mother's funeral that he was thinking of building a retreat centre for young people, I knew I had to get involved. I'd do anything for Jangler of course, but, more than that, I saw it as a way of trying to make my peace with Ben. I was determined the centre would be built, and that it would be the best it could be.

There was a lot of enthusiasm and support for the idea at the meeting, but it became clear that we had a lot of work to do to get the project off the ground. It was exactly what I needed to take my mind off things.

Jangler drew the meeting to a close bang on five o'clock as promised.

"So let's convene again after Christmas," he said. "In the meantime, to confirm . . . Alan and Finbar, you are going to progress the survey of other existing projects and facilities for young people . . . Bill and Melanie will speak to their contacts regarding expert mental-health advice." He looked at Mel. "It would be great if your friend – Katy,

278

wasn't it? – might consider coming on board."

I looked across the table at Mel again. I still couldn't believe she was there – it was such a coincidence. I probably should have been embarrassed to see her after all of that stuff we'd talked about the previous week, but I wasn't really. Her email, and then that phone call, had been a real turning point for me. And, all that aside, I'd forgotten just how good she looked. She'd had her black hair cut into a shorter, layered style – it suited her, made her a look a lot softer, not quite as stern. And, even though she was sitting down, I could tell she looked well in the dark green dress that matched her eyes so well.

"Richard, Peter and Declan will investigate additional sources of finance," Jangler was saying, "and Edward and I will put our heads together to come up with suggestions for suitable locations for the centre." He stood up. "Well, thank you very much, everyone. I wish you and yours a peaceful and happy Christmas. I may see some of you down at Ashvale on Monday night for Mass on Christmas Eve, and to everyone else I look forward to seeing you safe and well in the new year."

I stood as the meeting broke up.

"Well, well, well, this is a surprise," I said across the table to Mel.

She smiled and was about to say something back when Michael O'Toole came over to me to offer his sympathies. I thanked him and tried to get away as quickly as possible, but by the time I'd extricated myself Mel was talking to Ed.

"Don't let that woman leave!" I called over to my brother, then strode around to their side of the table. "I see you've met Mel, Ed. This is the whale expert I was telling you about."

She laughed. "Hardly an expert."

Ed looked at me blankly.

"Come on – you remember. I told you at the weekend – the girl who saw the whales in Norway? She helped – well, let's say, she inspired me somewhat in recent weeks."

"Oh right," said Ed, clearly not following what was going on at all.

I didn't bother going into it any further, just took Mel by the arm. "It's great to see you again, Mel. I was going to get in touch soon to arrange for us to meet up." I stood back and took a good look at all of her. "Of course if I'd remembered how good-looking you were in person, I'd have done it sooner."

Ed groaned. "Right, that's my exit cue. I've got to shoot off anyway, Rich – I need to pick up a few presents before driving Jangler back down to Ashvale."

Mel started to make a move. "Oh yes, you probably both need to get going – don't let me keep you."

"I don't have to go," I said. "Are you staying in town for a while? You don't fancy grabbing a coffee or a drink now by any chance, do you?"

"Sure. That'd be great actually. I'll just go grab my coat." She left us and went over to the coat stand.

"Will I get something for Sheila and Derek from both of us as usual?" Ed asked me as he put on his own coat.

"No, it's okay, thanks, man. I'm going to go shopping myself this year."

He looked surprised, then pleased. "Right so. Are you still coming down to Ashvale on Christmas Eve?"

"Yes, absolutely. I'm looking forward to seeing your

new set-up. I'll see you there," I said, and walked over to Mel.

"So how do you know Jangler?" I asked Mel as we walked over to the Fitzwilliam Hotel.

"He's on the board at The Mill," she said. "I've known him for years – he's a dote."

"Is he now? How did I not know he was on the board there?"

"Those journalistic skills of yours in need of a bit of sharpening up perhaps, Mister Blake? Maybe you were a little too long out there in the Pacific Ocean? Starting to lose the edge, are we?"

"Don't even go there, Miss McQuaid!"

She laughed. "Why do you call him Jangler anyway?"

"Nothing dubious, I promise you. It's to do with a big set of keys he used to carry around the school when he taught us."

I pushed open the door of the hotel bar. Inside it was already full with Christmas shoppers and office-workers starting on the beer early but, just as we walked in, a group of people stood up to leave the corner booth – their shopping bags alone nearly took up the whole bar.

"Grab those seats," I said. "I'll get the coffees in. Or would you prefer a real drink? I'm on the wagon myself, or I'd join you."

"No, no, coffee's great," said Mel. "Cappuccino please."

"So how's things at The Mill these days? That ol' Wright crone and her sidekick still giving you a hard time?" I asked, putting the cups down and sliding into the seat opposite her. "Have you finished raising that fifteen million yet?"

"Not quite, just a few cents more to go," she said with a smile. "No, to be honest, work is a hundred times better, thanks. I sorted things out with Marcus and Fenella. Let's just say we're all back on a level playing field again. It wasn't easy, but I got there in the end."

I held up my coffee cup. "Most excellent. Cheers to you for sorting that out!"

"Thanks, Richie," she said, taking a sip of coffee. Her whole face lit up then. "By the way, I absolutely loved your article last week." She sat forward in her seat and leant across the table. "It was so interesting to read about life on board the Greenpeace ship. Will you stay in touch with the crew, do you think? That guy Takumi sounded like quite a character, and I can't believe that couple went on their honeymoon on an anti-whaling expedition! Isn't the Mister Splashy Pants campaign brilliant? I've decided to do a sponsored swim on St Stephen's Day to raise funds for it. I just can't believe they're hunting humpbacks though – it seems crazy!"

"Whoa! Slow down there – take a breath, girl!"

She laughed and sat back. "I'm sorry – everyone tells me I'm obsessed by whales at the moment. It's sad, I know!"

I shook my head. "Not at all. There's nothing wrong with a bit of healthy whale obsession every once in a while – I've just spent a fortnight in the company of thirty whale enthusiasts. The *Illuminar* crew will be very impressed to hear of this fundraising idea – so how will that work?"

And she was off! Mel spent the next five to ten minutes talking about her St Stephen's Day swim: "My friend Katy is going to do it with me, and the lads from the local rugby club . . . Well, they do it every year just for fun, but this year Katy and me will be joining in – we're hoping to raise over a thousand euro for the whales. It should be good fun – everyone comes down to the beach in Greystones in Wicklow for St Stephen's Day morning – Katy's organising mulled wine, I'm doing mince pies . . ."

Her face became so animated and her eyes sparkled as she talked about it all, especially when she talked about the whales. She was definitely a very different woman from the one I first met all those months ago – the one who really needed to chill out and relax. This lady was clearly passionate about the cause, and her enthusiasm was quite infectious. I found listening to her very enjoyable – very enjoyable indeed.

"So since I started earlier this week I've already raised over three hundred euro, so I'm just under a third of the way to my target. Katy's aiming to raise five hundred and she's doing really well too. People have been so good at donating, and they've sent such lovely messages of support. I'm trying to persuade as many friends and family to come along to help raise awareness of the issue – we'll collect on the day too. I must remember to organise some buckets for that actually." She picked up her enormous handbag and started rooting around, eventually pulling out a bulging Filofax and a pen. She made a note, then popped the pen back in the Filofax and took what seemed like her first breath in the last half hour. "Anyway, Richie, enough about me," she said. "I've been going on about myself and whales for so long."

I shook my head. "No, it's great listening to you – all distractions are most welcome at the moment."

She smiled – a sympathy smile – I'd got very used to those over the last week or so. "But I haven't even asked how your mother's funeral went last week?" she said. "It must have been difficult for you?"

"Ah yeah, these have been a tough enough few weeks." I sighed and rubbed my forehead. "It's been a bit of an emotional rollercoaster – one minute up, next minute down. But I think it's been good for us all in many ways."

"You must be glad to be back talking to Ed now anyway? You seemed to be getting on well there today."

"Yeah, still some way to go, but it's a lot better now. Thanks for your advice on that, by the way. I did what you suggested and just said sorry – it really worked." I smiled. "I'll have to keep you around as my special adviser in future."

I'd swear she blushed a bit then – cute.

"He seems happier than I've seen him in – well – maybe *ever* actually." I paused, then took a breath before going on. "It's Lucy – my ex – that I'm still worried about. I need to make sure she's okay – need to try to put things right with her and her family."

Mel sat back in her seat. "Yes, of course. Have you been talking to her?"

"No – she won't take my calls. I did try to get in touch several times after the lunch that day, but she didn't want to know."

"Maybe you should try again now?"

"I did – I tried calling her last week after the funeral, but there was no answer. I left a message, but I haven't heard anything back. Ah – I treated her pretty badly, Mel – she's well within her rights to blank me."

"She'll come around."

"Well, there's a bit more to it."

"Oh?"

I paused for a minute. I needed Mel to know the full story about how I'd made such a mess of my relationship with Lucy, how I'd disrespected Ben's family. It wasn't going to be easy, but I wanted her to know the full truth about me. I definitely wanted to see more of Mel – she needed to have all the information to decide herself whether she wanted to be around me at all.

"Lucy's the sister of an old school friend of mine, Ben," I said. "He was my best friend when I was growing up. He took his own life not long after we left school."

"Oh Richie, I'm so sorry. That's the Ben you mentioned at today's meeting, isn't it?"

I nodded.

"It must have been awful when he died," she said. "And so young too – how do you get over something like that?"

I shook my head. "To be honest, Mel, I'm not sure I ever really did get over it. It was wrong to take up with Lucy as a result."

She looked at me for a few seconds, then took another sip of coffee before speaking again. "Do you think perhaps in some way you may have been *trying* to sabotage the relationship, Richie?" she asked. "I mean, one minute you were with your brother's girlfriend, the next you were getting engaged to Lucy. And that's just it – that day when I met you at the lunch, you didn't exactly come across as a man who'd just got engaged to the love of his life."

"Why? Because I was trying to pick you up on top of it all?" I laughed.

"Aha!" She pointed her finger at me. "So you *were* trying to pick me up!"

I smiled. "I don't know, to be honest, but I had spotted you earlier in the day. So, yes, I guess I may have been." I sighed. "What does that make me? I mean, Lucy's a really lovely girl. I liked being with her, and I liked being in a relationship, but we were very different really. And then there was all the pressure to get engaged. I suppose it was a lot to do with her being Ben's sister, and being around his family, his world, again. I just got lost in it all, and I didn't want to let her or her family down. But it was never going to work really – I know that now. Lucy and I didn't even share the same sense of humour. Imagine – she didn't laugh at my jokes!"

Mel feigned a look of horror. "Nooo! I find that quite impossible to believe."

"I know . . . right?" I smiled. "But look, even I know that there are better ways of ending a relationship than cheating on her one minute, and proposing the next. Let's just say I could have handled the whole thing better. A lot better."

Mel just nodded slowly, then finished her coffee.

It was hard to know what she was thinking.

I sincerely hoped I hadn't said too much. It was probably time to change the subject.

"But enough about my disastrous love life – what about you?" I asked.

"You want to know about my disastrous love life?" she said with a smile.

"Well, I don't know if it's disastrous, do I? Maybe you're blissfully in love now for all I know."

She sniffed. "I wish." She swirled her teaspoon around the foam at the end of her cup.

"When we first met," I said. "I got the impression from something you said that there was a bad relationship you had to put behind you?" I knew I was pushing it a bit, but I was genuinely interested. I wanted to know everything about this girl.

She took a deep breath. "I've only really told one other person the full story about Ian before – and that was just a couple of weeks ago."

"Oh sorry." I sat back. "I didn't mean to pry – you don't need to say anything."

"No, no, actually I'd like to," she said and leaned in on her elbow. "It'd be good to talk about it. There's actually been a development in the last week and I'm bursting to tell someone about it. Only I think we might need more coffees?"

She gestured to the waitress who took our order, and then she told me all about her right idiot of an ex.

"So I guess I'd been quite stuck for some time – perhaps without even realising it," she said. "But after meeting Ian recently, and finally getting the chance to say my piece, and then to walk away the bigger person, it feels great. I wish I'd been able to do it years ago."

"That's good to hear," I said. "I can't believe that guy though – he had an amazing woman like you and he treated you like that? Some guys just don't know when they have it good." Then I thought of Lucy. "I suppose I can't exactly talk, can I?"

"It's not the same," said Mel, her voice slightly shaky. "You never tried to change her, to take away her spirit, to hurt her physically. God, I was such a fool to put up with it for so long."

I reached out to touch the back of her hand, but before

I could, her phone buzzed on the table.

I pulled my hand back. "Looks like you've got an admirer there? That's the third text message you've got in the last five minutes. Are you going to go on ignoring him?"

"Him? No, I don't think so," she said. "But I'd better just check it's nothing urgent."

She picked up the phone.

"What?" she said after a few seconds, then she looked at me, a puzzled expression on her face.

"Everything okay?" I asked.

She looked back down at the phone. "My brother has just texted to ask if I'm cancelling my swim now that the whales are saved, and there's another one from Katy." She looked down at the phone and read out the text message: **"Great news about the humpbacks, eh?"** She looked back up at me, and a huge smile broke out across her face. "Is it off, Richie? Have the Japanese cancelled the hunt? Have you heard anything from the ship?"

"No, I haven't heard, but let me call the office."

I called the *Chronicle's* news desk.

"Hey, who's that? Trevor? Richard Blake here. Hi, man. Yes, thanks – we gave her a good send-off. Listen, can you check a story for me, Trev? Japanese whaling in Antarctica – anything about the hunt being called off? Thanks." I rested the phone down. "He's just checking it now."

I put the phone back to my ear. "What's that?" I listened intently. "Eh, thanks, man, that's brilliant. Great news, cheers. Yep, I'll be back in the office after Christmas. Catch you then."

I put down the phone and looked at Mel. "Japan has

yielded to international pressure – they've cancelled the hunt on the fifty humpback whales."

She put her head down in her hands for a few seconds, then looked back up at me – her eyes had watered up. If the damn table wasn't in the way I would have reached over to hug her.

"So there you have it," I said. "It seems the humpbacks of Antarctica will be safe for at least one more year."

"*Woooohoooo!*" she shouted and punched the air with her fist.

The whole bar stopped talking and turned to look over at us, but I didn't give a shit – the girl looked like her team had just won the Cup and the League in one go.

"I can't believe it, Richie! Isn't it fantastic? Mister Splashy Pants and the humpbacks are safe. Oh my God, it's like the best Christmas present ever!"

I laughed. You had to love this girl.

"It sure is, Mel."

"Of course they're probably still going after the fin and minke whales – it makes me so mad just thinking about it." She frowned for a second, before her face broke out into an adorable smile. "But hey, when you see the difference it can make when the world comes together and says no, you just think anything's possible, don't you?"

"You do indeed." I smiled.

She jumped up then. "I've got to go. I've got to tell my family and friends, and check the *Illuminar* blog. I need to send some emails too and update my fundraising page. Lots to do." She started to pull on her coat, then stopped for a second, sat down again and beamed at me. "It's just brilliant, isn't it, Richie? Fifty beautiful humpbacks are safe."

I smiled and nodded. "It is absolutely fantastic, Mel."

She got up again.

I stood up to help her with her coat. "So can I give you a call some time?"

"Oh yes, of course. I'd like that – you must let me know how things go with Lucy. I really hope it all works out for you. Happy Christmas, Richie." She gave me a quick peck on the cheek.

"Happy –" But she was off. I watched her leave and sat back down for a few seconds.

Dammit, I forgot to get her number.

I jumped back up, but she'd already gone. I looked around on the floor, half expecting to see a lone glass slipper somewhere – but my life had never much resembled a fairy tale.

I sat back down, and as I did I noticed a white woolly hat on the table.

I smiled as I put it in my pocket. Perhaps my luck was beginning to change.

Chapter 28

MELANIE

I was so excited when I heard the news about the humpbacks. It gave me such a boost that I cancelled my dinner plans with my mum and sisters, and spent the rest of Friday night and early Saturday morning either on the laptop reading the updates on the Greenpeace blog, or sending emails about my fundraising swim.

I had to peel myself away from it all on Saturday morning to collect my sister's kids for swimming. And, as I was being dragged out to do more wedding-dress shopping straight afterwards, Katy was coming swimming too – to make sure I didn't escape.

We were a bit early to collect them, and the kids were slow getting ready, so Nichola made Katy and me some tea and toast while we waited. I sat patiently waiting for her and Katy to get through the whole engagement congratulations and ring-admiring rituals before I could find a window to update them on the situation with the humpbacks.

"Wow, you're really into all this whale stuff, aren't

you?" Nichola said when I'd finished my excited ramble. "I can hardly keep up you're talking so fast."

"She's a woman on a mission," said Katy.

"Sorry. It's just great to see the campaign having this effect, and to be able to play my part in it – however small. I'm just a few hundred euro off my fundraising target now, can ye believe? The momentum from the emails I sent out after the announcement about the humpbacks last night caused another flurry of donations."

"Sounds good – well done, you," Nichola said, putting a plate of toast down in front of us. "By the way, Mel, not like you to miss our annual McQuaid girls' dinner last night. Who was the friend you mentioned in your text – the one you said you were with before you bumped us off?"

"Ah, sorry again about that, Nic. I'll give Mum and the others a call later to apologise about not coming to the dinner. It was Richie Blake I ran into earlier – you know, the guy I mentioned I'd written to on board the Greenpeace ship?"

"The journalist from Dublin?"

"Yes – his second feature article about it all is in the paper today as it happens – not that I've had a second to read it yet." I pulled the newspaper I'd bought on the way over out of my bag and put it on the table. "I bumped into Richie in town at a meeting late yesterday afternoon and we went for a coffee together afterwards. I didn't notice the time go by, then when I got a text asking if it was true about the humpbacks, Richie called the paper to confirm the news. After that, I just had to dash home to read about it all online. I would have been no use at the dinner anyway, Nichola, I was far too excited."

"It's all right, sure we got your text, and it's great about the whales. So . . . it went well with this guy then?" Nichola leaned over the table, looking like she was anticipating some juicy gossip.

"Ah no, it was nothing like that, Nic. He's a nice guy and very easy to talk to, but he's got a lot of stuff going on."

"Actually, Mel," said Katy, picking up the newspaper and pulling the supplement out of it, "I was talking to Frank about him, and he said the Blakes are both pretty sound fellas. Maybe I was wrong about this Richie. And hey," she pointed at the article, "he writes about whales? You two could be a match made in heaven."

I rolled my eyes. "Ha ha – very funny."

Katy raised her eyebrows. "I was actually being serious."

"Well, I haven't had the chance to read the article yet," I said, taking the supplement from Katy and flicking to Richie's piece. "But whales or no whales, I know Richie's a good guy underneath all the bravado and the baggage, and in many ways I do like him – but, as I say, we're just friends – keepin' it simple."

"Ah, Mel," said Katy, "I thought you said you were past all of that?" She looked at my sister. "I don't know, Nichola – I'm beginning to like the sound of this guy. Frank was in college with his brother – reckons Richie might need quietening down all right, but for the right woman he could be quite a catch."

"Really?" said Nichola, her eyes lighting up.

"All right, you pair – calm down. We're just friends who chatted for a while yesterday over coffee. It was nice – not exactly earth-shattering stuff."

"So how did you leave it?" Nichola asked.

"Leave what? There's nothing to leave – we're just friends, barely even that really."

But she was still staring at me. "The lady doth protest too much, methinks," she said after a few seconds.

Katy laughed.

They drove me nuts when they ganged up. I sat up straight in my chair. "If you must know, I found out about the humpback hunt being cancelled, so I suppose I left in kind of a hurry."

Nichola groaned. "Ah Mel! You're hopeless. Tell me you at least gave him your mobile number?"

"He didn't ask for it," I said, almost wishing we could go back to talking about wedding dresses and engagement rings. "He has my email address and he knows where I work – what more does he need? Anyway, you're both making way too much of this." I closed the supplement, planning to read the article later in peace.

Katy and Nichola smiled at each other.

A change of subject was needed, and quick.

"While I think of it, Katy," I said, "that meeting yesterday was about a new retreat centre for young people. Father O'Mara – one of our board members at The Mill – asked me to see if you could give us a bit of advice – we need a counsellor or psychologist to advise us on the whole thing."

"Oh yes? Sounds interesting," she said. "Tell me more."

So I told Katy all about the project.

"You should come to the next meeting in January if you're interested?" I said.

"Yes, I'll definitely come. I'd love to get involved in something like that."

"Sounds like a great project," said Nichola. "Other than Father O'Mara and Richie, who's behind –?"

But we were interrupted when my nine-year-old niece Jackie bounded into the room.

"Mom, I still can't find my goggles," she said, pulling a face.

Nichola sighed. "I thought your brother was helping you find them?"

Jackie folded her arms. "No, he's playing his computer game."

"What? Still?" Nichola went to the door and shouted up the stairs. "Aus-tin! *Do not make me come up there!*"

"Want me to go get him?" I asked.

"No, you stay right there and read whatever it is that journalist fella has to say for himself," Nichola said, nodding at the newspaper supplement. She turned to go, then looked back over her shoulder. "And hey, sis, don't rule the guy out for having a bit of baggage – we all have our issues, y'know? Nobody's perfect." She went off up the stairs.

"Wise words," said Katy before getting up from the table. "Sounds like they could be a while getting ready yet. Will I put more toast on?"

"Go on then." I sat back and opened up the supplement.

Richie's face grinned out at me from a photograph over the titles.

I began to read.

I'm told that when you look into the eye of a whale, you're looking through the window of your own soul. I think it might even be true. The trouble is, after experiencing such intense joy, exhilaration and brilliance

in one moment, you realise just what a disappointment life can be the rest of the time. But that might not be such a bad thing – for real change to happen, a catalyst is often needed. Could that moment with the whale have been the catalyst I needed?

"Woah, Katy – this article's about looking into the eye of the whale." I looked up at her. "That's what made me email him at sea."

"Really? Let me see." She leaned in over the table and we read through the article together. It was so beautifully written – very personal, quite sad and deep, yet hopeful all at the same time.

I knew Richie had been struggling with his mother's death and his words about her were particularly moving. What I hadn't realised was that he'd also been struggling with his friend, Ben's death too – and for so long. In the article he talked about how hard it was to finally have to face up to both deaths while alone and at sea, and then about the impact of an email he'd received from a friend who was there when he really needed her.

I wondered if it was me that he meant.

The last few lines really captured the sentiment of the piece: I leave the humpbacks, the *Illuminar* and its crew a very different man to the one I was when I arrived. It's been a turbulent voyage, but, thanks to the whales and a little help from a new friend, I've had my eyes opened and my soul serviced – and I'm finally ready to face back to the life and people I left behind.

I read the final words, sat back and looked up. "I think I'm the new friend he's talking about, Katy – that's so lovely." I groaned. "Oh God, did I make a mistake rushing off the other night?"

"Hard to say. I mean, I see what you mean about having baggage – it sounds like he's got more than a small airportful! But he's very honest, and he seems to have got a lot from being on the ship, from your friendship and from seeing the whales. What *is* it about those whales?"

I went to answer, but Katy held up her hand. "It's all right," she said. "I wasn't really asking the question. I'd like us to get to the pool, and eventually the shops at some stage today!" She laughed. "Anyway, as you say, you have his email address, and we'll see him at the next project meeting for the centre in January, won't we?"

"Hmm, true." I turned back to read through the article again.

The trouble was, I wasn't sure I wanted to wait that long.

As the day went on I tried hard to focus on swimming and on wedding dresses, but I kept finding my mind wander back to Richie. By the time I got home I was fed up just thinking about him – I decided the time for action had come. I needed to see if there was anything there between us.

After all, what did I have to lose?

So I sent Richie a quick email – this time no innuendo, no jokes. I suggested we meet up again soon. I didn't want to suggest quite when, with Christmas in a couple of days, but I really hoped it could be soon anyway.

Chapter 29

RICHARD

It was as close as I reckoned I'd ever get to being famous. My phone started to ring as soon as my second feature appeared in the supplement on Saturday morning, and it didn't stop all day with calls and messages from family and friends. I was a bit embarrassed when I saw my own words in print at first. It was the most personal piece I'd ever written, but it was what I wanted to say. I had nothing to hide any more. I just wanted to be myself.

After the article, everybody else got to see the real me as well – and from the sounds of the calls and messages they weren't frightened off.

Ed got genuinely emotional and choked when we talked about it on the phone. "It's made me see a whole new side to you," he said. "I hadn't realised you'd been struggling so much over the years, Rich. Sorry I wasn't there for you."

"Don't be an idiot, you had your own stuff going on."

"Even so, we're brothers. We need to be there for each other – especially now Mum's gone."

"Yep, you're right, man. Anyway, we're on to a new chapter now. It'll be better from here on."

Sheila was very touched about what I'd written about my mother, and Derek said he'd spoken to my father who was very proud. But it was Jangler who stayed on the phone the longest – he wanted to know everything about my encounter with the humpback whales and about this friend of mine. I'm not sure whether he realised it was Mel, I didn't mention any names.

The one person I didn't hear from on Saturday, though, was Mel. I checked my email a few times during the day, but no word.

I wondered if she'd got to see the article yet, and if she had, had she recognised herself in it? I guessed I should really have warned her about it coming out when we met, and I should have let her know just how much her email and that phone call meant to me – before she read about it in the paper. But there had been so much else for us to talk about when we'd met, and then she'd left in such a hurry. I just never got round to it.

Maybe I'll drop her a line myself later on, I thought.

I was on a high from it all anyway as I got ready to go out that night. It was going to be strange being out with the lads and not drinking. I was certainly missing the drink, but I was feeling a lot better in myself already, and I was just looking forward to be catching up with the lads again.

The phone rang just as I was buttoning up my shirt.

I picked it up and looked at the number: "**MacDonaghs**".

Woah. This was it.

I sat down on the bed, and let it ring one more time before answering.

"Hello, is that Richie?"

"Lucy?"

"Yes. Hi, Richie."

"Hi," I said.

"I'm sorry I'm only ringing now."

"Don't apologise Luce. It's me who should be apologising. I'm very sorry, I . . ." But my mind just went blank. "Shit, I've gone over this speech in my head a hundred times – but now that you're here, actually on the other end of the line, I can't remember a damn word of what I'd planned to say."

"It's okay," she said in a very quiet voice so that I could barely hear her. "I was so sorry to hear about Rose's passing, Richie. I hope you and Ed are okay. It's a big loss for you."

"Thanks, Lucy. Yes, it was a shock. I still can't really believe she's gone to be honest."

"I can imagine." She paused before going on; "I read your article today, Richie."

"Ah," was all I could think of to say. My brain had still not quite caught up with the situation.

"It was very nice," she said. "It sounds like the trip did you a lot of good?"

"Yes. It did, Lucy, it really did. It gave me plenty of time to think about things – especially about all that happened between us." I took a deep breath. "I'm just so damned sorry about it all, Luce."

She took a few seconds before she spoke. "Thanks, Richie, I appreciate that. It's taken me some time, but it's okay now really. It just doesn't seem to matter so much any more."

I was surprised. I never really thought Lucy would fully accept my apology, let alone say it didn't matter.

"Richie, I can't stay on the phone now," she went on, "but I'd like to see you if that's okay? I'm staying with my folks over Christmas. Can you come to Glenamara? I'm sorry, I know it is very close to Christmas itself, but I think it's important we talk."

I hesitated. "Eh *ye-ees* . . . I can . . ." I didn't mind going to Clifden, even on the weekend before Christmas, but I wondered why she wanted to see me in person? Why couldn't we have spoken on the phone? Or waited till she was next in Dublin?

Then a thought occurred to me. She didn't want to get back together, did she? She couldn't . . .

But I wasn't sure and, all that aside, I wasn't at all keen on running into Mr and Mrs Mac at Glenamara.

"Richie, are you still there?" Then as if she could read my mind, she added: "If you could make it tomorrow afternoon, my parents won't be here. They're going to Galway for a Christmas party and won't be back until Monday morning."

Well, that was something at least.

"Okay, I'll see you there at Glenamara tomorrow afternoon, Lucy."

"Good. See you then, Richie." And she was gone.

I stared at the phone for a minute, then went back in to the bathroom to shave.

"*Ouch!*" I nicked myself with the razor.

Nerves, I guessed. I was not looking forward to the next day but at least, whatever happened, it was a chance to try to start putting things right with the MacDonaghs.

It was just starting to get dark when I arrived into Clifden. It was raining hard, but the outdoor lights were on so I got the full effect of Glenamara's impressive façade as I emerged from the narrow avenue of pine trees which snaked up to house.

I parked the car on the gravel driveway in front and turned off the engine. The sight of the house I knew so well from my teenage years never failed to affect me. I stayed sitting in the car and looked up at it. Sitting there, looking at the flaky white-washed façade, and the red-framed window panes, I felt more nervous than I had ever felt. I'd have given anything to have been able to jump forward a couple of hours, to be turning on the engine to go back home.

The front door opened and Lucy stood in the doorway. She smiled a bit and waved me in.

I raised my hand to say hello back, then took the key out of the ignition.

All right, it was now or never.

I ran in to try to avoid the downpour.

"Would you like a cup of tea? Or coffee?" Lucy said when I was barely inside the door. "Or maybe a glass of wine? I know you're driving, but perhaps you could have a small one? I think Dad has a nice bottle of Rioja open –"

I could have really done with a drink to steady the nerves right then. It was getting harder and harder to stick to my new alcohol-free regimen, but I was determined.

"No booze thanks, Lucy." I said, shaking the rain out of my hair.

She looked surprised. "Okay Richie." She moved in the direction of the sitting room. "I'll put the kettle on then."

"Excellent. A cup of tea would be great, thanks, Luce."

I took my coat off and left it on the coat-stand, then walked on in. There was a fire already roaring in the grate and the room appeared very familiar, cosy and welcoming. Lucy came in behind me then and I watched her as she pulled over the curtains. She seemed very uneasy – which made two of us.

She puffed up a couple of cushions on an armchair then disappeared off in the direction of the kitchen again.

I was quite grateful for the few minutes to get myself together. I sat back and stared at the flickering flames, enjoying the warmth and comfort after the long drive.

A few minutes later Lucy arrived back with a laden tray.

"I was glad to get your call, Luce, thanks for getting in touch." I said, sitting forward as she set the tray down on the coffee table.

"Yes, I'd been meaning to get back to you for a while," she said as she sat down, "but I just couldn't bring myself to call you back. Then your mother died, and yesterday when I read your article . . . well, I knew I just had to get in touch."

"Ah, the article," I said.

She picked up the teapot. "I never knew you had that deeper side to you, Richie, or even that you felt like that about Ben. You never wanted to talk to me about him." She went to pour the tea, but partly missed the cup and the hot liquid splashed over the table.

"Damn!" She jumped up and ran out to the kitchen, then came back with a dishcloth. I helped her mop it up, but stopped her when she picked up the teapot again.

"Maybe we should just leave the tea for a minute, Luce?" I said. "Can you sit down?"

She put down the pot, came over and sat down on the sofa beside me. But it seemed she couldn't look at me – instead she sat up poker-stiff, and just stared straight ahead at the fireplace.

I thought it best just to get to the point. "Lucy, I'm sorry. I didn't mean to hurt you. I acted like an idiot and I treated you very badly. I feel terrible about what I did, about how I disrespected you and your family. I'm so sorry."

She swallowed, hesitated for a moment, then turned around to me. "Richie, I'm sorry too."

That caught me off-guard. I hadn't expected her to apologise.

I shook my head. "You've nothing to be sorry about, Lucy – you've done nothing wrong. I'm the one who cheated on you."

"It's okay, Richie, really," she said, looking back at the fire. "Sure I knew Sonya would get her claws into you eventually – she always fancied you, I could tell the first time I met her with Ed – the poor guy never stood a chance. She probably did us all a big favour anyway. You and I were never right together – we shouldn't ever have got together in the first place."

"What? No, that's ridiculous. C'mon, Lucy. We had a good time together – I really liked being with you."

"Yes, *liked*. You liked me a lot." She turned to me. "But you didn't love me, did you, Richie?" she asked, looking straight at me.

"Well, I –"

"See? That moment of hesitation – it says it all." She sighed. "Oh look, if I was being honest, I knew you weren't in love with me, Richie. We never really worked.

Sure, we were friends and we got on well enough, but you couldn't ever really let me in. I thought things might develop between us eventually, but you were always so guarded about your thoughts and your feelings. That's why I was so surprised yesterday when I read your article. I'd never seen that side to you before, never knew you felt like that about Ben's death."

"I'm sorry, Lucy." It sounded so lame, but I honestly didn't know what else to say.

"It wasn't your fault, Richie – I realise now that the reason you couldn't open up, or couldn't tell me you loved me was because you didn't feel it. And I was angry with you about that for some time, but I shouldn't have been – you can't choose who you fall in love with, can't decide who to let into your heart."

I had to strain to hear what she said next because she spoke in such a quiet voice as she stared straight ahead at the fire.

"When you proposed," she said, "I tried to forget all that. I pretended to myself that everything had changed – tried to believe that maybe somewhere along the line you had happened to fall in love with me. And like a fool, I got swept away with the idea of marrying you. I thought everything was going to be all right. It was stupid, I realise that now . . ." Her voice had tapered out to almost nothing.

"I did think I wanted to marry you at the time, Lucy, but I suppose you're right – I wasn't in love with you." I felt like a right shit.

She turned her face around to me, and I saw that she had tears hovering in her eyes. I moved closer to her, and she let me put my arm around her shoulder for a couple of seconds.

Then she pulled back, and wiped some stray tears away with the back of her hand.

"It's okay," she said, coughing to recover. "I was a mess after we broke up, Richie. I was single again, missing my life in New York, and utterly miserable. And of course I blamed you for most of it. It was hard, but it also turned out to be the best thing that could have happened. A few weeks after we broke up I went to see a counsellor and, after spending the majority of my time talking about Ben and my family, I realised that my problem wasn't about you, or about us at all." She took a deep breath, "My coming back to Ireland eighteen months ago, and seeking you out –"

I raised my eyebrows. This was news to me.

"You're surprised?" she said. "Well, it's true. It wasn't a coincidence we met, Richie – I went along to your twenty-year Ashvale reunion specifically to see you again. I was mad about you when we were kids, even thought I was in love with you then, but that was just a teenage girl's crush. By the time I started going out with you last year I think subconsciously it was all just a way for me to try to cling on to the past." She took a deep breath. "You know, I'd forgotten his face."

"Ben's?"

She nodded. "It was coming up to his twentieth anniversary. Mum and Dad were planning his memorial, discussing the different projects that his Foundation might support for the next few years – but all I knew was that when I closed my eyes I couldn't see my big brother's face any more. I think that's why I came back to Ireland from the States, why I sought you out. My counsellor suggested that I must have subconsciously thought that if I spent more time with the people who knew him best, that I would start to remember Ben again."

I knew what she meant. I'd been doing the same thing – going out with Ben's sister, clutching on to my Ashvale roots for dear life. I'd been trying to hold on to the memory of a friend, and a time and place that were long gone.

That much was clear to me, but what I didn't know was how to finally let it go – how to move on.

"My counsellor helped me to see that it wasn't that I'd forgotten Ben," Lucy was saying, "but rather that I'd been carrying around so much guilt about his death over the years that I almost wouldn't *allow* myself to remember him any more. His twentieth anniversary, everybody talking about him again – it all just served to magnify those feelings of guilt."

She turned away from me again and stared at the flickering flames in the fire.

"I've replayed that last Christmas with Ben over and over in my head at least a million times since," she went on, "each time searching for reasons, looking for ways that I could have foreseen what was going to happen, ways that I could have been nicer to him, got him to open up more. Anything that might have changed what happened."

I nodded – it sounded so familiar.

"What the counsellor helped me to do was to finally forgive him," Lucy said.

"Forgive Ben?" I said, startled.

She nodded, then turned back to face me.

"I had to forgive him for leaving us so suddenly – without any warning, any explanation," she said. "It was hard, but I worked through it with my counsellor. I hadn't realised how much anger I'd stored up towards him – it was quite a shock." Her voice had started to break.

I put my hand out for her, and she took it.

"Thanks." She took a deep breath and went on. "I made my peace with Ben. I forgave him fully and, once I did, I made peace with myself." She smiled at me. "Richie, you and I are the same. I can see that now from your article – we both felt guilty, and we were angry with him."

"I'm not sure, Lucy. I don't really think it is the same for me." I certainly felt guilty, and I'd been angry with everyone over the years – my father, my mother, even Ed, but the person I was most angry with wasn't Ben at all, it was myself.

"You know he called me that week, Luce? Just after Christmas – he called me at my mum's in London and suggested meeting up for a pint in Dublin in the new year – before we both started back to college. But I was seeing a girl, and I'd planned to meet up with her instead, so I told Ben I'd catch him another time. We'd been trying to meet for a few weeks already at that stage, but I was always too damned busy enjoying myself." I dropped my head and rubbed my forehead with the tips of my fingers. "I wish to God I could have that phone call back, I wish I had met up with him that week."

"Richie, you were eighteen years old. You can't be too hard on yourself." She stopped and looked thoughtful for a few seconds, before going on: "Although, I do know how you feel. Ben spent that Christmas with us here at Glenamara – and he didn't want to go back to college in Shannon after, he just wanted to be in Dublin with you and the Ashvale lads in college there. But Dad told him to

308

get hold of himself, and I teased him about being a wimp – those were my last words to him, can you believe it?" She put her head in her hands.

I moved in closer to her and put my arm around her shoulder. We just sat like that for a while.

"I realise now that I couldn't have known what was to happen, what he would do," Lucy said eventually. "Neither of us could, Richie. We couldn't have changed events and, even if we could have, we need to accept that we didn't. I needed to forgive Ben, but I also needed to forgive myself before I could move on." She took my hand and squeezed it. "And you need to forgive yourself too, Richie. It's okay to be the one alive, it's okay to be happy. Really it is."

I just nodded. It was a lot to process.

"I've been thinking of going to talk with someone about my mother, and about Ben – even about my relationship with my father," I said after a while. "It seems to have helped you."

She squeezed my hand. "It really has. You should do it, Richie. You're a good man – underneath it all." She smiled.

I smiled back.

"Really, though – you deserve to be happy, Richie. Do whatever you need to do to be able to move on." She sat up straighter then, and looked a little nervous. "Did I tell you I've started seeing someone?"

"No, you didn't. Anyone I know?"

"I don't think so – Craig Malloy, he's a doctor from Mayo, went to Mount Crescent College there."

"A Mountie? And I thought you had taste!"

She laughed. "He doesn't play rugby – he's more of a

golfer and hill-walker."

I smiled. "That's great, Luce. I'm happy for you," And I meant it. She deserved the best. "And how are your folks?"

"They're fine – in good form actually." She paused and looked at me for a few seconds. "You should meet them."

"No way! I'm sure Mr Mac still wants to kill me!"

She laughed. "I think he's mellowing. He's quite keen on Craig as it happens – they're in the same golf club – that's how I met him." She looked out the window. "Anyway it's pitch dark out there now, and the weather's awful. Why don't you stay here at Glenamara tonight, Richie? You could say hello to Mum and Dad then in the morning. I'm sure they'd like to see you and you'd still get home in plenty of time for Christmas Eve. I assume you'll all be going to Mass at Ashvale this year as usual?"

"Yes, can't miss it this year," I said. "Not now Ed's living down there."

"What?"

"It's a whole other story, Luce!" I laughed.

She smiled. "All the more reason to stay, Richie – you know how much I love to hear all of the Ashvale stories." She looked more serious then. "And to be honest, I think my folks would really like to sort things out with you – for Ben's sake."

And before I knew what I was doing, I was nodding, then telling her about Ed's new life and Jangler's new retreat centre.

It had been a long and emotional day, and I was glad to be upstairs settling in for the night in Glenamara's familiar guest room. I looked at my phone before turning off the light and read through the email I'd got late the night before from Mel. I'd been out with the lads when I got it and I hadn't had a chance yet to reply.

To: Richard Blake
From: Melanie McQuaid
Subject: Great article!
Date: 22 December 2007, 22.39 GMT

Hello, Mister Blake,

Great to bump into you again yesterday, Richie – sorry for rushing off. I just got a bit excited when I heard about the humpbacks being saved!

Just to say also I enjoyed your second article in the paper today – congratulations. This one was so special – very honest and moving. I loved the way you described looking into the eye of the humpback – it was the perfect description, and just made me want to go back and see the whales all over again. And what you said about your conversations with that new friend was very kind. I'm so glad to hear she helped you so much. I'm quite sure those chats meant a lot to her too ;-)

So I hope you've had a good weekend since we met, and that you got lots of good feedback on your article. I owe you a couple of coffees by the way – I ran off so quickly yesterday I forgot to pay. So let me know when you're free and it'll be my shout. Only thing is, Richie, after reading that article, I can't promise I won't have a go at chatting you up for real next time!

x Mel

I could almost hear Mel's voice and see her smile as I read her email.

And she seemed to be finding it harder to resist the ol' Blake charm, eh? Most excellent!

I couldn't stop smiling as I quickly typed my response with one finger.

Chapter 30

MELANIE

I must have checked my email over twenty times all through Sunday to see if Richie had replied. I knew I was being an idiot, but I couldn't help it – after reading his article and sending him the email on Saturday night, I just couldn't stop thinking about him.

I was checking my email one last time before going up to bed on Sunday night when I saw his response pop into my in-box.

Finally!

To: Melanie McQuaid
From: Richard Blake
Subject: Re: Great article!
Date: 23 December 2007 23:17 GMT

Hey there, Miss McQuaid,
Good to hear from you! Yes, you certainly disappeared fast on Friday night. Still, I suppose it would take some

man to compete with Mister Splashy Pants and forty-nine other humpback whales, eh?

Glad you liked the article anyway – I was keen to get back in your good books after that contentious piece about The Mill a few months back. This one was tough enough to write to be honest, but I'm glad I did it, and I have you to thank for helping me to see things more clearly. Hope you didn't mind me mentioning our conversations – they did indeed mean a lot to me – good to know they meant something to you too.

As for this weekend? Well, it's been a bit of a rollercoaster of a couple of days since I saw you as it happens – the big news is, I finally heard back from Lucy yesterday. In fact, I'm here at her home in Clifden at the moment. We've worked a lot out and things are going better than I could possibly have imagined – really great actually. I'm staying over tonight – will tell you all about it when I see you again – hopefully very soon.

Have a great Christmas in the meantime, and keep me posted on the swim progress.

Richie

PS: Put me down for a hundred euro for the swim – least I can do after borrowing your eye of the whale theory!

I had to read the email through a couple of times.

He seemed to want to see me again, but it was pretty clear he was getting back with Lucy. Why else would he be staying with her and it all be going 'better than he could possibly have imagined'?

Dammit anyway! I thought. He's getting back together with Lucy but keeping his options open with me. Well, you can forget that, buster! No way is that happening. I won't be anyone's back-up plan, or worse still – their bit on the side.

I sighed.

Maybe that wasn't it at all though. He could have just wanted to be friends? He'd never really said otherwise anyway – it was probably all just my overactive imagination – thinking there was more to it than there was. It was Katy's and Nichola's fault for spurring me on. After all, Richie was a born flirt – all the innuendo and talk probably meant nothing to him.

I slumped back in the kitchen chair – surprised by how disappointed I felt.

Oh well, it's probably for the best anyway, I thought.

The last thing I needed right then was a man in my life. It was time to get a grip and focus back on what was important – a nice Christmas break in Greystones with the family, and my swim for the whales on St Stephen's Day. After that, I thought I might even start looking at some travel ideas – a long break away from The Mill the following year was beginning to look like a very attractive option.

I glanced at Richie's email on the screen.

Away from The Mill, and away from all this.

At least he'd sponsored me for the swim – Richie's hundred euro would take me up past my target.

Argh! Stop thinking about him already! I snapped the laptop shut and went up to bed.

It snowed on St Stephen's Day – not a lot of snow, but enough to fill Katy and me with sufficient dread at the prospect of swimming in the sea. I wasn't looking forward to the cold water, but I was looking forward to the fun with the family on Greystones beach.

The beach was very busy – cars lined the street on the hill above, and onlookers leaned over the railings to see what mad fools were going swimming in such freezing cold weather. My nephew Austin and a couple of my brothers were tossing a rugby ball around on the pebbly beach, and a big group of lads from the rugby club were getting ready nearby. We swimmers were due to make a dash for the water at noon, and with just fifteen minutes to go there was a great buzz about the place – everyone was laughing and enjoying the Christmas spirit.

"Have a swig of this, girls – it'll warm you up before you get in," said Frank as Katy and I finished changing by the steps.

We each took a paper cup full of steaming mulled wine.

"What do you think, Mel?" Frank had put on a baseball cap with a stuffed whale of sorts attached to the top.

I laughed. "Yes, suits you, Frank. Very Save-the-Whale!"

He pulled a daft face. Then he peered behind me up the steps. "Hey, isn't that Ed Blake's brother?" he said, taking off the cap.

I swung around and looked up.

"You might be needing this later," Richie said when he reached us at the bottom of the steps. He held out a white, woolly hat.

My white, woolly hat.

"Thanks," I said, taking it from him and promptly feeling my cheeks flare up.

What was it about this guy? Why did I turn into a complete idiot whenever he was around? And why the heck *was* he around anyway?

"I, eh, wondered where that had got to," I managed to say.

"Richie Blake, isn't it?" said Frank. "I know your brother Ed from college."

"One and the same," said Richie. "Good to see you again, Frank. I remember you were on my brother's table at that lunch back in May."

I stood there in my little towel just watching as Richie, Frank and Katy became reacquainted.

"I liked those whale articles you wrote in *The Irish Chronicle*," Frank was saying. He nodded to me then. "Mel here liked them too – she must have read the last one at least ten times over. What was it you said again Mel? Something like they were the most moving pieces you'd ever read?"

Ground.

Please.

Open.

Richie grinned from ear to ear.

"Frank!" Katy poked her fiancé in the stomach to try to shut him up.

"What?" said Frank, looking all hurt.

Katy frowned at him, then turned to Richie. "So what are you doing in Greystones on St Stephen's Day, Richie?" she asked.

"Ah, I was just in the neighbourhood, so I thought I'd swing by and make sure you girls didn't chicken out of this swim." He gave me one of those annoyingly cute grins.

I pulled my towel tighter around myself, wishing to God I'd brought one of the bigger bath sheets. "Don't worry, Mister Blake," I said. "We'll make sure you donors get your money's worth."

"I should hope so, Miss McQuaid. I would expect nothing less."

We smiled at each other.

Katy coughed, reminding me where we were. "All right, Frank," she said. "Let's grab the gear and take it down a bit nearer to the sea. We'll need it as close as possible for when we get out." She raised her eyebrows and smiled at me as she turned to go. "See you down there, Mel?"

"Yes, I'll be down in a second."

Katy and Frank gathered up the gear and walked away.

"Alone at last," said Richie. "Although I think we may have an audience there?" He nodded behind me.

I looked over my shoulder to see my parents and my sister Nichola all watching us, each of them smiling broadly. I glared at them – and they got the message, quickly turning away.

I looked back to Richie. "Sorry about that, it seems my father hasn't given up hopes of packaging me off to the right man with a couple of heads of cattle and a few sheep. I haven't the heart to tell him you're a lowly journalist with no grazing land."

He raised his eyebrows.

"Not that you and me . . ." I said.

I needed to get myself together. We were just friends – I needed to remember that. There was nothing to be getting flustered about.

"Come on, Mel!" Katy shouted up to me. "It's time."

"You'd better go," said Richie. "I'll be watching remember? We want to see a nice, long, cold swim."

I smiled, turned and ran down the beach to join Katy while pulling my small towel down to cover the backs of my bare thighs.

"I can't believe he came today to see your swim, Mel," said Katy when I got to her. "Very impressive. And there seems to be a major spark between you two – look at you, all smiley and blushing." She poked me in my side as I threw my towel off.

"Hey, stop that! I'm not blushing – it's just the cold. Richie and I are friends – that's all. It was nice of him to come today to lend some moral support – but he's back with his ex."

"Ah pity," said Katy. "Oh well, nice of him to come to support you anyway."

"Mmm." I glanced back up at the steps.

"Ladies and gentlemen!" shouted the man with the starting pistol. "Please get ready to go!"

We lined up on the stony beach with the other swimmers, all of us just about five metres back from the shore. I was already freezing just standing there in my bathing suit, but I tried to block out the thought of how cold the next few minutes would be. The rugby players and other swimmers laughed and chattered excitedly, and the noise level was so high that Katy and I had to shout to hear each other.

"Good luck, Mel!" she said. "This is for the whales!"

"Absolutely. For the whales!"

The countdown started, and silence descended.

"Ten . . . nine . . . eight . . . seven . . . six . . . five . . ."

"Let's do this!" I shouted.

"... *four* ... *three* ... *two* ... *one!*
Bang!

There was a charge for the sea. Holding hands, Katy and I tip-toed as fast as we could in our bare feet over the pebbles. We were a bit behind the guys, so their cries warned us of what was to come.

"*Waah!* It's freezing!" Katy shouted out as the first small wave washed over our feet.

The cold water took my breath away, but I just kept going. "*Don't stop!*" I shouted as I hopped through the low icy waves. "Don't think about it! Just let's keep going!"

As soon as we'd got out to deeper water I took a deep breath, let go of Katy's hand and dived into a wave.

I quickly jumped right back up. "Whoa! That is *coooold!*"

Katy screamed too as she ducked below the waves. Once we got used to the extreme cold though it wasn't too bad and we managed to stay in the water for at least ten minutes before emerging shivering onto the beach. My mother and Nichola met us at the water's edge with our towels and flip-flops.

"Thanks, Mum." I wrapped my towel around me as I shivered beside her. I slipped my flip-flops on, then glanced over at Richie and Frank who were standing a few feet away chatting. Ah – that's nice that the two guys are getting on, I thought.

Richie caught my eye then and mouthed the words: '*Well done.*'

I smiled at him.

Then I gave myself a shake. All right, enough of this, McQuaid! You need to re-state your boundaries here quite clearly, so there's no room for misunderstanding – both you *and* Richie need to agree where you stand. No way can you go getting into any complicated love triangles. *Friends* is okay, *friends* is good even, but that's it.

I quickly got dressed in my warm fleece and tracksuit bottoms, then went over to join Richie and Frank.

Chapter 31

RICHARD

Christmas had been tough – no doubt about that. It had been very strange not having my mother around. I'd been at odds with her, or complaining about her for so many years that I never realised just how much I loved her, or how much I'd miss her when she was gone.

So yes, Christmas had been very sad. We'd all felt my mother's absence and the day was quite subdued as a result. By the time St Stephen's Day had come around I badly needed to get away, to get some time to myself. I'd left Sheila and Derek's place quite early to go down to Wicklow to check out my mother's old family house.

I couldn't believe the place when I saw it. It was big, and structurally it was sound enough, but inside it was a wreck. It hadn't been lived in for years and was going to take some amount of work to restore. And it was also a lot further down the coast than I'd expected. The setting was pretty incredible, but the location itself was quite remote – it was a good drive out from the nearest town of Wicklow. Ed and I would have to think long and hard about what to do with the place. It'd cost us a fortune to do it up to sell. I figured that maybe we could just sell it off for the land.

I checked the clock on my car as I drove into Greystones.

Excellent, just enough time to catch Mel's swim, I thought.

Despite everything else that had been going on, I'd thought about Mel a lot over the few days since we'd met again. So much so that I'd decided to just go for it – ask her out. She'd more or less asked me out in her email anyway, so I reckoned she'd be on for it. I didn't want to ask her out in an email though – so I went to Greystones to do it in person.

I'd asked a lot of girls out in my time, and it would be fair to say that my success rate was quite high, but this time was different. I was so damned nervous that it took me three attempts to get the car into a parking space on the road – not cool.

Mel had seemed a little on edge with me when she first saw me – she'd stood back and let Ed's friend Frank and his fiancée do most of the talking. I liked the way she always looked so flushed when I met her though – as if she'd just been doing something illicit.

I smiled as I watched her run off down the beach for the swim, pulling at her skimpy towel as she ran.

I joined Frank then, and we watched Mel and his fiancée brave the Irish Sea.

Mel came over to us afterwards. "Well, what did you think?" she asked.

"Great stuff! Well done, Mel," Frank said.

"You pair certainly have given us good value for

money," I said. "But the fellas hardly even got their hair wet."

"We aim to please," she said, with a smile.

"Was it cold?" asked Frank.

"Eh, *yeah*," Mel said.

"All right," said Frank, "I know when I'm not wanted. I'd better go congratulate herself anyway."

Frank walked off in Katy's direction, but appeared to get waylaid en route by the game of touch rugby that had started up again on the beach. I wouldn't have minded getting in on the game myself, but I had a job to do first.

I looked back at Mel.

"So how was your Christmas?" she asked, before I could say anything.

"It was okay, thanks. I only got back from Clifden on Christmas Eve. We all went to Mass down at Ashvale then, and we had Christmas Day and night at my aunt's."

"Sounds good." Mel drew on the sand with her big toe. "You mentioned Lucy got in touch – that's great that you got to see her in Clifden." She looked up. "In fact, there's something I want to –"

But just at that moment a rugby ball seemed to come from nowhere, hitting me hard on my right upper arm.

"Hey, you lot!" shouted Mel over her shoulder. "Be careful where you're throwing that thing!"

"Sorry, Auntie Mel!" shouted the teenager, running towards us.

"No worries, man," I said, throwing him the ball. "That was a good toss actually."

The kid looked pleased.

"That's Austin, and the rest of the men of the family," said Mel. "They do love their rugby."

I watched them pass the ball.

"Y'know, watching your nephew and the lads there reminds me a lot of when I used to toss a rugby ball around at Ashvale with Ben," I said. "We were only a few years older than young Austin there when he died." I stared at the lad for a few seconds.

"Actually, Richie, I wanted to talk to you about Lucy –"

"Hang on," I interrupted her. "That's it! I've just had the most excellent idea, Miss McQuaid – even if I do say so myself."

"What is it?"

I caught her by the elbow. "Are you free tomorrow?"

She looked a bit flustered. "Yes, but, Richie, I don't think it's a good idea to –"

But I couldn't delay to hear her out – this was too good an idea to allow to go cold. I wanted to act on it straight away. "I'll pick you up about lunchtime," I said, leaning in to give her a quick kiss on the cheek.

She just stood there staring at me.

"Oh, hold on –" I turned back and took out my phone, "I'd better take your number this time – I've run out of those woolly Cinderella hats!"

Chapter 32

MELANIE

I took my parents' beloved black-and-white spaniel, Harvey and two of the kennel dogs, Oscar and Sam, for a long walk down Brittas Bay beach early the next morning to try to clear my head. Just before we got to the end I let them off their leads and threw a stick for them. I gazed out to sea as they dived into the water to fetch it. But as I watched the three paddling resolutely through the waves for first prize, all I could think about was Richie. I couldn't stop thinking about him, in fact. It was all extremely annoying.

He'd said it himself: everything had gone great with Lucy. So why had I agreed to meet him again so soon?

I looked at my watch. Somehow or other, we were due to meet again in less than an hour's time.

I should have tried harder to talk to him about it. I should have tried harder to find out what he was thinking. I groaned. It was all so bloomin' frustrating.

I picked up the stick from where Harvey had dropped it at the water's edge. I had to jump back quickly as

Harvey, Oscar the small poodle-terrier mix and Sam the big black-and-tan shaggy mongrel shook themselves dry. Three pairs of eager eyes stared back up expectantly at me, as three happy tails wagged furiously. I obliged them with another throw, then sat down on the sand to wait as they battled through the waves again.

I should never have encouraged him to sort things out with Lucy. Now look what had happened.

I sighed. I should have been happy for him really. I knew I should – that's what a real friend would be. It was just that everything was so easy with Richie – he was so easy to talk to and I could really just be myself with him. I'd never been with anyone like that before.

I picked up a big pebble and flung it in the water, narrowly missing Oscar who'd given up on the stick and was on his way back. He looked at me, offended.

"Sorry, Oscar!"

He started to wag his little tail, before bounding over towards me. I jumped up before he could land on top of me with his wet paws.

"If only all males could be so uncomplicated," I said as I petted him. "No trouble understanding what you're thinking, eh, little fella?"

Oscar just looked up at me with his big happy eyes, tongue hanging out, tail wagging. He gave me a few seconds of quality time before bounding off to rejoin the other two who were just emerging triumphantly from the water, each holding either end of the stick. I laughed as I let them shake themselves dry again, then I put them all back on their leads and turned to walk back to the car park.

Oh well, I thought, maybe nothing can happen

between Richie and me, but at least we can be friends.

I could do that. I was sure I could.

And everything else aside, I was dying to know what his idea was all about.

My mother beat me to the door when Richie arrived to collect me at my parents' house.

"Mum, this is Richie Blake – he's the journalist from *The Irish Chronicle* I told you about," I said, introducing them. "You know – the one who wrote those articles about the whales?"

"Oh yes, of course, of course," said Mum. "I think I saw you down at the beach yesterday. How lovely to meet you! Very good of you to come to see Melanie swim. And again today? How nice!" She was literally beaming at Richie.

"Well, I was in the area yesterday so it wasn't any trouble," said Richie. He looked a little embarrassed, which I found quite amusing.

"Won't you come in?" Mum stood aside.

"I would love to, Mrs McQuaid, but I need to steal your daughter away as soon as possible. I have something very important to show her." He looked at me. "Maybe we could pop in when we get back?"

I shrugged my shoulders. "Sure." It wasn't like I knew where we were going anyway.

I zipped up my coat and grabbed my hat from the coat stand.

"Nice to meet you anyway, Mrs McQuaid." Richie shook her hand. "We'll see you later, hopefully."

Mum patted her hair, and smiled at him as she waved us off.

"At least I'm in with your mother," he said as we walked past the family's cars down the driveway.

I rolled my eyes. "So where are you taking me anyway?"

"I'll tell you both when we get there," he said, looking pleased with himself.

"Both?"

Richie nodded to the car in front of us by the roadside. I peered in and saw Father O'Mara sitting in the passenger seat and Ed in the back.

"Ed knows," Richie said, "but I'm afraid I have to keep you two in the dark for just another short while yet."

"You left poor Father O'Mara and your brother sitting out here in the car? You should have brought them in to say hello at least."

"Sorry, but we've no time to lose. Forgive me?" Richie said with a cheeky grin.

So cute.

Stop! Just friends remember?

It was a gate that I must have passed by hundreds of times on my way down to Brittas Bay, but one I'd barely noticed before. It was about nine foot high, with a bit of swirly detail at the top, and it was made out of some sort of metal – with rust and flaky olive-green paint competing for supremacy.

Richie opened it with an old key. "This is usually your department, eh, Father? Do you still have that massive key chain for Ashvale?"

"Not any more, Richard. Most of the doors take swipe-cards at Ashvale now." Poor ol' Father O'Mara didn't seem at all impressed at being dragged halfway across the county. "Now, Richard, I wish you and Edward would tell me what is going on."

I turned to Ed myself. "Yes, come on. What's this all about?"

He shook his head. "Sorry, it's all Richie's idea, but he talked to me about it yesterday and I think it's a great plan, but I'm sworn to secrecy for another few minutes at least." He looked at Father O'Mara. "I promise, you're going to like it though, Father. Trust us."

"C'mon then, you lot." Richie had already walked on through one of the creaking gates and was holding it open for us.

Father O'Mara and Ed walked on ahead down the dark, mucky path that was almost completely enclosed by overgrown trees and bushes. I waited for Richie to close the gate behind us. Once he was ready, I turned around to follow the others, but as I did I tripped over a low branch that was sticking out. I grabbed for Richie, and he caught me before I fell.

"Thanks," I said, steadying myself again.

"Mind yourself there, this path is quite slippy." He put his hand on the small of my back and guided me down the rest of the way. We didn't speak on the way, but I was so aware of his hand on my back, and of him beside me, that I almost forgot Ed and Father O'Mara were with us at all.

"What's this?" asked Father O'Mara, looking up at the crumbling old building that had been hiding around the corner at the bottom of the path.

"It's very big," I said – mainly because I didn't really know quite what else *to* say.

The place was an absolute wreck. It looked like it might once have been a big old farmhouse. It was three stories high, and made of grey stone – possibly granite, but it was hard to make out for all of the ivy and overgrown bushes covering the walls. A small section of the slate roof had fallen in, but otherwise it looked relatively intact structurally. Tucked in just beside the building was a beautiful old oak tree, but underneath it a pile of discarded beer cans and a patch of scorched earth.

We were standing at what looked like the back of the house, and could just make out the remains of what was possibly once an old vegetable patch or garden in front of us. There was a small structure just outside the main house, which looked like it had once been a shed for animals, or an outhouse. Most of the windows were smashed or missing their glass, but the frames were still there and the back door was closed and still on its hinges.

Father O'Mara came over to us. "It's a fine plot of land, Richard, and a grand big house." He put his hand on Richie's arm. "Tell me what you're thinking, son."

"Well . . ." Richie looked at Ed, then back to Father O'Mara, "I would like to present to you, Father – your new retreat centre!"

Father O'Mara just looked at Richie. I couldn't tell what he was thinking at all.

Richie went over to Ed and put his arm around his brother. "We want to donate this place – our mother's family house – to you, Father, for the young people. It's the perfect location for the new centre."

Father O'Mara just nodded thoughtfully.

Ed stepped away from Richie and looked back up at the house. "Rich, are you sure about this? I mean, now that I see it for myself, it's clear the place is falling apart. It'll cost us an arm and a leg to do it up."

"I know it doesn't look much now," said Richie, "but that's where Dec and his construction firm come in. I talked to him yesterday, and he's a hundred per cent behind the project. We'll probably need a couple of other guys to come in on it too, but we'll find them." He walked back over to Father O'Mara. "Just think of this place after it's been given a complete overhaul, Father."

"That'll need to be some overhaul!" said Ed. "Even with all that help, Rich, would it not be cheaper to build somewhere from scratch rather than renovate this place?"

"Not necessarily," Father O'Mara finally interrupted. I'd been beginning to wonder if he was ever going to say anything. "I like it actually. In fact, I think it's the best of all the buildings we've seen so far, Edward. It has a certain character about it."

I smiled. "Yes, I think it could work too," I said. "It's very charming, and if we can get all the building costs covered . . ."

"Right." Richie held his hand up. "Hold that thought – wait till you see the best bit. Come on!" He strode off around the side of the house.

Ed looked over at me and raised an eyebrow. "We'd better go see what else he has in store for us."

As we came out into the open at the end of the side passage of the house, a gust of wind forced me to close my eyes. When I opened them again and wiped the few tears from the wind away, I immediately saw what Richie was talking about. Stretching out in front of us, less than fifty metres away across an overgrown grassy field at the front of the house, was a jagged cliff-edge – we could hear the wild Irish sea crash up against the rocks at its feet.

The place was alive.

"So, what d'ye think?" Richie turned around. "Not bad, eh?" he asked with a grin.

I glanced at Father O'Mara beside me – he was clapping his hands, and bouncing up and down on his toes.

Richie came over to stand between us. "I think he likes it," he said.

"I most certainly do, Richard," Father O'Mara said. "It's incredible, but –" He looked over at Ed, who was smiling and staring out at the sea. "Are you quite sure you boys want to do this? Rose left this place to you. It's an amazing plot of land – you could do a lot with it, and Rose obviously wanted you both to have it."

Ed turned around to us. He smiled at Father O'Mara, then nodded to Richie.

"We want you to have it now, Father," Richie said. "We want you to go on helping young people find their way in life, the way you helped me, Ed and the other lads." He put his hand on Father O'Mara's shoulder. "All I ask is that we name a small part of it in memory of Ben . . ." he looked at Ed, "and another part for our mother."

Ed smiled and nodded.

Father O'Mara took Richie's hand in both of his. "Of course we can do that. Thank you, Richard." He took a step over to Ed. "Thank you both. This is truly a wonderful thing that you're doing. I am humbled by your generosity." He put a hand on Ed's shoulder then. "Shall we take a look inside the house?"

Ed nodded and took the keys from his brother.

"I've never seen Father O'Mara look so happy," I said to Richie as I watched them walk off towards the house.

But Richie seemed distracted. After a couple of

seconds, he took deep a breath in and took my hand. "Let's walk a bit, will we, Mel? I'd like your expert opinion on the sea view from down there."

The wind whipped around us as we walked hand in hand down to the cliff edge. I stole a glance at Richie – he looked quite serious, almost lost in thought.

I should really try to talk to him now, I thought, find out exactly what's going on with Lucy – and why he's been making such an effort to see me.

But something stopped me as I felt his hand in mine.

Just a few more minutes couldn't hurt, could it?

"So did you have any more thoughts on your travels next year?" he asked. "Any more whale-watching on the horizon?"

"Yes, most definitely," I said, "I mean I haven't quite worked out where or when yet, but I'm thinking of taking a few months off together at some stage next year. Try and see a bit of the world, do some diving, and hopefully see a lot of whales along the way."

He stopped by the cliff edge. "What about Japan? You could volunteer with Greenpeace?" He turned around to face me. "In fact, that's a great idea – I could introduce you to my mate Takumi, who works there on the whaling campaign when he's not at sea. Or to Ray, who's with the International office – you'd love it, Mel."

I smiled. "Sounds great, I might take you up on that."

I let go of his hand.

I needed to do this. I had to stop things before they went too far and I wasn't strong enough any more.

"Richie?"

But he held up his hand. "Mel, before you say anything, there's something I've been trying to ask you –

if I don't do it now, I never will." He took a deep breath. "I just wondered if, in between all that travel and saving the whales, whether you might be able to find time to squeeze me in for an oul' coffee, or a bite to eat – even a bit of whale-watching or whatever it is you whale-lovers like to do?" He rubbed the back of his neck. "I'm asking you out, Mel."

He looked so nervous, so genuine, that I almost gave in.

But I couldn't risk it. I looked down at my feet. "Richie, you're a great guy, and I hope we can be good friends, but I don't think any more than that would work between us."

He looked surprised, and hurt. "Why not? We'd have as much chance as the next couple. Why not let go of the 'single' thing, Mel? Give a guy a chance."

"It's not that, Richie. I need to be able to trust the man I'm with."

He nodded slowly, then looked down. "All right – I get that. You know my faults better than anyone, Mel, I could understand you not wanting to get involved with me." He looked back up. "I just hoped that you would at least give me a chance. I wouldn't mess up this time, I promise. I can honestly say I've never felt like this about anyone before."

I looked into his eyes – his lovely dark, brown eyes. He looked so genuine, I really wanted to believe what he was saying.

"You can't do this, Richie," I said. "You can't stand here and say these things to me, then go home to Lucy."

His whole face changed. "What would make you say something like that? Lucy and I finished months ago – you know that, Mel."

"Just a couple of days ago you were staying over with her – now you're here saying all these things to me." I took a step away from him and looked out over the sea.

Richie followed me and put his hand on my arm. "Mel, you've got the wrong idea. I stayed in Lucy's on Sunday night to meet her parents to sort things out with them too – they were away until Monday morning. And yes, Lucy and me sorted a lot out this weekend, but we are well and truly over. In fact, she's seeing some guy from Mayo now – it's good, I'm happy for her."

He turned me around to face him. Holding on to both of my arms, he said, "I'm moving on, Mel. With or without you, I'm moving on." He put a finger under my chin and lifted my head up so I was looking straight at him. "But I'd really like it to be *with* you."

"I don't know, Richie . . ."

"What are you afraid of, Mel?" His eyes searched mine for an answer.

I looked at the good man reaching out to me. I wanted so badly to go to him, to be held by him, kissed by him, to look into those eyes again and again.

I took a long, deep breath in – the fresh sea air reminded me so much of Norway and that precious moment with the whale. And my fear melted away.

"Mel?"

I smiled at him. "It's nothing, Richie, I'm not afraid of anything – not any more."

And I stepped into his arms.

Epilogue

To: Richard Blake
From: Melanie McQuaid
Subject: Missin' you already :-(
Date: 14 September 2008, 23.12 GMT + 9 hours

Hello, Mister Blake,

I'm sitting on my futon as I type, wishing you were still here beside me grumbling about my tiny Tokyo apartment or fighting me for the laptop to check the news on Reuters. By now you should be winging your way back home, probably watching a science fiction movie, or maybe even trying to finish off *Moby Dick*? Remember you have to finish it *before* getting home to win the bet :-)

I just opened the card you must have left by the bed this morning. It was such a lovely surprise – but you really shouldn't do that to a girl, y'know – I'm bawling here reading it! I love you too, you soppy, romantic fool. And I'm going to miss you too – so sooooooo much! It was really brilliant having you over here on holiday – two months was way too long to go without snuggles – let's never do that again, eh?

I know you said not to worry a bit, but I'm really sorry we were so busy on the campaign while you were here. It was great that you were able to help us out in the Greenpeace office with the media though – thanks again for that. Takumi was very impressed by my powers of persuasion! I'm really gutted that it's not looking so good for the whales though, especially with two of our own people detained for trying to expose the corruption within the whaling industry. Hopefully the truth will win out in the end. I just wish we could get through to more Japanese people, make them see the harm whaling does :-(Still, I have three more weeks left on my volunteer placement – maybe something will give soon.

Do give everyone my love when you get back home. Katy rang for a chat not long after I got back from the airport – apparently the first pilot retreat with the young people at the new centre went great this weekend. My nephew Austin was on it, and Dec's daughter Tara. Katy said they all seemed to get a lot from the experience. You'll be pleased to hear they loved Ben MacDonagh Park – they played rugby, soccer and rounders there over the weekend apparently. Isn't that great? I have such a good feeling about the place, Rich – I think the little Wicklow Retreat Centre for Young People is going to be something quite special. Good luck with the builders tomorrow – say hi to Dec for me. Gosh, it's hard to believe it's just three weeks now to the official opening – it really has all happened so fast, hasn't it? And then Katy and Frank's wedding the following week – it's all very exciting! I'll be so sad leaving Tokyo and all of the team here, but I'm already counting down the hours till I get home for it all. And of course, until I see you again xx

Right, I'd best get off to sleep. It's late here and I can't believe I won't be waking up to look into your sleepy eyes beside me in the morning – boo :-(

Love you

xxxxxxxxxxxxxxxxxxxxxxxxxxxxxxxxxxxxxxxxxxxxxxxx
xxM

To: Melanie McQuaid
From: Richard Blake
Subject: Re: Missin' you already :-(
Date: 15 September 2008 16.27

Hello there, Miss McQuaid,

I'm just home. Wrecked. Bloody connecting flight from Abu Dhabi was delayed by two hours. The only good thing about it was that I had plenty of time to read, and so yes, I did indeed finish *Moby Dick* – once I got into it, it was pretty good actually – I quite liked that Ishmael guy and the whale action was impressive. But the best bit is that I can now look forward to watching my entire *Doctor Who* box-set collection with you on your return – a deal's a deal after all!

I'm sure you've seen on the news, but all hell is breaking loose on the international markets today after the Lehman's collapse earlier. I should really go to bed, but I'm glued to the box.

Great to hear about the pilot retreat. I won't be able to take tomorrow off now after all, so I'll have to get Jangler to follow up with Dec and the builders about the centre's snag list instead – hopefully they'll be nearly finished by now anyway.

Right, best go check out what's left of the markets before I collapse into bed. Keep fighting for those whales, Miss, they need all the help they can get.

I'll miss your cute snoring beside me tonight, but call you tomorrow.

Your devoted love slave,

Rich

To: Richard Blake

From: Melanie McQuaid

Subject: Re: Re: Missin' you already :-(

Date: 15 September 2008 00:35 GMT + 9 hours

Oi, you! I do not snore! Cheek!

Great you're home now, and hey, don't worry about calling – I know you're going to be really busy with the Lehman's thing over the next few days. Talk when you can. Hope the jet lag won't be too bad tomorrow.

Gotta go sleep now, my eyes are closing as I type – long day today, they work us poor interns hard here!

Did I mention I miss you? Well, I do – LOTS!

Love you xxM

PS: Oh God, *Doctor Who*? Beam me up, please, Scotty!

To: Melanie McQuaid

From: Richard Blake

Subject: Re: Re: Re: Missin' you already :-(

Date: 16 September 2008 13.50 GMT

Greetings, lowly intern,

Beam me up, Scotty? Tell me you are joking, Miss McQuaid. You do realise that's from *Star Trek*, not

Doctor Who? It sounds like I will have to dust off another of my box sets as you appear to be in dire need of a full and proper science fiction education, Miss. What's that you said again? Oh yes – '*a deal's a deal after all*'!

What a difference a day makes. First day back, and it's been non-stop all morning – it's absolutely manic in here, so no time for jet lag. I've a meeting with Edith in ten minutes. I'm expecting her to have baked me a massive big humble pie – seems I was right about the economy after all: first it was Lehman Brothers, now it looks like AIG is in serious trouble too. I've even been given a front-page slot for my piece on it all.

Anyway, I've a few minutes before Edith gets here to tell me what she hates about my article, so I just wanted to drop you a quick line in case I don't get time to call later. I've some news I think you'll be very happy to hear: I rang Jangler this morning about the snag list – he's on to it now by the way. Sounds like things are going well there – apparently not only have Dad and Dec covered all the centre's building costs, but since the pilot retreat went so well for young Tara, Dec offered yesterday to cover the running costs of the place for the next five years as well. Proper order really, he made a killing by selling off most of his property portfolio a few months back – at least one person took my economic predictions seriously.

But the big news is that Jangler's just been promoted to chairman of your Millennium Centre! Yep – that ol' Cruella crone stepped down. Word on the street is that hubby's property business is starting to look very shaky. No surprise there, eh? Anyway, Jangler was asking me when you'll be getting back to work – he wants to talk to you about getting Marcus and the board to agree to scale back that oversized development project at The Mill. So expect to be busy when you get back, Miss.

Funny thing though, the first thing Jangler asked about was my trip over to see you – before we even got on to the topic of the Centre. So I told him how well it had all gone and how great it was to see you and spend some quality time together. Then he said something like: *"That's wonderful to hear, Richard. It certainly does the soul good to witness a plan come together."* I didn't want to sound rude by asking what he was talking about, but what do you reckon he meant – what plan?

Oh shit. Edith's early, she's just outside – face like a bull. And I don't see any pie.

Love ya, Miss – hurry home, will ya?

R

THE END